Hearts *racing.*
Blood *pumping.*
Pulses *accelerating.*

Falling in love can be a blur...
especially at 180 mph!

So if you crave the thrill of the chase—on and off the track—you'll love

THE ROOKIE
by Jennifer LaBrecque

The reasons Maddie Felton was off-limits could fill a book.

First and foremost, racing was Tucker's passion but it was also his business, and Maddie and—more important—her father were a major part of that business equation. That aside, Maddie hailed from one side of the tracks and he was definitely from the other.

She was a puzzle. He'd pegged her as a spoiled rich girl before he ever met her, but every time he was around her he realized Maddie Felton's puzzle had many more pieces than he'd first thought.

He knew his ability to compartmentalize, the ability to put everything else aside and focus on the task at hand, made him a good driver. But Maddie Felton refused to be compartmentalized. He was drawn to her and she refused to leave his head.

Maddie was a mystery...and Tucker always had to figure out a mystery.

Dear Reader,

I'm going to share a secret—I'm a late bloomer. I must confess that I wasn't always a NASCAR fan. Much like my heroine Maddie, I used to think, "It's noisy and they drive really fast around a track for a long time." Then one day I sat down and actually watched a race with my family. Wow! I was a convert. And then there was the first time I went to a race. Talladega in the spring. It was incredible, overwhelming and totally awe inspiring—all of it, the fans, the cars, the drivers, just the entire NASCAR experience.

I was thrilled to be given the opportunity to write for this series. I'm fascinated by all the people that make NASCAR racing the exciting sport that it is—the drivers, crew members, owners, engineers, hauler drivers, sponsors and fans. They are everyday people taking part in a larger-than-life sport. Behind the glamour, grit and sweat, they are real people with real problems. They get up and put their pants on the same as you and me every day.

I hope you enjoy watching Maddie and Tucker fall in love during their rookie NASCAR NEXTEL Cup Series season. I love to hear from readers. Please visit my Web site at www.jenniferlabrecque.com or drop me a note at P.O. Box 298, Hiram, GA 30141.

Happy reading,

Jennifer LaBrecque

NASCAR

THE ROOKIE

Jennifer LaBrecque

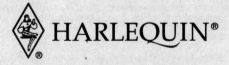

HARLEQUIN®

TORONTO • NEW YORK • LONDON
AMSTERDAM • PARIS • SYDNEY • HAMBURG
STOCKHOLM • ATHENS • TOKYO • MILAN • MADRID
PRAGUE • WARSAW • BUDAPEST • AUCKLAND

ISBN-13: 978-0-373-21777-9
ISBN-10:   0-373-21777-3

THE ROOKIE

JENNIFER LABRECQUE

writes contemporary romance. Named 2001 Notable
New Author of the Year and 2002 winner of the
prestigious Maggie Award for Excellence, she is also
a two-time RITA® Award finalist. A Georgia native and
University of Georgia graduate, Jennifer lives in suburban
Atlanta with her husband and daughter, rabid race fans
who have converted her, as well. Jennifer's husband
currently races throughout the southeast on the Outlaw
Racing Street Car Association (ORSCA) circuit.

First and foremost, this book is dedicated to the men and women who make NASCAR what it is today. And to my husband and daughter, who love racing almost as much as they love me...well, maybe more.

CHAPTER ONE

"…NASCAR SPONSORSHIP."

Madeleine Felton zoned her father out. Yeah, it was her first time sitting in on a family business meeting, and she was excited to be here, but she wasn't in the least interested in anything to do with NASCAR. She'd pay attention when it came to her part.

She surreptitiously studied her thumbnail on her left hand. Dang. After this meeting she needed to call Nadine for an emergency manicure. There was the slightest tear in the corner of her nail, and if that sucker went it was going to hurt—

"She doesn't even know what you said." Doug, Maddie's oldest older brother, tossed a sheaf of papers on the polished mahogany boardroom table dominating Felton Enterprises' inner sanctum.

"I'm the one who should be handling this. Maddie's gonna screw it up," Steve said. Her youngest older brother, four years older than her, shot her an apologetic look, "Sorry, Maddie, but you will."

What had she expected? That her big brothers might actually be glad she wanted to contribute something to the family business. "What? I'm not going to mess anything—"

Doug, who fancied himself an expert in everything, cut her off. "What do you know about NASCAR?"

NASCAR? Pretty much nothing. She vaguely recalled something last year about Daddy expanding Sleep EZ's market share in the midrange motel-accommodations market through NASCAR sponsorship, but she hadn't paid much attention.

It didn't particularly bode well that Daddy, Doug and Stevie were bringing up NASCAR in conjunction with her joining the family motel business.

She didn't like the sound of this. At all. And she hated when Doug patronized her. "NASCAR? Let's see." She touched her finger to her lip and pretended to ponder. "It's noisy and they drive really fast around a track for a long time."

She was being sarcastic, but really she didn't know a whole lot beyond that. And the most salient point was that she didn't want to, either. Noisy, dirty and a surfeit of testosterone and speed—no thanks, she could just drive around Atlanta's beltway if she needed some of that.

"That's insightful." Doug shook his head.

"Enough," her father boomed, standing and planting his hands on the expensive tabletop. "I don't want to hear any more, boys."

Doug and Stevie always firmly put her in her place as the baby sister. They indulged her, patronized her, didn't take her seriously...and she played right into it. If she wanted them to treat her like a capable adult, and she did, then she'd act like one. She shoved her hand with the torn nail into her lap and focused on her father.

"Your sister came to me a few days ago because she wants to be more involved in the business."

Stevie snorted and rolled his eyes. "Sure, Dad. She'll show up for work until there's a sale at Neiman's."

She narrowed her eyes but otherwise ignored Stevie's jibe. Her brothers weren't bad guys. They'd just all slipped into roles when her mother died. Her mother had been delicate, fragile, and in the end, had shattered. Maddie, nine at the time, was the spitting image of her mother. Her father and brothers had been determined to coddle and protect Maddie, as if she might shatter the same as her mother.

Alone, confused, lost without her mother, afraid her brothers and father might abandon her the same as her mother had, unsure she wasn't cut from the same cloth as her mother, Maddie had fallen into the role handed her. No responsibility. Nothing too taxing. No stress. No challenge. She'd just floated along, like a piece of flotsam carried downstream by the current, directionless, her path determined by others, but actually no path at all.

It had taken her years to figure out that despite the physical resemblance, she wasn't like her fragile mother. Or at least she didn't think so. Likewise, she'd come to realize that her childhood fears of abandonment if she didn't go along with her father and brothers that had carried over into adulthood, were unfounded. At least she thought they were. In both cases there was only one way to find out. The proof was in the doing. It was time for Maddie to take control of her own destiny, prove what she was made of, time for her to take on a job that would challenge her, test her mettle, other than the do-nothing jobs she'd had since college.

Both her brothers were important to the smooth running and growth of the family business. Maddie wanted to take her place in the ranks. Unfortunately, Maddie was the only one who realized it was time for a change.

"This job comes with flex hours so she can work it around shopping," Daddy said.

And didn't she just love being discussed as if she weren't in the room?

She had a degree in marketing with an emphasis on advertising and public relations that she never used. She'd interviewed for, and landed, a couple of entry-level jobs at ad agencies when she graduated from college, but Daddy had always nixed them before she'd ever gotten started, deeming them too taxing. And she'd gone along with him, playing the role she'd always played.

But she'd found out a lot about herself and her capabilities when she'd renovated and moved into the carriage house on her father's property. It had done wonders for her self-confidence and fueled her ambition. She was ready to contribute to something more than her closet and Neiman's bottom line. But NASCAR? Thanks, but no thanks.

"I thought I'd be working with Sherman, Reichman and Burkholtz on the new ad campaign." At least that's what she'd proposed to her father. SRB was the ad agency on record for Felton Enterprises and Maddie had looked forward to collaborating with them.

"Well, princess, you will be indirectly. The best way to facilitate expansion is to grow our customer base. You can't run with the big dogs if you stay up on the porch. Felton Enterprises and Sleep EZ are fully committed to our NASCAR sponsorship."

"NASCAR?" She was not feeling good about this.

"Yeah. We've got one of those noisy cars that goes fast around the track for a long time," Doug said.

Her father ignored Doug's sarcasm and sat back down in his oversized leather chair—the veritable king of the boardroom.

Doug and Stevie were younger replicas of their father. All three Felton men shared a square jaw, thick neck and a short, broad build. They could've been extras in a 1930s-era movie on pugilists. Everyone always said it was fortunate that

Maddie'd inherited her mother's refined features. She supposed, but it had taken her a long time to realize her personality ran more along the lines of her father's.

He cleared his throat. "Maddie, I want you to take over from Stevie as Felton's liaison and spokesperson with NASCAR."

"Me and NASCAR?" Could there possibly be a worse fit than her and stock-car racing? She knew nothing about racing and she was pretty sure if she did she wouldn't like it. "I'll be doing a lot of phone work to set up interviews and stuff?" she asked hopefully.

"Some of that, of course. You'll be working with Kelsi Morris. She's Chalkey Racing Enterprise's handler for Team Three." She felt as if he were speaking a foreign language. It must've shown on her face. "Team Three drives the Number 76 car that we sponsor. You'll host the prerace events and the skybox in addition to arranging driver appearances at our locations and coordinating driver ad shots. Stevie's been handling this, but at the rate we're expanding I really need him focusing on overseeing the new training program. He can turn over the files to you when we're through here. And you'll have an assistant who'll coordinate your travel arrangements and general administrative work."

Travel arrangements? "You mean, I'd actually have to go to the races?" She'd envisioned a nice office job—meetings with Creative, interfacing with media, overseeing implementation. She had never, ever envisioned herself as part of NASCAR racing. This was so not her cup of tea.

"Maybe it's too much." Doug exchanged a concerned look with their father.

"I can keep working it. I'll figure out a way to do both," Stevie chimed in.

This was familiar territory—her father and brothers decid-

ing what was best for her, making sure nothing was too difficult. It'd be so easy to let everyone fall into the roles they'd
played since her mother died and her brothers and father began to treat Maddie like a piece of rare Dresden porcelain.

Her father shot her a questioning look.

It'd be simple to slide out of the race track thing, but
where'd that put her except right back where she'd started?
She'd wanted the opportunity to prove herself and this was
definitely a challenge.

"No. It's not going to be too much." She stiffened her spine
and pasted on a smile. "I'll do it."

Ack.

TUCKER MACRAY GRIPPED the steering wheel and fought to
bring the car down going into the sharply banked Turn Three
at the Atlanta track. It was too tight and he rode it too high.
He completed the test run and rolled past the NASCAR track
official posted at the pit road and into the garage area. He un-
buckled, climbed out of the car, pulled off his helmet and ran
his hand through his hair. He welcomed the cool, early spring
air after the heat of his test run.

"Still pushing coming out of Turn Three?" asked Mike
Snellings, his Chalkey Racing Enterprises crew chief.

"Not as much, but it's still there," Tucker said, stepping
away from the car, getting out of the way of his team, who
were intent on doing their job. Out of the garage and off the
track, these guys could kick back with the best of them, but
at work they were all about the car and getting the team to
Victory Lane.

Tucker and Mike crossed from the garage to the Number
76 Chalkey hauler parked opposite the garage in line with
all the other haulers. He and Mike didn't always agree, but

Tucker was relieved that they both trusted and respected each other and their commitment to winning. Tucker knew respect and trust between a crew chief and driver could make all the difference in a winning season. Mike knew his business.

"The steering felt tight going into the turn. It was hard to get it down on the track," Tucker said.

"I noticed you were higher on the top than you like to be," Mike said, following him down the short chrome aisle that cut through the back of the hauler. Davey, Tucker's hauler driver, stood cleaning the already spotless drawer fronts in the alcove before the front of the hauler that housed what Tucker always thought of as "the war room."

"Good run, man?" Davey asked.

Tucker shrugged. "It was all right. It's gonna get better."

"Right on."

Tucker walked into the war room and put his helmet on the table in the center of the room. What had one of the guys called it? Techie paradise. It was decked out in state-of-the-art. Four plasma screens mounted on one wall, DVD and stereo equipment on another, computer with wireless Internet on the third. Pit seating horseshoed around the table. It was tight but comfy quarters—home away from home where he and the rest of the team could grab a moment of privacy and downtime at the track.

"How's it hanging, Tuck?" Marcus Chalkey asked from the corner where he sat surfing the Internet.

"Good." Tucker pulled a cold ginger ale from the mini-fridge and automatically passed a diet cola to Mike. "Want a drink, Marcus?"

"I'm good, Tuck, I'm good," Marcus said.

Dan Chalkey owned the team and Marcus was his one-and-only offspring, which was the one-and-only reason Tucker let the guy call him Tuck. That nickname came loaded with bad memories.

Tucker wasn't sure whether Dan sent Marcus along to keep an eye on things because Tucker was the rookie driver on the team or if Marcus just came along for the ride because he didn't have anything else going on in his life. Maybe it was a little bit of both. Regardless, Marcus pretty much stayed out of the way. He'd commandeered the one corner of the war room and sat parked in front of the computer, Internet-surfing most of the time. Aside from calling Tucker the annoying nickname, Marcus seemed okay. Heck, half the time Tucker forgot Marcus was around. He was sort of like another fixture in the hauler.

Tucker popped the top on his ginger ale and he and Mike sat opposite each other.

"Okay, we'll look at the track bar adjustment. Anything else?"

"That's it. I couldn't get it to come down, but I think that'll take care of it."

"I'll have Larry take a look at it. We'll have you set. You've got a good shot at the outside pole at Bristol." They'd spent the day testing and tuning at Atlanta, home to Chalkey Racing Enterprises, in preparation for the upcoming race at Bristol this weekend.

"Yep. If we can get it down on the track, we'll give 'em some racing." Running at Bristol was like dropping in on an old friend. The short, tight track frustrated some of the drivers, and tempers were almost guaranteed to flare, but Tucker had raced many a Saturday night at tight short dirt tracks throughout the southeast before he'd hit the NASCAR Busch Series and now the NASCAR NEXTEL Cup Series big leagues. He'd take an Atlanta or New Hampshire any day over Talladega.

Mike nodded. "We'll have it by the time you're through with the advertising people."

This was the part he didn't like, didn't want—the advertising. Tucker loved stock cars and everything about racing. Racing was an out game. Every time he got behind the wheel his goal was to out the competition: outsmart, outmaneuver and outdrive the field. Just as simple and just as complicated as that.

He could drive. He loved getting behind the wheel, hurtling along, with all his energy and focus on the track and the moment. Talk about a rush. Not a day went by that he didn't thank God for racing. Ad shoots were another story.

"I just want to drive and work on the car," Tucker said. "That's not exactly true. I want to drive and I want to win."

Snellings laughed. "We're kicking ass and taking names."

Tucker grinned. They were doing okay. Six races into the season an article by a noted sports columnist had tagged him as one of the top two contenders for the NASCAR NEXTEL Cup Raybestos Rookie of the Year title. And he knew he wouldn't be on his way if it weren't for Snellings's and the rest of the crew's experience, and it didn't hurt that he was a little more seasoned from the circuit than some of his rookie counterparts.

On any given day when his personal world was going to hell in a handbasket, he could get behind the wheel of a race car and for that length of time, all was right with Tucker Macray's world.

His two favorite places to be were behind the wheel or under the hood. But now he was about to do his obligatory time in front of the camera while Mike worked out the kinks. "I'll check back in with you when I'm done."

"Not necessary, but whatever you want to do," Mike said. They both knew Tucker would show back up at the garage afterward. It'd been an adjustment for both of them. The Number 76 driver last year had been very hands-off. Tucker was used to working on his own car and was just the opposite. It wasn't a matter of not trusting Mike and the team. It was just the way he was made. If he'd been a cowboy, he'd have never turned his horse over to someone else's care.

Tucker stood. "I'll see you later."

"Yeah. Smile pretty for the camera." Mike smirked. "And why don't you see about getting a decent haircut on the way?"

Tucker laughed and ran a hand over his head. "What? And break a tradition? Race fans wouldn't recognize me and it'd deprive the announcers of filler material."

"There's that."

It'd been the second race of the season and he'd driven the hell out of the Daytona track, barely avoiding a spinout ahead of him that had taken six cars off the track that day. Afterward, one of the TV announcers had jokingly commented that if he kept driving like that, maybe he could earn enough money to get a decent haircut or at least a good brush. He'd been officially, publicly dubbed Bed Head Macray.

He liked the place he'd been getting his hair cut for the past fifteen years. So what if he had a little bit of a cowlick. He wasn't doing one of those slick, pretty-boy salon cuts and he wasn't doing hair gel. And the craziest thing had been all the letters from fans telling him they liked his "bed-head hair."

One day, in the annals of stock-car racing, he wanted to be known as the best NASCAR NEXTEL Cup Series driver on the circuit. But everyone had to start somewhere, and for now he was known as the Number 76 Sleep EZ driver with bed-head hair.

CHAPTER TWO

Maddie pursed her lips from her vantage point in the back of the room where they were shooting the photos for the new print ads featuring Tucker Macray endorsing Sleep EZ. Mr. Hotshot Race Car Driver could use a good haircut. Maybe she could hook him up with Chantal. A snip here and a clip there and Chantal would whip his hair into shape in no time.

She'd offer to make an appointment for him when she met him afterward. She'd slipped into the photo shoot late, courtesy of a flat tire on the way. Of all the lousy timing, not that there was a particularly good time for a flat. She'd fully intended to arrive early to introduce herself, offer a few pointers and give Mr. Macray his new prop. Oh, well, all in good time.

She studied Tucker Macray in his less-than-fashion-forward racing jumpsuity thing. The first word that popped in her head was *average*. Average height, average build, average weight. She'd guess somewhere between five-nine and five-ten. He didn't appear to be muscle-bound and bulky, nor was he a beanpole. Just an average guy. Not drop-dead gorgeous, but he wouldn't make small children cry, either.

He reminded her of someone even though she'd never

seen him before. It suddenly came to her. The roadside assistance guy who had shown up to change her tire. Macray looked like the kind of guy who'd fix her car, drive a tow truck, show up to change a flat. Tucker Macray looked like an average guy.

The ad shoot ended, and while all the people who seemed to actually have a job concerning lights or cameras or whatever milled around, she scanned the passes that doubled as name tags—she'd had to pick one up herself before being allowed in—for Kelsi Morris.

She couldn't remember Kelsi's exact title, but she was Maddie's contact at Chalkey Racing Enterprises and the equivalent of a handler for all things that related to Tucker Macray. Maddie had called and introduced herself yesterday, explaining that she'd be stepping in as Felton's liaison. Stevie had described Kelsi as bubbly and vivacious. Maddie had found her professional but a tad cool over the phone.

She finally spotted her, tall and thin with a really good, very expensive blond dye job. She looked more like a Project Runway model than a handler, but then again, Maddie didn't exactly know what handlers looked like, anyway, and she supposed there wasn't a rule against them being tall, thin and gorgeous. She approached Kelsi, offering her hand.

"Hi, Kelsi. I'm Maddie Felton."

Kelsi offered a brief handshake. "Awesome." Her smile didn't quite reach her eyes. "Glad you made it. We were actually expecting you *before* the shoot." She smiled brighter. "We stick to a strict schedule."

Whoa. It was subtle, but the other woman had just taken her to task. Maddie might lack a lot of experience, but she was pretty good at reading people, and right now she was getting some not very welcoming vibes from Kelsi. Either Kelsi had taken an instant dislike to Maddie or she was one of those women who didn't get along with other women.

"I had a flat on the way here," Maddie said, offering an explanation but not an apology.

"No problem." Uh-huh. "Why don't I introduce you to Tucker, now that he's through?"

"Sure."

Even in three-inch heels Maddie felt dumpy and stumpy next to the willowy Kelsi. They made their way through the people—Maddie could swear that now that the shoot was over, the number of people on the scene had doubled.

Tucker Macray was busy scribbling his name on a glossy photo of himself, leaning against his car for a thirtysomething brunette wearing a snug T-shirt and even snugger jeans.

They'd almost reached Macray when the photographer stopped them. "Hey, Kels, we need you over here for a minute."

Kelsi looked at Maddie, obviously unsure whether Maddie had enough sense to get to Tucker Macray without further assistance.

Maddie waved her on. "Go ahead. I'll introduce myself," Maddie assured her.

"Okay. I'll be over in a minute or two," Kelsi said.

Maddie had almost reached Macray but held back a bit to allow him to finish his autographing. Unfortunately, the room wasn't that large, and while she didn't mean to eavesdrop, there didn't seem to be an alternative.

The woman gave him a folded paper and an arch look. "The next time you're in town, call me. We could hook up and you could look under my hood, check out my chassis."

O-kay.

The brunette shot him what Maddie supposed was intended to be a sultry look. "And I'll make sure all your pistons are firing."

Puh-leeze. Maddie didn't want to hear this, but it would be equally awkward if she turned around and left.

Macray offered the woman a thin smile, and Maddie was unsure whether to interrupt and rescue him, to laugh or simply to continue standing there. He took the decision out of her hands when he glanced past Ms. Chassis to where Maddie stood waiting. "Excuse me, but I believe this lady needs me."

That answered that. He wanted rescuing.

The woman looked over at Maddie, totally unfazed that her come-on had been overheard. She turned her attention back to Macray. "Don't forget." Her husky laugh grated on Maddie's nerves, which were already on edge thanks to being late for her first liaison task.

"Certainly," he said.

The woman left, casting a final come-hither look over her shoulder. Sheesh. Desperate women were pathetic.

Macray turned to Maddie. "Yes, ma'am?"

She stood there like an absolute moron because all coherent thought flew out of her head when Mr. Average Guy fixed anything but average hazel eyes on her. The impact of his gaze rippled through her from the top of her head to the tip of her toes and all spaces in between.

"Can I help you?" An unmistakable note of amusement crept into his voice.

Maddie wasn't used to amusing people. Especially not people who were for all intents and purposes working for her. And how embarrassing that she was standing here gawking at him like some groupie on the heels of the Check-Out-My-Chassis woman. She lifted her chin and looked down her nose. "I'm Maddie Felton…with Felton Enterprises."

"Ah, Ms. Sleep EZ." Now, why did that send a little tingle down her spine? He held out his hand. "Tucker Macray. Pleased to meet you."

She grasped his hand and a sensation sizzled through her. His callused palm rubbed against her softer skin—the hands of a working man. He had a nice firm handshake. Her father had always maintained you could tell a lot by the way a person shook hands.

"It's nice to meet you, as well," she said, extricating her hand as soon as decently possible. Hel-lo. What was wrong with her that a mere handshake left her feeling all warm and jittery and slightly off kilter?

His celebrity status didn't impress her—quite frankly, driving a car around a circle to see who could get there first didn't make a whole lot of sense to her. No, it was the sheer force of presence he exuded, the buckle-her-knees force of his eyes. So much for being average.

And she'd better get a grip before she totally blew her first day on the job before she even really got started. "I'll be working with you on behalf of Felton Enterprises for the remainder of the season."

"Good deal. I heard you were taking over for Steve." Macray nodded, his smile friendly enough but dismissive. "It was nice to meet you."

First Kelsi admonished her for being late and now Macray was blowing her off? What the heck? She hadn't even gone over her list. "There are a couple of things I need to go over with you first."

"Yes?"

Arms crossed over his chest didn't exactly engender open communication. News flash. If he didn't like her peremptory tone, he shouldn't have dismissed her that way.

She shifted. The toes on her right foot were numb because her shoes were too small but they'd been perfect with her suit and the store hadn't carried her size. Such was the sacrifice to look professional. Which brought her to her first point. "I wanted to talk to you about your hair. I have a stylist that I could set an appointment with for you."

Macray ran his hand over his head, which simply made it worse. "I like my hair."

"It's nice enough—" it was a cowlick disaster, but she was aiming for diplomacy "—but you have a couple of cowlicks and Chantal could work with those."

Amusement lightened his eyes. "Have you watched any races, listened to any broadcasts, read any articles with me in them?"

Maddie squirmed. She'd meant to. Honestly, she had. She'd been cable-surfing on her way to the race channel when she'd been sidetracked by a makeover show on the style channel. NASCAR NEXTEL Cup Series racing or *Fix My Face?* In retrospect, it appeared she'd made a poor choice. "Um, not really."

"You either have or you haven't."

Humph. She wasn't sure what it was he found so funny. "No. No, I haven't."

"I didn't think so."

What? Had she missed some secret handshake? "Why do you say that?"

"Because the media has nicknamed me Bed Head Macray and we wouldn't want to muck around with that."

"Ooh." That explained a lot. "I get it now. You *want* your hair to look bad."

"Hey, don't get carried away. I wouldn't call it *bad.*"

Maddie eyed his head. Obviously perspective was everything. "Okay. Then on to the second thing. I have something for you." She tried not to preen over her stroke of marketing genius. She delved in her purse. "I'd like this to become part of every appearance you make, on and off the track." It wasn't in the zippered pocket. Now, if she could just find it.

MADDIE FELTON WAS A PIECE of work. *Spoiled daddy's girl* was written all over her, from the top of her well-cut cinnamon-colored hair to her designer suit complete with three-inch heels, to the expensive scent that sent his mind wandering to sitting in the dark on a porch swing on a warm summer evening with the sound of crickets filling the night.

Odd that she should conjure up that thought. Maddie Felton didn't strike him as a porch-swing kind of woman. Furthermore, Tucker couldn't exactly recall the last time he'd spent a summer night with a woman curled up beside him on a swing. Definitely not since his divorce. Heck, it'd probably been before he and Darlene had gotten married. Back when Darlene was more of a girl than a woman and he was still a green boy.

He didn't have time for porch sitting now, and, bigger issue yet, Maddie Felton looked like trouble to him. Clueless and in charge struck him as a bad combination. Even if she did have golden-whiskey eyes and a cute little upturned nose that she was more than willing to look down. Actually, especially because of that.

"It was right here…give me just a minute," she muttered while she rooted through one of the ugliest and biggest pocketbooks he'd ever seen.

What the heck did she have for him? At least he was ninety-nine percent certain it wasn't her number and an invitation to fire his pistons. Talk about embarrassing. He hated it when women did that kind of crazy stuff. Unfortunately, it happened often enough. He'd had every sexual innuendo in conjunction with a car tossed his way more than once. He was hard-pressed not to roll his eyes when it came his way, but fans were important, and if some of them got carried away once in a while, he tried to just ignore it and cut them some slack. Still, that kind of talk was a turnoff, even when the woman was pretty like the brunette. He knew he was kind of an old-fashioned guy, but it embarrassed him.

"Here it is," she said, pulling out a...what exactly was it? She handed him a plastic key ring emblazoned with *Sleep EZ With Us Tonight* and a 1-800 number. All right, then. "This is the marketing piece I'm supposed to carry with me all the time?"

"Sure. We give them to every Sleep EZ guest. Put your race car key on it and fans can identify with it. They'll see you with your Sleep EZ key ring every time you're getting into your car."

Tucker bit back a smile. "Let me get this straight. The key to my race car goes on this key ring? And I'm supposed to wave it at the crowd on the way to my car?"

Her eyes sparkled her approval. "That's right. If you can get some on-camera coverage, that'd be great. If you ever win a race, you know, make sure you have it in your hand."

Now, there was a vote of confidence. *If he ever won a race.* He should tell her. He should tell her now before it went any further and got any worse. She was going to blow a gasket when she found out, but the temptation to let Ms. I'm-the-Boss prattle on...he couldn't resist.

"Should I hold it up like this?" He held up his hand, the key chain dangling from his index finger, and pretended to wave.

"Great. If you're actually holding it in your hand, no one will see the Sleep EZ logo and the whole idea will be lost."

He nodded. "Not a problem. I'll practice before the race this weekend."

"Good." He would've told her then and there but she looked so smug, he couldn't.

Kelsi strolled over. "Sorry about that. I see you two have met."

Kelsi was one of those women that would've never given him the time of day a couple of years ago, but now that he was a NASCAR NEXTEL Cup Series driver... She hadn't been as obvious as the woman who'd given him her number and offered to make sure his pistons were firing. She was more sophisticated and a little more subtle, but it had been the same message.

First and foremost, he wasn't looking to get involved with anyone. He wasn't good relationship material. Second, he anticipated a long career in NASCAR. If he decided to get involved, he wasn't interested in a woman that only wanted him for what he did rather than who he was.

"Definitely. We've definitely met," Tucker said.

"We've addressed a few of my ideas," Maddie said.

"Oh, really?" Kelsi looked questioningly from one to the other and then back at Tucker, speaking to him. "Great. That's super. Let's hear 'em."

He'd really rather not, but there was no getting around it. "She recommended her beautician—"

Little Ms. Bossy jumped in and corrected him. "Stylist."

"Stylist. But I told her we couldn't mess with my bad hair because that would kill my Bed Head persona."

Kelsi nodded with such solemnity Tucker almost laughed aloud. It struck him as absolutely insane that three adults were standing around discussing his hair. "I agree. One hundred and ten percent. It's in our best interest to keep your bad hair. It's branding."

Maddie shot Tucker an I-told-you-your-hair-was-bad look and said, "We shelved the stylist idea, but I gave him this

Sleep EZ key ring and he's going to incorporate it into all of his appearances and his driving experience."

"How?" Perplexed, Kelsi frowned.

"He'll use it for his race car key," Maddie said.

Tucker leaned back slightly, preparing for Maddie Felton's impending spontaneous combustion. He figured about thirty seconds.

Kelsi glanced from Maddie to Tucker and back to Maddie. "Right. That's very funny. Everyone knows race cars don't have keys."

Maddie narrowed her eyes. "What?"

"The driver flips a toggle switch," Kelsi said, laughing at Maddie, definitely not with her.

Whoosh.

Good thing his driver's uniform was made to withstand fire.

CHAPTER THREE

"I UNDERSTAND YOU MET Tucker Macray today. What'd you think?" her father asked. Louis Felton cut an imposing figure behind the expanse of his mahogany desk. Except Maddie knew he was one big teddy bear inside.

An image of laughing hazel eyes and mussed hair popped into her head. What'd she think? She bit her lip. If she uttered the word that immediately came to mind, her father would have an apoplectic fit since cussing was reserved for the men in her family. Tucker Macray had made a total fool of her today. Instead of calling him what she wanted to, she settled for another *A* word.

"Average." She firmly put the memory of his eyes out of her head so she wasn't technically lying. "Just sort of an average guy."

Her father nodded his approval. "That's what I thought, too. He comes across as kind of laid-back and easygoing." Louis grinned. "But when he's on the track, that boy's hell on wheels. Wait until you see him drive."

Oh, joy. *Never* suited her just fine. She'd be thrilled to never darken a race track and never cross paths with Tucker Macray or smug Kelsi Morris again.

"I can hardly wait." She'd developed fabulous avoidance tactics but was a terrible liar.

Daddy peered at her from beneath heavy gray brows. "Is this too much for you, princess? You just say the word."

Maddie almost had the sense that her father wanted her to say the job was too much so that she could go back to shopping and he didn't have to worry about her, manage her. She immediately felt guilty for entertaining such thoughts about her father.

A knock on the heavy office door interrupted them and Sharon came in. "Sorry, Mr. Felton, but if you don't sign these contracts, it'll be too late for the courier to get them there tomorrow."

Sharon handed him a sheaf of papers and turned to smile at Maddie. Both women knew better than to say anything. When Louis was reading a contract, a proposal or even an e-mail, he liked it quiet. Sharon mouthed a hello at Maddie.

Maddie offered a silent greeting in return. Sharon had been her father's personal assistant for what seemed like forever but was actually more like the last twelve or fourteen years. Once or twice in the past couple of years, Maddie thought she'd caught a look from Sharon, a vibe, and she'd wondered if Sharon might have more than a professional interest in Louis Felton, but Maddie'd written it off as too much imagination on her part.

Maddie, for want of anything better to do while her father scanned the documents, surreptitiously studied Sharon. Not for the first time, Maddie thought that she'd love to do a fashion intervention/makeover for the older woman. Sharon had good bone structure, but she also possessed a real penchant for frumpy. A new hairstyle, updated makeup and something other than gray suits would take ten years off of her and turn more than a few heads.

Louis scribbled his signature, handed them back to Sharon

and returned his attention to Maddie. "Do you want me to put Stevie back on the NASCAR sponsorship?"

The door closed behind Sharon and Maddie drew a deep, quiet breath. One day she had to address it. But it wasn't time yet because actions spoke louder than words. She could tell Daddy all day long that while she might look like her fragile mother, inside Maddie was more like him. But words were cheap and she'd been guilty of perpetuating the myth.

Mary Beth Felton had been emotionally fragile. When she'd died, the Felton men had devoted themselves to coddling Maddie, as if by doing so they could "save" her even though they'd lost Mary Beth. Her father and her brothers had wrapped her in a cocoon and she'd let them. It seemed to be what they all needed at the time.

One word was all it would take to ensure she and Macray never crossed paths again. Her face burned as she thought about how idiotic, how peremptory she'd looked demanding he use a key ring for a nonexistent key.

Okay, he hadn't made a fool of her. He'd definitely aided and abetted, but she was the true culprit. She hadn't done her homework. She'd set herself up with her own ignorance. Well, she could say one little word and her ignorance, along with Tucker Macray, would become a nonissue.

But to coin one of Stevie's favorite phrases—*actions talked louder than words.*

Maddie gathered her resolve and shoved a strand of hair behind one ear. "Daddy, it means a lot to me that you've given me this to handle. Of course it's not too much."

His smile didn't quite clear the trepidation, or was that aggravation, from his eyes. "If you're sure."

"I'm positive. Really."

First she'd order every book available on-line about

NASCAR. Second she'd…well, she didn't exactly know what she was going to do next. She was winging it.

What was certain, however, was that the time was coming when she had to clear the slate with Daddy.

She knew the truth about her mother.

TUCKER CROSSED THE blacktopped parking lot of Chalkey Racing Enterprises to his '73 Dodge pickup. Some of the guys gave him a hard time about driving his old truck when he could easily afford something new, but he liked his truck. He caught his reflection in the window while he was unlocking the door and grinned at himself. He liked his truck the same as he liked his hair—his *bad* hair. He didn't plan to change either one any time soon, thank you very much, Ms. Maddie I'm-the-Boss Felton.

He pulled out of the parking lot and headed north. Before he hit the first traffic light he speed-dialed his surrogate parents' familiar number on his cell phone.

Jack Matthews answered on the third ring. "Hey, you on your way?"

"Maybe half an hour," Tucker said, turning left at the light.

"Sounds good."

"Are Andy and Charlene there?" Tucker asked.

"No, but the kids are here. Charlene's got Andy painting the den so we're doing the grandparent thing and babysitting," Jack said.

Tucker grinned. Jack could sound long-suffering all he wanted to, Tucker knew Jack and Edna adored their grandchildren. Occasionally Tucker missed what Andy, his best friend from high school and beyond, had. Andy'd married Charlene Tibbs a couple of years out of high school. They had a good marriage, a house that needed a ton of work and two of the cutest kids Tucker'd ever laid eyes on—not that he was biased or anything. But, hey, he'd tried that route with Darlene and found it just wasn't for him. Racing was in his blood and owned his heart.

"I'll catch up with Andy tomorrow, then."

"He'd like that. Edna and Bobby caught a mess of fish for dinner." The older man laughed. "Take your time. They've just finished cleaning them. We won't be eating for a while." Jack's tone had grown far too casual. Tucker knew what was coming. "Plenty of time to stop in and check on your folks on the way out."

"Nah. Maybe some other time." He'd sent a check last week. As far as he was concerned, he'd more than fulfilled his familial duties.

"All right then," Jack said, letting it go. Jack always made the suggestion. Tucker always turned it down. And that was that until the next time Tucker came in from the road when they'd replay the same conversation. "We'll see you when you get here."

Tucker turned off his cell phone and cranked the Toby Keith CD, keeping time on his steering wheel with the music. His mind wandered as his old truck rolled down the familiar highway that carried him out of Atlanta and into the north Georgia foothills, past the towering north Georgia pines and bare-limbed oaks.

He deliberately kept his eyes trained on the blacktop as he passed the turn that would've taken him to his parents. He felt Jack's quiet disapproval, but he wasn't going there. Never again.

Tucker credited racing with saving his life, but that wasn't exactly accurate. Jack Matthews had saved his life.

When he was a kid, he'd been so ready for something to

take him out of the dismal realities of his life—an old man who liked to beat the hell out of him if Tucker happened to look at him wrongly, or depending on just how much beer or bourbon had been consumed. Sometimes just the fact that Tucker was breathing seemed to be enough provocation for Henry Macray to beat the crap out of his son while his mother turned a blind eye. Drugs or alcohol could've so easily provided the outlet he sought.

Yep. By thirteen he'd reached critical mass. He shuddered when he thought about what a close call his life had been. But he'd been lucky. He'd never, ever forget the night that had changed his life forever. It'd been that summer between seventh and eighth grade and Andy, a kid he'd known from school, had called and asked him if he wanted to come over for the weekend. Anything was better than home and he'd jumped at the chance.

Andy was into midget racing and Tucker had discovered a new love. From that night forward, every weekend found him at the track with Andy and his dad, Jack, cheering Andy on and working on Andy's car. Then there'd been the weekend that Andy had broken his leg. Jack had offered Tucker a shot at midget racing. The entry fee was already paid and the car was ready. Why not? It had been one of those moments in life that you never appreciated its significance until later.

Tucker could drive. Not only was he damn good at it, he loved it. His life had never been the same from that day forward. He'd discovered something that provided a rush far better than drugs and alcohol but was equally addictive and didn't reduce him to the level of his parents—an alcoholic or a druggie.

Jack had fronted him a midget racer and he'd moved through the ranks. Midget racing. Sprint cars. Super-late models. Jack had backed him every step of the way—had pushed him and encouraged him and taught him to believe in himself, both on and off the track.

Tucker turned off of the highway onto the dirt road that was hard-packed red Georgia clay.

Jack and Edna Matthews were more like parents than Tucker's parents had ever been. When the farm next to them had come up for sale last year, Tucker had jumped at the chance to buy it. Most of the time when he was home, he ate Edna's home cooking, hung out with Jack and Andy in the shop out back and gave Andy and Charlene's two kids piggyback rides.

He pulled into the driveway flanked by waving pampas grass and parked behind the crew cab beside the Matthewses' rambling farmhouse. Napoleon, the rat terrier who belonged to him but stayed with Jack and Edna when he was gone, raced from the barn, barking a greeting. He bent to greet the little dog. "Hey, guy. I missed you, too."

The screen door on the back flew open and four-year-old Bobby hurtled down the steps, letting the door slam shut behind him. "Uncle Tucker, Uncle Tucker, we caught some fishes for you to have for dinner."

Napoleon, being a smart dog, pranced out of range of the four-year-old body rocket as Bobby launched himself at Tucker.

Tucker caught him and held him at eye level. From the dirt smeared on Bobby's face, Tucker'd guess Edna had caught dinner while Bobby played with the worms. "Is that right? Are they all for me?"

"Nope. You got to share them with me and Papa and Nana."

"What about Melanie? Shouldn't I share with her, too?"

Bobby regarded him intently, his dark brown eyes seriously considering whether his two-year-old sister deserved fish for dinner. "She's sleeping, but you should when she wakes up. If you don't, Nana will give you a time-out."

"Time-out's bad?" The crush-'n'-run gravel crunched beneath his feet as he headed toward the house.

"It ain't good. I don't like time-out."

"Hmm. I probably wouldn't like it, either. I think I'll share my fishes with Melanie, too." He whispered into Bobby's ear, "And don't say *ain't*. It makes your Nana crazy."

He carried Bobby in the back door. Edna stood at the counter, dredging fresh catfish in cornmeal. She looked up, a welcoming smile on her laugh-lined face. "Well, looks like trouble found trouble," she said with a laugh.

"Uncle Tucker's gonna share his fishes with all of us so you don't give him a time-out."

Edna nodded and winked at Tucker over her grandson's head. "He'd better or he'll find himself in that corner chair in the living room."

Bobby wiggled and Tucker put him down on the linoleum floor. "Thanks for the heads-up, little guy."

"Welcome." Bobby scampered out, passing his grandfather on his way in. Jack propped against the counter. His big frame dwarfed the kitchen—a gentle giant. In all the years Tucker had known him, Jack had never raised his voice or his hand to anyone.

"How'd it run today?" Jack asked.

Tucker recounted the day's practice session. He and Jack drank sweet tea and talked racing while Edna fried the fish to a golden, crisp finish.

Edna pulled a bowl of potato salad out of the fridge and passed it to Tucker. Yum, just the way he liked it—new, red potatoes, eggs, celery, mayonnaise, a dab of pickle relish and just enough mustard to color it pale yellow. He put the bowl next to a plate of red sliced tomatoes on the round oak table tucked into the kitchen's bay window.

While Edna covered the fish to keep them warm and dropped hushpuppy batter into the hot oil by the tablespoon, Tucker recounted the key-ring incident. Edna turned from the stove and slanted him an admonishing look. "You ought to be ashamed of yourself, Tucker Macray, embarrassing that poor little girl that way."

"She embarrassed herself. All I did was let her." Okay, so maybe he did feel a tad guilty over that. He could've stopped her at the onset or before Kelsi got involved. Instead, he'd egged her on. So, maybe he ought to be a little ashamed of himself, but no way, no how, could Edna classify her as a poor little girl. "And that poor little girl's daddy could buy and sell me a couple of times over."

"You were raised better than that," Edna said, and turned the hushpuppies to brown on the other side.

There'd been no niceties, manners or otherwise, in his life until Jack and Edna. "Well, technically—"

"Don't sass me. And I don't care how much money her daddy's got. I read an article in the *Southern Regional Power* magazine on the Feltons. Her mama died years ago. Every girl needs a mama and she doesn't have one. That makes her a poor girl."

His parents had sucked, but he'd found Jack and Edna and he'd turned out okay. He knew firsthand you didn't have to share DNA to experience family bonds of love. "What about a stepmother?"

"Her father never remarried," Edna said.

Tucker knew a twinge of sympathy. He didn't want to think about bossy, fiery little Maddie Felton without a mother.

"You need to send her some flowers to apologize," Edna continued.

Sympathy flew out the window. "What?"

"You heard me." Edna didn't bother to look up from where she stood transferring the hushpuppies with a slotted spoon to a paper-towel-lined plate.

"But I don't think my punishment fits my crime. Sending her flowers is way over the top."

"Don't *but* me, Tucker Macray." Her mouth took on a stubborn set. "It's the right thing to do." Edna carried some very old-fashioned ideas about propriety and gallantry. She hung her apron on a hook inside the pantry, dismissing the topic, and Tucker knew arguing with her was useless. "Ya'll get that on the table while I get the kids." She nodded toward the platter of fish and hushpuppies and headed for the door. "I'll take care of it tomorrow if you don't have time," she said to Tucker.

Jack grinned. "I'd send those flowers if I was you."

He still thought it was an over-the-top gesture, but Edna had spoken and he'd pretty much walk through fire for Edna. So he'd send flowers to Maddie Felton even though it was just inviting some of that red-haired trouble his way and he didn't need it. "What if she gets the wrong idea?"

"I suppose that depends on what you have 'em put on the card, now doesn't it?" Edna's eyes gleamed. "You want me take care of it?"

"No." Not just no, but hell no. More than likely, Edna'd put some groveling message on it. Or worse yet, something lifted from those romance novels she was so fond of reading. Nope, he'd send them…and then make sure Maddie knew Edna made him. "I'll call the florist tomorrow." And he would be-cause Edna would check up on him.

"Good. And don't you let that girl know it wasn't your idea."

Damn. There went that plan. He'd never been able to get anything past Edna. He'd never let Maddie Felton know he'd sent her an apology bouquet under duress because somehow Edna would find out and his life would be a misery.

"Fine. As far as she's concerned, it's all my idea."

"Smart man," Jack muttered as Edna sailed out of the kitchen, satisfied that she'd got her way.

Tucker wasn't sure just how smart it was. It felt like trouble to him, but then again, Maddie Felton had pretty much spelled trouble from the second he'd looked down into her whiskey-colored eyes and felt a jolt of attraction from simply shaking her hand.

CHAPTER FOUR

THE FRONT DOORBELL RANG, startling Maddie. She set aside the book on NASCAR history and padded across to the front door, the original flagstone entryway cool beneath her bare feet.

Jess, who bore the title *housekeeper* but who was as close to a mother figure as Maddie had known since that summer evening fifteen years ago when Mary Beth Felton had died, stood on the stoop.

"These just came for you. I took the delivery at the main house," Jess said, holding a professional arrangement of iris, daisies and pink roses scattered among green fern and baby's breath. "Who's sending you flowers?"

Maddie took the vase. "No clue. Come on in and let's find out." Jess closed the door behind her and followed Maddie into the carriage house's den.

Jess made herself at home in the overstuffed armchair between the fireplace and the love seat. A couple of times a week she usually wandered over to the carriage house for a visit or Maddie stopped by the main house. However, a flower delivery was never part of the equation.

Who was sending her flowers? Maddie wasn't dating anyone. It wasn't her birthday. As far as she knew, she didn't have any event or occasion to celebrate. Her day suddenly seemed much brighter. It almost didn't matter whom they were from, there was something special and uplifting about getting flowers.

Maddie placed the vase on the coffee table, plucked the envelope from the clear plastic holder and slid the card out.

Sorry about the other day. I was a jerk…with bad hair. T. Macray

Maddie couldn't contain the smile that spread over her face or the laughter that welled inside her. And her heart beat a little harder and faster. Okay, maybe he wasn't so bad. She could picture his eyes, those eyes, alight with humor, and she supposed his hair wasn't really all that bad….

"Heh-hmm." Jess cleared her throat, pulling Maddie out of her reverie. "Who's it from? Must be sorta special, seeing as how you're laughing and smiling and you have a funny look on your face."

That was enough to smack the smile right off her face. Maddie shrugged. "No one special. Except I definitely see the potential for him to be a special pain in my—"

Jess cut her off with a quelling look.

"Do you want something to drink? Maybe an orange soda?" Maddie offered. Orange Crush was Jess's favorite and Maddie kept a supply on hand for when the older woman dropped by.

"You shouldn't wait on me," Jess protested.

Maddie'd learned a long time ago how to handle this. "I'm not waiting on you. I'm just offering because I need to refill my water."

"Well, if you're going to the kitchen, anyway, and you've got one to spare…" Jess leaned back in the chair and Maddie suspected Jess's arthritis was acting up again.

Leaving her resting, Maddie ducked across the hall into the

kitchen on the other side of the front door. Her carriage house, tucked onto the back of her father's estate, was tiny, but it was cozy and she'd made it her own.

She returned and gave Jess the drink. Sinking onto the love seat upholstered in a warm chocolate-brown, she offered a quick rundown of her racing faux pas and the apology flowers.

"He sounds precious," Jess said.

Maddie snorted. "*Precious* never came to mind."

"He's a hottie, isn't he?"

Maddie laughed to cover the flush that rolled through her. Tucker Macray wasn't exactly what she'd call a hottie…but those eyes. "What do you know about hotties, Jess?"

"Enough. I hear my granddaughters talking. Twyla goes crazy over your Macray."

"He's not *my* Macray." And it was sort of weird to think of Jess's fourteen-year-old granddaughter with a crush on Tucker Macray. Maddie'd witnessed the woman propositioning him after the photo shoot, but Twyla carrying a torch for him really brought home Macray's celebrity status. It was just plain weird because he was just an everyday guy—with bad hair and, she had to admit it, a sense of humor. Not every man had the ability to laugh at himself, especially not a guy associated with a macho sport like stock-car racing, but he'd definitely been poking fun at himself with that card.

"He's Sleep EZ's Macray." A thought occurred to her that diminished her pleasure in the flowers. "That's what this is all about. He wanted to make sure he didn't upset the money that keeps him going around that track."

Jess settled her glass on the end table and crossed her arms over her ample bosom. "I don't know that *I was a jerk* sounds like a corporate apology." Jess nodded toward the books stacked on the end table. NASCAR, NASCAR and more NASCAR. "Decided to do some homework?"

"Crash course, no pun intended." If only she'd skimmed the books before that initial meeting she would've known stock cars turned on with a toggle switch instead of a key. It would've saved her a boatload of embarrassment. Instead, she'd made a fool of herself in her first appearance. Good job. Screwed up first day on the job. It was useless to cry over spilt milk but she'd be prepared this weekend. "Better late than never."

"Your Tucker is favored to win the NASCAR Rookie of the Year."

Well, that was good, she guessed. Daddy had said he could drive like nobody's business. "How do you know that?" He definitely wasn't *her* Tucker, but she let it drop or Jess might begin to think that Maddie doth protest too much.

"Because if there's a NASCAR race on, our TV's tuned into it. Bart's a die-hard fan and Cissy's just as crazy about it as he is."

Jess had moved in with Bart and Cissy, her son and his wife, and their two girls after her husband had died in a hunting accident a few years ago.

You could've knocked Maddie over with a feather. Jess, who could double for Aunt Bee on *Andy Griffith,* watched NASCAR? "I just can't see you sitting down to watch a NASCAR NEXTEL race." She tossed out the question she'd been dying to ask someone. "Don't you think it's kind of…well, boring?"

Jess's blue eyes lit up. "Oh, no. Once you learn a little about the sport and the drivers and then watch one, it's anything but boring. You'll be on the edge of your seat. Cissy's worse than Bart." Her smile took a sheepish turn. "And I'm almost as bad."

Maddie'd had no idea Jess and her family were fans. And she'd bet her father was equally clueless. An idea bloomed in the back of her mind. "Have you ever asked Daddy for tickets?"

Jess looked as shocked as if Maddie had suggested Jess strip down to her underwear and climb into the hot tub attached to the pool. "Good gracious, no. I don't talk to Mr. Louis about stuff like that. He's got enough on his plate without an old woman asking him for race tickets."

Jess was always doing for everyone in the Felton household. Finally, Maddie could do something in return, and quite honestly, she'd managed to goof her first encounter and she was nervous about her first trackside appearance. It'd be nice to have a familiar, supportive face nearby. "If I got you, Cissy, Bart and the girls tickets to the race at…wait a minute and I'll find out where the next race is—" She had it on a sheet of paper somewhere.

"Bristol," Jess supplied without blinking. "It's in Tennessee this weekend."

"Yeah." Maddie snapped her fingers. "That's it. Bristol." Guess Jess did know her NASCAR. "If I got everyone tickets, would you come?"

"Honey, we don't belong at something like that with you. You're the corporate sponsor and I'm the housekeeper. It doesn't look right."

Maddie shook her head at the woman who was as close to a mother as she'd known since she was nine. Jess had talked her through boy troubles, mean-girl troubles, teen acne and everything in between. "That's the craziest thing I ever heard. You're family. You're all going to come, and tell Twyla she's going to meet Tucker Macray in person."

"Maddie—"

"Nope. My mind is made up." She crossed her arms over

her chest and shook her head. She could be stubborn and dig in her heels.

Jess relented with a laugh. "Okay. If you clear it with Mr. Louis."

"I know he won't mind." Maddie'd make sure he didn't. "So, you'll come?"

"If Bart doesn't have to work." Jess grinned, her excitement evident. "Twyla's gonna be beside herself."

Oh, boy. Another swooning female in action. Maddie supposed she'd better get used to it, because it looked as if it was standard for women from fourteen to who knew how old. "Tell her to prepare herself. His hair is even worse in person."

Jess dropped her a wink. "She likes his hair."

Go figure.

RACE DAY AT BRISTOL, Tennessee. Maddie quietly drew a deep breath to keep her nervousness at bay. This place was a madhouse. The excitement was nearly palpable and somewhat infectious. The noise level alone was incredible.

Announcers blasted over the loud speakers. Generators attached to motor homes and haulers hummed as a backdrop to the roar of 790-horsepower engines starting up—she'd done her homework—times forty-three vehicles amplified by the high walls of aluminum seating ringing the oval track. And then there was the sheer volume attached to more than 160,000 people thronging about—yes, it was a sold-out event. People milled about and the majority of them left her in no doubt as to their favorite driver because they wore shirts, jackets and caps, carried coozies and coolers, you name it— if it could be driver-branded they were either wearing it or carrying it.

She'd felt an unanticipated sense of pride at being part of

something bigger than herself when she'd seen strangers walk by sporting Tucker Macray and Sleep EZ paraphernalia.

Maddie brushed her hand over the side of her dark blue skirt. She'd had to invest in a wardrobe of coordinated dark-blue-and-yellow outfits. No way she could show up for a race day sporting anything except the Sleep EZ team colors. Not that shopping was a hardship.

She glanced around. Things had come a long way since her early arrival this morning when the Sleep EZ space, sectioned off in the long line of the white hospitality tents, had been nothing more than folding chairs and tables. Now Sleep EZ colors festooned the tent while a large, life-size photo of Sleep EZ's newest location hung as a backdrop across the entire back tent wall—all in place thanks to a crew under Maddie's direction. Yellow-and-blue-checkered cloths draped the round tables. A posy of fresh spring flowers in short, round glass vases graced the center of each table. A mix of upbeat pop music piped through speakers mounted in the corners of the tent topped off the fun atmosphere.

Sleep EZ customers, mostly families, and the Tennessee-area managers milled about. Registered guests had entered a draw when checking out after a stay at a Sleep EZ. Each week Sleep EZ drew tickets for a race and the opportunity to meet Tucker Macray on race day. And Jess and her family were here, as well, all decked out in Sleep EZ Macray T-shirts and hats. Everyone seemed to be having a good time, laughing and eating.

The caterer had done a nice job—chafing trays of wings, ranging from mild to nuclear, a veggie tray, a platter of cold boiled shrimp and a build-your-own hoagie station, complete with a cold cut/cheese bar. One of the biggest hits was the ice-cream sundae bar in the far corner. It'd been intended for the kids, but an equal number of adults seemed to enjoy it, as well.

Maddie'd made the rounds with all the guests, customers and employees alike, introducing herself and thanking them for coming to today's event. She had been nervous at first, but she genuinely liked people and everyone was thrilled to be here. She could guarantee that the folks here today would definitely be repeat Sleep EZ customers and encourage their friends and family to stay at a Sleep EZ, as well.

So far, so good. She hadn't goofed up anything…yet. Of course, the day was still young. Really young, in fact, considering the race wouldn't start until this afternoon.

"Hey, Maddie."

She turned. A man stood behind her. He was a little on the short side, only slightly taller than her, his dark brown hair cut short and neat, and he wore a pair of starched khakis and a Chalkey Racing Enterprises dress shirt. He looked vaguely familiar, but she couldn't quite place him. She tried faking it. "Hi. How are you?"

Disappointment and irritation flashed across his face. "You don't remember me, do you?"

Dang, this was embarrassing. She opted for honesty as the best policy. "I'm sorry, but I don't. You look familiar but I can't quite place you. Did we go to school together?"

"No. I'm Marcus. Marcus Chalkey."

Right. Duh. That explained the CRE shirt and his familiar face, except, in her defense, she'd only met him once, years ago. "Oh, yeah. It's been a long time. How've you been?"

"It's been six years. We ran into your family at Cape Hatteras when we were both on vacation. We all went to dinner together and you had a crab salad with key lime pie for dessert. I've been fine. And you?"

O-kay. Either Marcus had a much better memory than she did and was better prepared or he seriously needed to get a life if he could remember the exact when and where and what she ate. Now that she thought about it, after that dinner in Cape Hatteras Doug and Stevie had deemed Marcus a dweeb.

"I've been fine, too. So…are you looking forward to today's race?" It seemed like the thing to say when you were standing around at a race track and it had served her well all morning as a conversation point.

"Yes. We're definitely excited about tonight's race. We're expecting great things from Macray here at Bristol. Especially after his second-place showing last night in the NASCAR Busch Race." Marcus could've been repeating a sound bite he'd practiced in front of his mirror at home. In fact, she was pretty sure that was the case.

"Have you met Tuck yet?" he asked, sounding a little more normal or at least a little less like an advertising automaton.

"I met him last week at a photo shoot for our new print ad." The less said about that, the better. She wasn't big on proclaiming her ignorance. In fact, she was relieved to know that her key chain incident hadn't made the CRE circuit with her as the butt of the joke. But it obviously hadn't since Marcus didn't seem to know anything about it.

"Tuck's a good guy. We're friends. We hang out at the track together." Marcus put his hands in his pockets and puffed up with self-importance. "Even though we both have to remember I'm in charge—you know how awkward that can be with the hired help sometimes." He smiled as if they were royalty among lesser beings.

"Um," Maddie uttered noncommittally. How about Marcus Chalkey was a freak—a pompous freak, to boot?

"Yeah. My dad and I talked about me driving for the

team—" what, driving them all nuts? "—but we decided my strength was really in the managerial role."

Based on this two-minute conversation, Maddie had a sneaking suspicion that Dan Chalkey had parked Marcus with Team Three to let him think he was running the show. She bet he couldn't manage his way out of a wet paper bag. But it was her job to get along with Chalkey Racing, be it crewmembers, driver or owner.

And she wasn't much better. Daddy had essentially parked her here, probably thinking it was the least likely spot in the company for her to goof up. Maybe she and Marcus were operating out of the same wet paper bag. She pasted on a smile. "That's impressive. It's a big responsibility."

"Tell me. Here's Tuck now."

Maddie had positioned herself next to the flap of the hospitality tent so she could intercept Macray when he came in since it was her job to hostess the event. He joined them, his cowlick at that odd angle.

"Mornin'." His greeting included both Maddie and Marcus. Certainly there was no reason for the slow heat that wound through her at his hello and his easy smile.

Marcus clapped him on the back. "Tuck, ready for the big race?" It was just a flicker in his eyes but Maddie was 99.9 percent sure that Tucker Macray loathed being called Tuck. "I hear you've met Maddie. She and I go way back."

"Marcus's dad and my father are friends," Maddie said, explaining away Marcus's implication that she and he were something of an item. Not. Ever.

Tucker nodded. "Okay. How about I meet some fans and then go race?" Tucker said.

Great. She was busy trying to disassociate herself from freaky Marcus and here Tucker had to cue her to do her job.

She mustered a smile. "Sure."

Marcus, mercifully, excused himself to attend to "something important."

Half an hour later, despite herself, Maddie had to admit Macray impressed her. He'd afforded everyone he met his unstinting attention, really focusing on the conversation and seemingly pleased to meet each and every person. Jess had insisted her family be introduced last, after the obligations to "paying Sleep EZ customers" had been met. Fourteen-year-old Twyla had nearly swooned.

The announcer boomed over the loud speaker and the noise level in the tent seemed to have increased exponentially. Tucker said something to her as they walked toward the tent opening. Maddie didn't have a clue what it was other than she caught the word *Jess* and *yours*. She leaned in close to hear him. She wasn't sure what she'd expected, but Macray smelled good. Not good like her past boyfriends who were fond of designer fragrances. No, this good was the faint scent of soap and man. And he'd said something she hadn't caught. "I'm sorry. I couldn't hear you."

They stepped outside. Despite the sun's warmth, an April breeze still chilled the air. It was almost as loud out here.

"Jess is a friend of yours?" Tucker asked Maddie, leaning close to her ear, his breath warm against her skin. A shiver danced through her.

"Yes. She's a very good friend." Maddie spoke equally close to his ear and there was an intimacy to inhaling his scent on her indrawn breath that set her pulse fluttering.

Macray sent her a sharp, quizzing look.

"What?" Maddie said, noting that he'd missed a small spot below his right ear shaving. She knew he wasn't married, but didn't he have a girlfriend around to point that kind of thing out to him?

"She and her family seemed a little blue-collar to be a close friend," he continued at her indignant look. "I can say that because I've got blue-collar roots. I ran cable before I started driving full-time."

She didn't care what he did for a living before, it struck her wrong. She planted her hands on her hips and treated him to her most withering look. "They're fine people."

He remained decidedly unwithered. In fact, he bordered on amused. "Most blue-collars are. I'm just surprised you're friends with them."

Of all the... "Either you're a snob or you're implying I am."

He shrugged. "Neither. I'm just curious."

"Jess is our housekeeper. She has been for years. Since before my...for a really long time."

"Seems like a nice lady."

Well, that was better. "She's the best."

This was the first opportunity she'd had alone with him, and it was about to be over in about thirty seconds and she still owed him a thank-you. He might irritate the ever-living daylights out of her, but first her mother and then Jess had drilled good manners into her. "Thank you for the flowers. Not necessary but appreciated."

"So you got them?" Now it was his turn to look uncomfortable.

Would she thank him for them if she hadn't gotten them? Ha. It was nice to see *him* stick *his* foot in his mouth. She simply raised her eyebrows and a faint red crept up his face. "Yeah. I guess you did if you...well, okay. Glad you got them. I've got to go."

Having gained the upper hand, she felt almost magnanimous. Plus, winning was good for Sleep EZ. "Good luck, Macray," she called to his back as he walked away.

He had the outside pole position. Unfortunately, she didn't quite remember what that was, and she wasn't about to ask anyone except maybe Jess if she could catch her alone, but she was sure it was pretty good.

He turned around and waved, his Sleep EZ key ring in his hand, his equanimity obviously restored, his eyes alight with devilment. "Got my good-luck charm."

How could he irritate her one minute and have her laughing the next? And she should've known, flowers or not, that her mistake wouldn't die so easily. She opened her mouth to yell but caught herself just in time. Instead she drummed up the most pleasant smile she could muster. "Let's hope it works."

He laughed, obviously not in the least insulted, and turned back around. A cowlick stuck straight up in the back of his hair. Funny, even though he was sort of obnoxious and irritating, his hair was sort of growing on her.

CHAPTER FIVE

"WE JUST SERVED THE LAST of the turtle cheesecake squares, Ms. Felton," said Emma, the caterer for the suite.

"That's fine." The race was close to over, anyway. "You all did a great job! Thank you."

"It was a pleasure to work with you." Emma smiled and left through the service door.

Maddie stayed where she was, next to the counter that doubled as a drink and dessert bar in the Sleep EZ skybox, and slipped her right foot out of her shoe. Her feet were killing her. She flexed her toes. Oh, that felt good.

Note to self—sponsor hostess performing trackside required comfortable shoes since it was mostly time spent on her feet. She sucked it up and slid her foot back into her pump. She'd finished up in the hospitality tent and then moved to the suite, which overlooked the track.

They'd had nearly fifty people in the hospitality tent. Sleep EZ's skybox accommodated far fewer. Maddie, not being a sports enthusiast, had never been in any kind of skybox. This was much nicer than she'd expected. The back of the carpeted room contained a small L-shaped counter on one side and a cloth-draped buffet table opposite it. She'd been relieved, no pun intended, to discover private men's and ladies' restrooms. A counter with stools separated the serving area from the stadium seating, which consisted of upholstered chairs, reminiscent of a theater, overlooking the oval track. A television screen mounted in each front corner of the front glass wall offered a close-up of the action and the voice-over from the announcers.

She'd heard Macray's name, well, car number mostly, plenty of times today. Once or twice she'd even glanced at the television screen but was pulled away again by hostess duties.

The suite guests were mostly business affiliates rather than customers. Chad Mackenzie, the contractor handling Sleep EZ's Tennessee and western North Carolina renovations, sat in the front row with his wife and two small sons. Both the boys were beside themselves with excitement. Then there was Todd Thompson, the district director who handled the Tennessee operations, and his girlfriend, Mallory, a flight attendant.

And, of course, her brother Stevie had shown up. Ostensibly he was here to watch the race and also because he was in charge of the location renovations. And while that was true enough, she also knew he was here to check up on her and evaluate her job performance.

As if her thoughts had conjured him, he excused himself from the guy with the bright red hair he was sitting next to and headed her way. Chad Sweeney was the vice president of the regional material-supply company Sleep EZ contracted with for renovations and new construction in Tennessee and most of the Carolinas. Chad had left his wife and three children home, bringing his father instead to enjoy a day at the race track.

She was about to find out if she'd passed muster today.

"Nice job, kiddo," Stevie said, his eyes assessing her despite his light tone.

She smiled at the compliment. Stevie wasn't effusive in

handing out praise so she'd willingly take his *nice job.*
"Thanks. I think everything went well today."

Actually, she rather felt like basking in her job well done.
There'd been a few minor glitches, and she felt as if she'd run
her butt off all day trying to keep things organized, appear
calm and gracious and remember people's names at the same
time, but by George, she'd done it.

And she couldn't wait to zone out on her couch and soak
her feet, but she'd never tell her well-intentioned, but highly
overprotective, brothers or father. As ridiculous as it sounded,
her family snatching her off the job because her feet hurt
wasn't that far-fetched. Stranger things had happened.

She remembered all too well being a frustrated ten-year-
old in ballet class. She just couldn't get a particular sequence
of moves down. Daddy had yanked her out of class. Nothing
and no one was allowed to upset her apple cart.

"Have you seen any of the race?" Stevie asked.

"Not really. There hasn't been time." She'd wanted to make
sure everything was perfect and she certainly didn't want to
look as if she was neglecting her hostess duties.

"Cut yourself some slack." He grinned at her and seemed
to know what she was thinking. "Even the hostess gets to
watch a little of the race."

She laughed and it released a measure of the tension she'd
carried throughout the day. "Okay. Let's watch some racing."

Rather than go down the steps to where Stevie had sat with
Chad on the second row, they perched on two empty stools at
the eating bar.

The cars seemed to literally fly around the track. Macray
passed below her in second place, all of the cars moving at
what seemed to her an impossibly fast speed. Guess that's
why they called it racing, she silently chided herself. Okay,

so if she were honest she'd have to admit that she'd welcomed the distraction from the television screen earlier. Maybe she was a wuss but this seemed like a disaster waiting to happen. Maddie thought her heart might pound out of her chest.

The announcer's voice-over came through the speakers with the background noise of the cars hurtling along the track. "The Number 63 car is getting ready to make his move with twenty laps left. Coming out of Turn Three is about the only hope he has of taking the second spot from the Number 76 car. Macray's been holding him back, but he's running on old tires and the Number 63 car picked up two left fresh ones on that last pit stop." The announcer's voice took on a note that pitched the excitement further. "Can Macray fend him off?"

Could he? They came out of the incredibly tight turn. The other driver made his move. Maddie's breath caught in her throat. She wasn't even sure what happened. In the blink of an eye cars spun out of control, smoke obscured the track, the impact of car against car, car against wall, came through the sound system and Maddie thought she might hyperventilate right then and there. The bottom fell out of her stomach and she felt almost sick. Was Macray part of the wreck?

"Five…no! Six cars out. Danny Tomlinson in the Number 63 tried sending Sleep EZ's Macray to the wall. Tomlinson spins out and ends the chances for third, fourth, fifth and sixth spots for Ruger, Jacks and Mullins."

Maddie released her fists, unaware until that moment that she'd had them clenched so tightly she'd dug nail marks into her palms.

"Macray's still holding second place under the caution. That was some driving from a rookie just then. Hats off to the Number 76 car and a really tough break for the other guys."

The Sleep EZ skybox erupted into cheers, echoing the stand fans. Maddie found herself clapping along with everyone else, but stopped short of a woo-hoo.

"So, as soon as we come out from under the caution, we'll see if Lambert and Macray can hold on to the first and second spot."

"Tomlinson's car's off the track and he's being checked. Let's hear what the Number 63 crew chief, Ron Marcette, has to say."

Maddie zoned out Tomlinson's crew chief. Macray was okay. Not only was he okay, he was still in a good position. She wasn't sure whether she wanted to cheer or wring his neck. It was one thing to see all the drivers hurtling along the track, trying to outmaneuver one another, but when it looked as if he'd crashed she'd felt almost physically sick. Her concern encompassed all the drivers, but particularly Macray because she personally knew him. Was he crazy to do this week after week? Were they all crazy?

Her pulse galloped out of control.

"It looks worse than it is," Stevie said with a smile.

"I know. I've read about all the safety precautions and equipment. It's just different when you're actually seeing it happen."

He nodded. "Pretty exciting, isn't it?"

"Exciting. Terrifying." How had she ever thought it would be boring? Definitely not boring. "I think more terrifying than exciting since I'm a neophyte."

Stevie nodded and his laugh crinkled his eyes. "A couple of races from now it'll be all about the excitement. Who knows, you might even develop race fever," he teased her.

She hadn't wanted to work the NASCAR job and she remained convinced she'd be better suited to another position at Sleep EZ, but today hadn't been as awful as she expected. Fan enthusiasm had proved contagious, and she had a newfound respect for drivers and their teams. She might've gotten caught up in the action on the track, but race fever? She didn't think so.

This was her proving ground, her opportunity to show her family, and perhaps herself, that she was capable. That a measure of responsibility wouldn't cause her to crumble as it had her mother. Then, at the end of this racing season, when actions had spoken louder than words, she'd ask her father to transfer her to another role in the company. Bye-bye NASCAR NEXTEL Cup Series racing.

She grinned back at Stevie. "I'm sure I'll be a die-hard fan by the end of the season." Not.

"GOING TO GREEN NEXT LAP," Terry Snow, Tucker's spotter, said into the headset.

Tucker gripped the wheel and kept a cool head. Team Sleep EZ was a shoe-in for second place. Barring a natural disaster, which seemed unlikely at this point, or another move like Tomlinson's, the 76 team owned second place. And that was great, except he and Mike Snellings had talked through it via their headsets the last two caution laps and they didn't want second. They wanted first.

And he'd bet Lambert, who'd been holding first since his inside pole position start, fully expected Tucker to challenge him when they came out of caution, because that's exactly what Tucker would do if the situation was reversed. Tucker'd been running on the bottom all throughout the race. Lambert would expect Tucker to drop down and kick it in to pass.

"Show 'em what we've got." Snellings's voice came over the headset.

Tucker grinned. The green flag dropped. Tucker didn't

hesitate. Everything happened within seconds, but then in situations like this, everything seemed to slow down, as if he and the other cars moved in slow motion. A tremendous sense of calm and clarity filled him. What looked like split-second decisions on film were deliberate, considered actions. Foot to the gas, he ripped through the gears and shot high. He was even with Lambert. Turn approaching. He held tight and pushed the car as hard as it could handle coming out of the turn.

"Clear low," Terry, his spotter, instructed.

Tucker dropped to midtrack, sliding into first place, trapping Lambert behind him. Lambert wasn't giving it up without a fight.

"Left," Terry said.

Tucker had picked up fresh tires but held off on extra fuel, knowing he'd need every weight advantage if he was going to slip into first and keep it.

Seven laps to go.

"Number 53 on your right," Terry announced.

Where the hell had Randolph in the Number 53 car come from? It didn't really matter as long as he didn't get past Tucker. Did he have enough fuel to fight off both Randolph and Lambert?

Only one way to find out. Tucker moved up and Randolph dropped back. Lambert took advantage and pressed from behind. Tucker held the lead.

Six. Five. Four. Three. Two.

"Left," said Terry.

Lambert wanted it bad. So did Tucker.

Quarter lap. He inched out ahead of Lambert. Almost there. Done!

"We did it!" he shouted into his headset, his calm flying out the window with the wave of that checkered flag. In the stands the fans cheered wildly.

Adrenaline surged through him.

"That was a helluva race," Mike Snellings replied to him.

Hot damn! His first NASCAR NEXTEL Cup Series win and Maddie Felton with her golden eyes had been here to see it.

What the heck? Why had she popped into his head?

He realized she hadn't just popped into his head, she'd been hovering in the back of his mind, just outside his focus and concentration the entire race. Exactly where she had no business being. He firmly put her out of his mind.

Tucker smoked the tires and the crowd went even crazier.

"This one's for you guys. I'll meet you down front." He laid rubber and took his lap to Victory Lane.

Pandemonium greeted him before he even got out of the car. Cameras clicked, mike booms were shoved at him and he openly shared his elation with the world. He didn't think he could quit grinning even if he wanted to.

"How's it feel winning your first NASCAR NEXTEL Cup Series race? Especially after your second place last night?" the anchor, the same guy who'd dubbed him Bed Head Macray, asked.

He thought about saying it didn't suck, but decided that wasn't quite what he should broadcast around the world. "It's sweet. It would've been nice to pull a double but we'll take this today."

"So what brought today's victory?"

"It was definitely a case of everything being right. Our team did a great job having the car ready for this track and Mike made a good call on fuel during the last pit."

Tucker reached into his pocket and pulled out the key ring Maddie'd given him. "And the other deciding factor in today's race…I had my lucky race charm, compliments of Sleep EZ motels."

He dangled the key chain from his finger the same way he had that day he'd "practiced" when Maddie had given it to him. The anchorman chuckled. "Well, it worked like a charm today. I'm sure Sleep EZ's pretty happy with today's win."

"I hope so." Corporately they should be pleased, but what did she personally think of his win? Damn. Since when did it matter to him what Maddie Felton thought?

CHAPTER SIX

"SO, WHAT'D YOU THINK ABOUT our win on Sunday?" Kelsi Morris asked Maddie as she and half-a-dozen excited Sleep EZ customers were ushered through the lobby of Chalkey Racing Enterprises, CRE, for their corporate tour. The tour had been Maddie's brainchild. She'd discussed it with Kelsi, who'd cleared it with the executives.

Maddie wanted to do more than simply step into Stevie's empty spot as corporate sponsor liaison. She wanted to bring fresh new ideas to the job that would maximize Sleep EZ's corporate sponsorship of the Number 76 car. A CRE tour had felt like one step beyond the hospitality tent and skybox, and had been well received by both CRE and her father.

Maddie hung in the back with Kelsi while Marcus Chalkey and Sam Whitfield, head of CRE public relations and a twenty-year racing veteran, led the group.

"The race was…interesting," Maddie said. Which was the very sanitized version of her heart being stuck somewhere in her throat while those maniacs raced around the track so fast they sounded like a swarm of angry bees.

"Tucker was brilliant the way he avoided the wreck and then took first place," Kelsi said. Maddie couldn't particularly put her finger on any one thing, but she had an underlying impression Kelsi didn't especially like her. It was just a second sense, a prickle that ran down the back of her neck and maybe a faint note of censure in Kelsi's comment. Maybe Maddie's *interesting* comment hadn't been enthusiastic enough to suit Kelsi. Maddie let the matter drop.

They entered a large open area that struck Maddie as a cross between a racing tribute and a museum.

"Have you seen this before?" Kelsi asked.

"No. I've never visited the offices at all." Mainly because she hadn't even known CRE existed a month ago. She certainly hadn't expected anything so sophisticated as the glass-and-chrome spotlessness of CRE's corporate offices.

"You'll enjoy this. Sam does a great spiel."

They caught up with the rest of the group. Sam stood beside a full-sized race car. "We retired this car after Daytona last year. You can look through the windows to get a feel for what it's like to be a driver. You definitely have to be okay with tight spaces." He smiled, revealing a chipped front tooth. "Of course, it's all designed to optimize the driver's safety."

"Any chance we can sit in it?" asked a woman named Margaret Coolee. Margaret hailed from Aiken, South Carolina, and had shown up for the tour this morning decked out in Number 76 from head to toe—from the blue-and-yellow 76-imprinted ribbon around her ponytail to the licensed laces in her sneakers and everything in between.

Sam shook his head and smiled in apology. "I'm afraid not. Guests aren't allowed in the cars, but you can certainly put your head through the window. We do ask, however, that you don't take anything off or out of the car."

Why would someone take something off the car?

"You'd be surprised," Kelsi murmured beside her, obviously reading her expression.

Maddie hung back and waited until all the guests had taken a turn checking out the car's interior. She'd read her books and been at the track, of course, but hadn't actually seen a car up close.

Sam's explanation of the various safety features knotted her stomach. Maybe because rather than a nameless, faceless driver, Macray came to mind.

When he'd won last week, she wasn't sure whether she wanted to kiss him or shake him. Part of her joined in the excitement of his win, the other part of her remembered nearly hyperventilating when the cars had wrecked and she didn't know if he was involved.

Of course, she'd done neither. She'd seen him at a distance and then smiled for the camera when she was brought over for her five-second photo-op. Even with all the excitement of his win and the noise, her heart had thumped a little harder when she'd congratulated him on his win. What was it about Tucker Macray that elicited such passionate emotions in her?

She shook off her thoughts and stuck her head through the open driver's-side window. Mild claustrophobia gnawed at her. This wouldn't work for her at all. Talk about tight quarters.

Dual channels for the driver's legs ran from the seat to below the steering wheel. On the back of the seat a tethered brace accommodated the torso and neck. According to Sam, they were all designed to keep a driver in place in case of an accident in addition to the five-point harness, a neck brace and helmet. She couldn't imagine driving at high speeds, mere inches separating you from the next car, focused for hours on crossing that finish line first or the best position you could jockey into, all the while confined so completely in such a small space.

Maddie swallowed a lump of trepidation and straightened. She'd seen enough of the inside of a race car.

"Ready?" Kelsi asked.

Maddie nodded and they caught up with the rest of the group. They joined them at a soaring two-story wall that showcased CRE's current season drivers with larger-than-life photos and bios.

"Here you'll recognize CRE's drivers," Sam said. "And of course, the reason you're all here today—your favorite driver, Sleep EZ and CRE's Number 76, Tucker Macray."

Maddie's heart flip-flopped at the picture of Tucker sporting his easy smile and cowlick, his helmet casually tucked beneath one arm, his eyes seeming to smile into hers. Before she realized it, her mouth had curved into an answering smile. Idiot.

Self-consciously, she looked away, feeling awkward at her response to a picture on a wall. Maddie surmised a gleam of speculation and naked dislike on Kelsi's face as the other woman studied her. Maddie quickly glanced away, but she knew what she'd seen. There wasn't a woman alive who wouldn't recognize that territorial no-trespassing look. It definitely explained the vibes she'd gotten from Kelsi earlier. And maybe for a second there she'd lost her mind and smiled back at Tucker Macray's photo, but Kelsi was way off the mark.

Luckily, Sam chose that moment to usher everyone forward. "Now we'll head over to the garage where the magic really happens." They exited the building into a rear parking lot toward a large building on the other side of the pavement.

"So, this must be a pretty cool job?" Maddie said, determined to win Kelsi over...or at least find out if the other woman did, in fact, have a thing for Macray.

"It is."

No one would accuse Kelsi of being a chatterbox, that was for sure. "Must be hard to date anyone seriously with your schedule."

"My schedule's not bad, and actually, I'm surrounded by lots of single men in this business." Kelsi looked at her as if she were a moron.

Maddie was good at giving people what they expected from her. She played the simpleton. "Anyone special?"

"I'm working on it. I think he's about to come around."

Hmm. That didn't really tell her anything, but her gut told her the other woman was talking about Macray.

"You're gorgeous." Maddie wasn't above throwing out some flattery. And, anyway, it was only the truth. "It's hard to imagine anyone wouldn't be interested in you."

Kelsi preened a bit. "Well, he pretty much has his choice of whatever woman he wants. Sometimes men need a little help seeing what's right in front of them. But I have no doubt he'll come around."

"Good luck."

"Thanks. I plan to get my man."

Okey-dokey. She'd bet her classic Chanel suit that Kelsi had set her sights on Macray. And it was none of Maddie's business. Nope, her business was to get along with everyone and do her job. Message received.

They moved as a group into a large building with a lobby, a reception area and a locked door with a scanner next to it. Sam checked in with the receptionist, scanned his credentials card and they gained entry into the garage.

Wow. Noise and activity buzzed throughout the room, which was actually the size of a warehouse, yet everything seemed organized and it was all immaculately clean. All the guys wore work uniforms with their names emblazoned on their shirt-front, and after a brief glance in the group's direction, they were all busy and seemingly engrossed in what they were doing.

Sam led them through explaining how each team worked

on a different component or aspect of the car, fielding questions as they moved through. One group cut sheet metal to body part specs, another group welded chassis components. Then there was the area where it was all assembled, as well as a decaling site.

As they moved into a different section of the building that housed the paint shop, Sam explained that the motors were built off-site and "imported" for each car.

They passed an area with a mock car and a camera mounted overhead. "This is where the pit teams practice daily. Each practice is filmed, then each film reviewed for where the team can perform more efficiently. A tenth of a second can make a huge difference in winning or losing a race."

Even with the "homework" she'd done, Maddie hadn't realized just how much work and precision went into getting a car on the track. She mentally winced when she remembered her comment to her father and brothers about cars going really fast around the track.

They were just entering the final section of the building when Tucker Macray joined them. Maddie, through Kelsi, had arranged for Tucker to be a participating part of the last leg of the tour.

He joined them as they were heading into the building housing the car he'd be driving in Martinsville in an upcoming race. For a brief moment his gaze snared hers and Maddie felt a connection as strongly as if a minor jolt of electricity had passed through her.

There was something wrong when a three-second glance left her breathless.

Maddie had arranged for a photographer to snap photos of the Sleep EZ customers throughout their garage tour. Now Marcus marshaled them all together. "Photo-op."

He took Maddie by the shoulders. "Here you go. Sleep EZ needs to be front and center." He plucked her day planner from her hands. "Let's just put this over here till we finish with the pictures."

He slid in beside her and Maddie forced herself not to move away from his hand in the small of her back. Poor Marcus. He was just such a dweeb. He was even carrying a briefcase on the garage tour, as if to prove he was the boss and someone important. A dweeb with a lot of money, but a dweeb nonetheless. There were certain things that money couldn't buy in life, like eyes that could pierce you and leave you feeling more alive than you'd ever felt in your life.

It was subtle, but she didn't miss the hint of speculation in Macray's eyes as he noted Marcus next to her. No! No way. Not in this lifetime, she wanted to shout, but she could hardly go there. Instead, she plastered on a smile for the camera, but she would set Tucker Macray straight on the Marcus Chalkey front at the next opportunity. Let Kelsi think whatever she wanted.

After the photos, both group and individual, Tucker took the floor. His passion for the sport spread among the group as he talked them through the car and then showed off his helmet, uniform, gloves and pointed out the microphone in his helmet that allowed him to stay in constant contact with his crew chief and his spotter.

"And what happens if you can't make contact with your spotter?" Margaret asked.

"That's a serious problem. At that point I'm driving half blind because, while I can see what's ahead of me and in the front half beside me, I have no idea who's on my rear or back quarter panels. It's not just dangerous for me, it's dangerous for the other drivers, as well, so you can see the spotter's crucial. He's the guy who tells me where I can go and when I can go. He's sort of driving remote control."

Tucker's answer surprised her. He had a captive audience all ready, willing and definitely well on their way to worshipping at his feet, yet he'd downplayed his role in the driving equation.

They finished up and headed for the final lap of the tour, a walk through Macray's hauler. Halfway across the pavement Marcus dropped back to where Maddie was bringing up the rear.

"What time do you have penciled in for the meet-'n'-greet in Talladega?" he asked.

That was four weeks away and she honestly couldn't remember. "Let me check…" With a start, she realized she'd left her day planner. Actually, it was Marcus who'd whisked it out of her hands and put it aside, but the last thing she wanted was him to offer to accompany her to retrieve it. She definitely wasn't looking for alone time with Marcus. "I left my day planner behind. Go ahead and I'll catch up with the group in a minute."

She turned on her heel and retraced her steps. This section of the building was empty now that their group had left. The murmur of male voices drifted from another area, but she didn't see anyone.

Her heels echoed on the concrete floor and a creepy feeling slithered down her spine. Where the heck was her day planner? Where had Marcus put it? There, on a tool chest. She snatched it up and practically ran out of the building.

She stepped out into the sunshine, relieved to be out of the garage. She crossed the pavement to the hauler. Marcus stood outside the rear door, his back to her, deep in conversation on his cell phone.

"I'm not sure who you think you're dealing with on this," he said. He glanced over his shoulder, obviously hearing her approach, and then turned his back to her again, just as obviously dismissing her.

"You need to take care of this immediately," he continued. He wasn't exactly shouting, but it was close. "Today, if you don't want to lose our business."

Now was apparently not a good time to look up and give Marcus the Talladega info. Maddie opened the rear hauler door and slipped inside. She closed the door behind her.

Lots and lots of shiny, spotless chrome.

The back was a narrow chrome-floored aisle flanked by lockers and drawers. It was all spotlessly clean and well organized, considering the labels fronting each drawer.

The group was at the other end of the hauler. She walked up the aisle. The passageway bottlenecked and then opened into a fairly large room. However, it was tight quarters with a dozen people inside.

In the crush she wound up between the wall and Macray. One of the tour guests, Travis Baumgarten from Topeka, a middle-aged salesman with a hearty smile, edged past her, sandwiching her between the unyielding hauler wall and the hard planes and heat of Tucker Macray—and his scent and those eyes....

"We were wondering where you were, Ms. Felton," Macray said, so close she noticed distinctive flecks of green in his hazel eyes.

"I...uh...forgot my..." How the heck was she supposed to think when they were in such close proximity? What was the question? "Oh, yeah...my day planner. I left it in the garage and had to...uh, go back and get it."

For what felt like forever but was only a few seconds, Maddie absorbed his heat, his energy, the bone-melting force of his gaze up close. Macray shifted and Maddie managed to breathe again. "You don't want to throw a party in here. These are some tight quarters," she said to the group at large. She even managed a seminormal, light laugh.

Everyone laughed along with her. Maddie surreptitiously glanced around for Kelsi, looking for the other woman because they'd been tour partners thus far. The leggy blonde wasn't there.

Sam, the PR head, grinned. "Definitely not party central, but some of the guys call it Command Central or the War Room. It offers a place to retreat and relax when they're waiting on the car or the race at the track. They can come here to relax or to strategize or discuss the car."

Tucker nodded. "Definitely. It becomes our home away from the motor home."

"So, what do you like to do in your downtime at the track? Computer games, TV, tai bo?" Margaret asked. She had also inquired about the spotter.

Good question. What did Macray do when he wasn't doing the car thing or playing spokesperson for Sleep EZ?

He braced one hand against the doorjamb and Maddie noticed a small scar on his little finger. "I don't talk about it much because the other guys give me a hard time, but I love to knit while listening to classical music."

Knitting to classical music? You could've heard a pin drop in the silence that followed the pronouncement. Not that there was anything wrong with either one. She just hadn't thought that Macray... Wow, apparently neither did his fans.

Travis, the Topeka salesman, cleared his throat. "Really?"

Macray's eyes danced with humor. "No. But I had everyone going, didn't I?"

Maddie bit back a giggle and the whole group laughed, as if relieved that their favorite driver wasn't knitting sweaters or booties in his spare time. The look on everyone's face had been priceless—the knitting NASCAR driver.

Tucker grinned. "Seriously, when I have some downtime, my two favorite things outside of being under the hood of a car are fishing and reading."

"I'm a librarian," said Jane, a tall woman sporting short bobbed hair and round glasses. She'd been quiet the entire tour, but now the mention of books seemed to break through her reserve. "What do you like to read?"

Who'd have figured a librarian as a NASCAR fan? But Maddie was quickly learning, racing aficionados came in every shape, size and background.

"I read a variety of magazines, but I really like a good mystery and political thrillers." He named the book he was currently reading.

Maddie piped up without thinking about it. "I read that last month."

Tucker wore the same surprise the group had when he'd announced he knitted. What? Did she come across as illiterate? "Did you like it?"

"Yeah, except…wait, I can't say or it'll give the book away." She ought to just for that stunned look that she'd read his book.

"Don't."

Darn it. He had the most disarming smile. Sort of left a woman feeing all soft and gooey inside. And it was impossible to stay annoyed with him when he smiled like that.

Jane shot her a reprimanding look. "You can't give away the ending."

Maddie laughed. "I won't."

They wrapped up the hauler portion of the tour. When they exited the trailer, Marcus was at the rear, still on his phone. He ended his conversation and flipped his cell phone closed.

"Did you get the time?" he asked Maddie.

She relayed the information to him. "I would've told you earlier but you were on the phone."

"I'm busy."

Sheesh. Not only was he a dweeb, he was a dweeb with attitude.

TUCKER SHOOK HANDS WITH all of the guests outside the hauler. This was where he got off of the CRE tour.

"It was a pleasure to meet you," he said to the last one, the librarian. Tucker had truly enjoyed meeting them all. For the most part, fans were nice people and he enjoyed meeting people who shared his love of racing.

Sam led the group across the pavement, back toward CRE's corporate headquarters. Tucker watched for a minute or so until he realized he wasn't watching *the group,* but Maddie Felton. The sun glinted in her cinnamon hair, picking out sparks of deeper red.

He shook his head. He had lots to do other than stand around watching Maddie.

Just because Maddie had read the same book he had. Just because for one dangerous second when he'd been looking into her eyes, with her sweet scent wrapped around him, he'd nearly forgotten the other people milling around in the hauler. For one moment of nearly crushing lunacy he'd been tempted to steal a kiss, to just brush his mouth over the fullness of her lips, to sift her cinnamon hair through his fingertips and see if it felt as silky as it looked.

Nope, that was all best forgotten. Anyway, Maddie Felton and Marcus Chalkey seemed a likely item. They'd stood together during the garage photos earlier today. It would make sense—about the same age, similar backgrounds, their fathers were friends. It made beautiful, logical sense. And what the hell difference did it make to him? Why did he feel like breaking something at the thought of Marcus's arm around Maddie's waist? Why did some crazy territorial feeling kick in at the thought of Marcus nuzzling the tempting curve of her neck? A better question was why was he wasting brain cells speculating on Ms. Felton and Mr. Chalkey?

He shook his head to clear it and headed back to the garage. The reasons Maddie Felton was off limits could damn near fill a book. First and foremost, racing was his passion but it was also his business, and Maddie—and more important her father—were major parts of that business equation. The Chalkeys were another major part of the equation. That aside, Maddie hailed from one side of the tracks and he was definitely from the other. She could also be a tiny tyrant when the mood suited her. She was a spoiled, rich daddy's girl. He needed his head examined because sometimes when he looked at her he thought he glimpsed a vulnerability. By all accounts her father and two brothers were overprotective, so the notion that she needed someone to look out for her was ridiculous.

He damn near ran over Mike Snellings outside the garage door.

"Whoa. Easy," Mike said.

He'd walked right into Mike because he was so busy burning up brain cells speculating about Maddie. He'd known she was trouble. Now she was distracting him on the job.

"Sorry."

"Was the garage tour that bad?" Mike teased.

"Nah, it was fine."

"Hey, the guys made some adjustments earlier today."

Tucker and Mike walked over to the car. Even though it

was black on black, Tucker spotted it immediately. He knew his car like the back of his hand so anything that didn't fit stuck out like a sore spot. He leaned in the window and picked a dead rose off of the seat.

"What the hell?" Mike said.

He twirled it between his thumb and forefinger. "It appears to be a dead flower."

"Yeah, I got that part. Where'd it come from?"

"No idea." Tucker thought hard for a moment. "It wasn't here earlier when the tour group came through. I would've noticed."

"Looks like one of your fans has a weird sense of humor."

"None of the people that came through this morning could've left it because I was with them the entire time they were in here and afterward, as well." Except Maddie Felton. Maddie had shown up late to the hauler. And she'd told him she came back to the garage.

Crap! He'd been busy thinking he'd like to kiss her and she'd been busy pulling this prank.

"What?" Mike said. "You've got a funny look on your face."

"I think I figured it out." He filled Mike in on sending the flowers and then Maddie's subsequent return to the garage earlier today.

A frown bisected Mike's forehead. "I'm sure she didn't mean it maliciously, but she doesn't understand how superstitious race teams are. You want me to talk to Mr. Chalkey about it?"

Part of him was disappointed she'd done something so childish. He'd like to ignore it, not even give her the satisfaction of acknowledging it, but Mike was right, the team didn't need this. However, Tucker really didn't want to bring it up to Mr. Chalkey.

"I don't see the need to involve Mr. Chalkey." He headed toward the garage door, reaching for his cell phone. "I'll handle it. I'll be back in a while," he tossed over his shoulder to Mike.

He called the CRE main receptionist. "Margo."

"Yes, Mr. Macray?"

He still winced every time he heard that. "Mr. Macray" sounded like his old man.

He took a deep breath and tamped back his anger. He felt like a total fool that he'd ever given Maddie Felton the benefit of the doubt, but this was a business situation and he'd handle it in a business manner. "Is Ms. Felton still in the building?"

"She's right here."

"Would you ask her to wait a minute? I'm on my way over. I need to discuss something with her."

"Certainly."

Before he'd ever met her, he'd pegged her for a spoiled rich girl who knew nothing about racing. She hadn't done much to indicate otherwise when he first met her. Then he'd seen her hostessing at the track, seen the way she'd defended her housekeeper when she thought Tucker was maligning the woman's status and he'd begun to think he might've misjudged her.

He looked down at the black, crumbling rose. Apparently not.

CHAPTER SEVEN

"I'LL SEND HIM IN WHEN he gets here, Ms. Felton. Can I get you something to drink while you wait?" Margo ushered her into a small conference room with floor-to-ceiling windows that overlooked the CRE "campus."

"No thanks. I'm fine."

Margo closed the door. Maddie bypassed the round, glass-topped table and its four chairs, electing to vent her nervous energy by pacing.

Why did Macray want a private audience with her? Today's tour had gone extremely well. Maybe he wanted to tell her he was pleased to be working with her. Maybe he wanted to discuss an upcoming event. Or perhaps he wanted to ask her how the book she'd read last month ended. Maddie couldn't contain her smile. No way she was telling him. He'd just have to read it for himself.

He rounded the corner of the garage building and she watched him cross the parking lot. A light wind ruffled his hair—not that it made any difference because his hair was a mess in general. His stride wasn't arrogant. Instead he moved with a surety of purpose. In her book that was an important distinction.

He entered the building and she smoothed her hair in a sudden onslaught of self-consciousness. Maybe she wasn't the only one that had felt something pass between them in the hauler, despite the other people present. Her heart beat faster as she simply thought about his nearness, the brush of his arm against her shoulder, the faint feathering of his breath against her hair.

The door opened and Macray stepped inside, closing it softly behind him.

Her breath stuck in her throat and the room seemed to shrink to a cozy intimacy. "Margo said you wanted to see me?" Maddie said to break the silence and because she had only been alone with him within the confines of a crowd and now a sudden nervousness engulfed her.

Macray crossed the room, an affable smile on his face, but a glint in his eyes belied the curl of his lip. Maddie knew in that moment what made him a formidable opponent on the track.

"I wanted to return something." He pulled a crumpled dead flower from his pocket and held it out. "You misplaced this."

O-kay. He had a sort of twisted sense of humor and he'd definitely got her with the knitting joke earlier, but he didn't appear to be joking at all. In fact, it felt rather awkward.

She tried to laugh it off. "I'm not sure where you got that, but it's not mine."

He didn't laugh back. "This was left in the seat of my car. I know it wasn't there when the tour left the garage because I double-checked to make sure nothing was switched on." He shrugged, and the blue polo shirt with the CRE logo clung to the rise and fall of his shoulders. "You went back, you were the only one alone with the car, and then this shows up."

Two black petals drifted to the floor, dark, accusatory spots on the otherwise pristine beige carpet.

What? "You think I left *that*—" she nodded toward the crumbling black flower in his hand "—in your race car?" She shook her head. "Why would I do that?"

"I'm guessing it was a joke, but race teams can be superstitious."

He was serious. His accusation stung as if he'd slapped her. If she had left the flower—and she most assuredly hadn't—it would've been an incredibly childish move. Did he really think she was so immature and unprofessional? Obviously he did.

She straightened her spine and stared him dead in the eye. "I didn't do that." She was proud of how dignified and calm she sounded.

"You really didn't?"

Wasn't that what she'd just said? She lifted her head a fraction higher and hoped he didn't miss the chill in her tone. "I really didn't."

"But if you didn't…it just fit…the flower after I sent you flowers…and no one else was there…" he puzzled aloud, a perplexed frown knitting his dark brows.

Maddie gripped the back of the upholstered chair, her temper beginning to simmer. "I don't know what to tell you other than I would never jeopardize my job by doing something like that," Maddie said, winning her struggle to stay calm instead of yelling at him. He wasn't quite quick enough to hide a flash of skepticism. "What? You think because I work for my father it wouldn't really matter? You have no idea how important this job is to me. I'd never risk it for a practical joke."

Speculation gleamed in his hazel eyes. Great. Her temper had led her to say more than she'd meant to. This job's importance to her was none of Macray's business.

She relinquished her grip on the chair.

"I apologize, then," he said, something else replacing the speculative look. It took her a moment to realize it was respect and admiration. She'd been on the receiving end of looks that coddled, indulged, loved and protected, but she'd never been the recipient of respect and admiration. It went a long way to assuage the earlier sting of his accusation.

"Apology accepted. Let me know if you figure out who did it because I agree, the timing is weird." It hovered on the tip of her tongue to say that it was almost as if someone wanted Macray to think Maddie had left the flower there. However, she withheld comment because she didn't want to be labeled paranoid. But then again, there was more than one way to convey an idea. "Under the circumstances I would've thought the same thing." Maybe because someone wanted him to think that very thing.

He ran his hand through his hair. His smile struck her as both rueful and sincere, a disarmingly potent combination. She also thought, rather inanely, that his eyes were more green with brown flecks than the other way around. Before she got too weak at the knees, she reminded herself that Macray put on a race face the same as she'd always played to her own audience.

"Thanks," he said. "I kind of feel like a jerk."

"No harm done." So, it had hurt her feelings a tad that he'd think she would do something like that. She'd get over it. She was already over it. "But I'd be interested if you figure it out." She stepped around him and walked to the door. Maddie paused when a detail popped into her head. She turned to face Macray. "It may not mean anything, but Kelsi wasn't with the group when I joined you in the hauler."

He rubbed his finger over his forehead as if warding off a headache. "I hadn't thought about it, but she wasn't, was she?"

Considering the nasty look Maddie had intercepted from Kelsi, a purely feminine part of Maddie delighted in the fact that he hadn't noticed the other woman's absence. "No, she wasn't. I specifically looked for her when I rejoined the group because I'd sort of partnered up with her for the tour."

"But why would Kelsi do that?"

Maddie was sure his question was more a matter of him thinking aloud than actually asking, but she tossed his own explanation back at him. "Probably a joke."

Macray shook his head. "I don't think Kelsi has much of a sense of humor."

Maddie wasn't so sure that Kelsi was going to snag Macray anytime soon. Of course, a lot of men didn't care about a sense of humor when a woman looked like Kelsi. And it was absolutely none of her business.

"I don't know her that well. But I'd be interested if you find out who it was."

"Sure, I'll let you know."

Maddie closed the door behind her, leaving Macray in the room to puzzle it out. She offered Margo a distracted goodbye on her way out the door.

She couldn't shake a gut feeling that someone wanted to cause trouble for her in this position. She crossed the parking lot, unlocked her car and got in. She sat there for a moment, her hands on the steering wheel, a queasy feeling in the pit of her stomach.

She didn't know what to think. About anything. The whole thing with the flower was weird. The idea that someone was sabotaging her on the job was crazy—and given her mother's history, Maddie didn't use that word lightly—but she couldn't shake the feeling.

Then there was this "thing" with Macray. Every stinking time he was around, her heart beat faster and a breathlessness stole through her. She even had some crazy—there was that word again—notion that there was a connection, a sizzle between them, which made no sense.

He wasn't her type. She couldn't say precisely what her

type was, but she knew it wasn't a race-car driver. So what if they'd read the same book. She couldn't imagine that they'd have a thing in common...except that spark that shot through her whenever he was around.

Maybe she was cracking up. Maybe her father and brothers had been right all along. She shoved aside the idea. She was not like her mother. She was not and would not crack under the pressure of a real job.

She clicked her seat belt in place and cranked her car. She'd prove it to them. She'd prove it to herself.

THAT EVENING, TUCKER WALKED into his house and tossed his truck keys onto the kitchen table. Napoleon darted in before the back door closed and danced circles around him. He scooped Napoleon up and scratched the dog beneath his chin.

"How was your day? Mine turned out sort of crappy." Napoleon licked Tucker. Tucker laughed. "Hey, at least one of us had a good one. Now, if you figure out who left that flower on my seat, let me know, huh?"

His concentration this afternoon had been shot to hell all because of that stupid flower. He'd learned his lesson with Maddie. Instead of charging in and accusing anyone, he'd sort of chatted around and it hadn't gotten him anywhere. No one had seen anyone coming or going. When he'd mentioned to Kelsi that she'd missed the hauler portion of the tour, the blonde had told him she'd had a phone interview to set up with a radio station and been extremely flattered that he'd noticed her absence. Encouraging Kelsi wasn't a desired outcome.

It was only a dead flower and he ought to just let it go, but he wasn't made that way. That's why he read mysteries, because they were solved and resolved in the end. The *who* and the *why* behind the dead flower would drive him nuts until he figured it out. It was one of his idiosyncrasies that had driven Darlene crazy about him. Tucker couldn't stand a loose end or an unsolved puzzle.

Napoleon wiggled and Tucker put him down. Tucker snagged a ginger ale and tossed a frozen burrito into the microwave. He poured a serving of dog food into Napoleon's bowl and then cracked a raw egg over it. Napoleon didn't warrant a bad day just because Tucker was out of sorts.

The little dog gobbled his dinner.

The microwave dinged and Tucker settled at the table with his burrito. He tried to lose himself in his book while he ate but he finally gave it up, closing the book and tossing half his burrito into the garbage.

He turned off the kitchen light and wandered down the hall to the den. Napoleon followed, his nails a familiar click against the scarred hardwood floors. Tucker stretched out on the couch and grabbed the remote. Napoleon curled up next to him, offering a satisfied sigh when Tucker clicked on the TV.

Tucker smiled, same as he did every time he turned on the television. Sixty-inch LCD flat-panel HD TV. Yeah, baby. The whole house might desperately need a remodel but he'd bought the TV as soon as he had a place to put it. Not too shabby for a poor boy who'd grown up with the electricity cut off half the time because his parents had used the power-bill money to get drunk or stoned.

He channel-surfed till he found the show where they built custom bikes. Five minutes later he was channel-surfing again. Okay, the truth of the matter was the dead flower was bugging him, but Maddie Felton was the real distraction.

She was an enigma, a puzzle, a mystery. He'd pegged her as a spoiled rich girl before he ever met her, but every time he was around her he realized Maddie's puzzle had many more pieces than he'd first thought.

He knew his ability to compartmentalize, the ability to put everything else aside and focus on the task at hand, made him a good driver. If it was hot in the car, he mentally tuned it out. If another driver pissed him off, he shut down the emotion and focused on the race. He had dear old dad to thank for that particular ability. When he was getting the hell beat out of him, he'd developed the ability to shut off the emotions, remove himself from the pain and focus on something else. But dammit, Maddie refused to be compartmentalized. She refused to go away. Instead, she danced in and out of his head. He wasn't even sure that he particularly liked her, and it shouldn't matter whether he liked her or not as long as they both did their jobs. But he was drawn to her and she refused to leave his head. He'd carried her with him all afternoon, like a relentless refrain that played through his senses. Her scent, the glint of sunlight in her hair, the golden whiskey of her eyes, the brush of her body against his in the hauler, the curve of her lips, the melody of her voice. Try as he might to shut her out, she lingered in his head, refusing to be tuned out. And now could he even enjoy his sixty-inch HD TV? Hell, no, because Maddie Felton was an even bigger mystery than the dead flower.

And Tucker always had to figure out a mystery.

"WOW. I'M AMAZED. YOU HAVEN'T screwed up the NASCAR gig yet," Doug teased Maddie across the conference table. Doug, Stevie and her dad met weekly to review the business, the past week and the upcoming week. Now she was a part of those meetings, as well.

His tone teased but his words hurt. She realized that Doug

did that often—made teasing comments that held barbs, that undermined her competency. She doubted he even realized it. But the important thing was that she was aware of it. She recalled the look of admiration and respect Macray had sent her way yesterday and it bolstered her resolve. Doug could only treat her like his incapable little sister if she allowed him to. And she wasn't playing that part.

"No disasters thus far," she said, interjecting a cool note in her tone, something she'd never done before with Doug. This was business.

Doug slanted her a look but Stevie interceded. "Maddie did a damn fine job at the Bristol race. I was impressed," he said…and then ruined it by reaching over and patting her on the head as if she was a pet poodle who'd performed a new trick. Would they ever let her grow up, see her as a responsible human being instead of a fragile hothouse flower?

Patience. She drew a deep breath. "That's nice to hear. I thought it went well."

Daddy shot her a speculative look. "How'd the CRE tour go?"

"Great." Technically the tour had. Customers were happy. It was just the post-tour part when things had slid downhill. She'd cut out her tongue before she'd breathe a word about that. She hadn't left the flower and certainly there was no reason to pass along that Macray thought she might pull that kind of stunt.

"We've had lots of positive feedback on Macray pulling out the Sleep EZ key chain after his Bristol win. That was a great idea to give him that key chain, Maddie," her father complimented her, which was nice, but he looked surprised, as if he hadn't expected that out of her.

Macray had pulled out his key chain on TV and everyone had loved it. No one in this room had to know that she'd been sincere rather than tongue-in-cheek when she gave it to him.

"Thanks. It seems to be a big hit. Sharon said there's been a run on them and we've had to reorder."

Stevie spoke up. "Customers are going crazy for them. I've put in a rush order."

"We can have Macray autograph the back of the key chain with a permanent marker," Maddie suggested. As it stood, Macray currently autographed whatever fans brought in or a stat picture. "Then fans could carry his autograph around all the time."

"That's a damn good idea, little sister," Doug said from the other side of the table. "You're starting to scare me. And here I thought you only knew how to shop."

Because that's what he and Stevie and Daddy had wanted to think. Spending her days shopping was safe. That's where they'd wanted her and that's where she'd gone. And she could get angry with Doug or she could let his comments roll off her back. She laughed, "I might be capable of a little more."

This was the opening she'd been waiting on. She jumped in with both feet. "I actually have a few ideas I'd like to throw out to maximize our exposure with our NASCAR NEXTEL Cup Series sponsorship." She didn't give anyone the opportunity to object, although she was pretty sure from the looks on their faces, she'd caught them by surprise, perhaps even rendered them speechless. If it weren't so insulting it'd be funny. Well, it was actually pretty funny regardless. She swallowed a laugh as she pulled out and passed around three copies of her proposal.

"My first suggestion is that we create a NASCAR presence in the lobby of each of our locations." She had their attention. "As it stands, we have a small box at the registration desk with a small sign. I'd like to see us come in with a display easel or, in the smaller operations, a wall unit. We have photographs of our customers at all of our events, anyway. We obtain waivers when we're issuing the tickets or passes. Each week I can have Tamara—" her assistant was worth her weight in gold "—e-mail all our locations with photos of Sleep EZ customers from the weekend race or an autographing at a store location or a special event like the CRE tour. It's my understanding that all of our locations have color printers. Tamara e-mails a mock layout and the photos. Each location prints them and displays them in the lobby. It offers exposure and should generate a lot of interest for a minimal investment. You'll find the numbers on the cost of putting display boards in all of our units on the second page. I think you'll agree that the exposure benefit offsets the investment. And it also fits in with the moderate, family-oriented image we project on-site and in our advertising."

"When would you implement this?" her father asked, obviously impressed.

"We have the money in the budget. I'd suggest right away. The manufacturer could ship first of next week. We could have the promotion operational in a week and a half, tops."

Her father glanced around the table. "Doug? Stevie? What do you think?"

"I like it. Good idea, Maddie," Stevie said.

Doug rolled a pencil between two fingers. She'd known Doug would be the harder sell. "I think it has merit. It definitely has merit. It's not a huge investment, but—" Maddie had fully anticipated a *but* from Doug "—I'd suggest we test it in a couple of locations in each state to get feedback on customer response and implementation."

"PR's hard to measure," Maddie stated. "How will you decide whether it warrants a total location rollout? And how long do you think is a reasonable test period?"

She could've announced she'd been snatched by aliens and returned after a trip to their planet and she was pretty sure it would've elicited the same stunned expressions.

Her father recovered first. He shot her a piercing look, nodded and directed his attention to Doug. "She has a point. It's not easily measured like a registration software beta test." He glanced down at the figures she'd supplied. "And it's not a costly investment. Let's move forward on it."

Maddie wanted to leap from her chair, whoop and punch her fist in the air—all of which would wipe out the impression she'd just made. Instead, she allowed herself a small smile. "Thank you. I'll work with Tamara on implementing it right away." The men all looked as if they were ready to move on, so she plowed forward. "I'd also like to see us introduce a program where we offer a ten percent discount to any guest who presents a NASCAR ticket stub at check-in or checkout. Sort of a race car fan rebate. Page three gives the break-even/profit analysis."

Stevie spoke up. "I see you don't have Macray slotted to promote this."

"No. It shouldn't be specific to our sponsored car number. We want to be identified as welcoming all NASCAR fans. We may sponsor the Number 76 car—" hey, she was beginning to pick up the lingo "—but we want to be known as the NASCAR lodging choice."

They discussed some of the particulars before ultimately deciding to run with both of Maddie's recommendations.

"Anything else?" her father asked her.

"Just one more thing."

Her father raised his brows in question.

"I've scheduled myself for a garage-tour race morning before the Phoenix race. I'd like to look into setting up cold-pass garage tours for Sleep EZ customers in the future."

"Who would conduct the tour?" Daddy fired the question at her.

"Tamara'll handle the wrap-up in the hospitality tent this time, but I should be able to handle it after that."

"Are you sure that won't be too much for you?"

She was going to be running her butt off…and she was looking forward to the challenge. "It won't be too much." Better to move along than allow them to start hovering and questioning her. "That concludes my part."

"As long as—"

"No, sir. It will be fine."

"We'll see." Daddy made a notation on his sheet and switched gears. "Steve, how's the remodel going on the Memphis location?" He looked at Maddie again. "You don't need to stay for this since we're done with your part."

"I'd like to stay," she said quietly. And she would. She wanted to know what was going on in other aspects of the business. It was pretty heady stuff to realize that she could positively impact Sleep EZ's business. Plus, she wanted them to know she was serious and that meant learning all aspects of the business.

They were just getting into Stevie's update on the remodels when Sharon brought in sandwiches, standard practice on meeting day.

Maddie lifted the plastic dome off her chicken salad on whole grain with mixed field greens and tomatoes. She glanced up. The room's windows acted as a mirror.

Sharon paused at the door, looking at Maddie's father with undisguised longing. Maddie quickly glanced back down at her sandwich, gob-smacked by the glimpse of stark, naked longing on the other woman's face that was gone almost as soon as it had appeared.

She'd been so caught up in the day-to-day on Planet Maddie she'd overlooked what had been obvious in one unguarded minute. Little things from the past began to fall into place. Sharon never dated. The occasional "vibe" she'd picked up from the other woman.

Was Sharon in love with her father?

CHAPTER EIGHT

"WHY DIDN'T DADDY EVER remarry?" Maddie settled at the granite kitchen counter in the "big house" and asked the person who knew her family the best, Jess.

Jess looked up from where she sat at the opposite end, polishing a silver sugar dish. "I suppose he never met anyone that interested him."

Maddie picked up another polishing cloth and the matching creamer. She'd always loved the monthly silver polishing ritual, ever since she was a small girl. Jess had allowed her to help and it was one of those rote tasks that encouraged conversation. Mind you, no one ever used the silver tea and coffee service, but Jess insisted on a monthly polish—the third Wednesday of each month at 4:00 p.m. Jess ran a tight ship.

"But he never even dated. You know, the first couple of years after Mama died I was terrified he was going to remarry and I'd have a stepmother. I think I was so relieved he didn't date that I didn't think about how lonely it must have been for him." And she'd been, even until today, so wrapped up in her own insecurities that she'd never examined it too closely.

"What brings this up now?"

"I'm pretty sure Sharon's in love with him." Maddie blurted the news as she worked the cloth along the intricate pattern adorning the creamer's feet.

Jess quirked a white eyebrow. "Is she now?"

"I caught her looking at him. You only look at someone that way if you love them."

"And you know this how?"

It was true enough Maddie had never been in love. She'd kept things light with the boyfriends she'd had and when said boyfriend started getting serious, it was time for a changing of the guard. But just because she'd never walked that path, it didn't mean she didn't recognize it when she saw it. "I watch movies. Read books. Now, if we can just get him to notice her."

"You *want* him to notice her?"

"Well, yeah. She's nice and Daddy must get lonely. I was thinking if I did one of those impromptu makeovers—"

Jess cut her off. "You're wasting your time."

"Why? She has potential. With a new haircut and some different clothes…" Maddie petered out as Jess sat shaking her head.

"First of all, your daddy's the last man on earth who'd ask out his secretary. Not that he's a snob, but he wouldn't want to make her feel uncomfortable. And second, even if she wasn't his secretary, he wouldn't ask her out."

"Why not?"

Jess stared steadfastly at the sugar bowl, now tarnish free, her expression guarded. "I just think after your mother…"

Now. Now. After all these years, just say it. Say it and let it out. "Because she killed herself? Because she committed suicide instead of dying from a heart attack?" Maddie said, clutching her polishing cloth as if it was a lifeline.

Resignation and no small measure of relief followed Jess's initial start of surprise. "Who told you?"

Thank goodness she didn't deny it. It had been hard enough

to give it voice. Maddie wasn't sure she could have argued it with Jess. She wasn't sure she could endure yet another pretense around it now that she'd spoken the words aloud to another human being. "No one told me. I've always known."

"But you never said a word."

"That night…I'd gone into their room because I'd had a bad dream. Daddy was still downstairs in his study—lots of times he fell asleep down there and I'd come get in bed with Mama." It replayed through her head, as if she were watching a movie segment stuck in replay mode for the past fifteen years. "She always left the bathroom light on for him. At first I thought she was just asleep, but I couldn't get her to wake up. And then I saw the empty pill bottles next to the note on her nightstand and I knew." Even now, it could've been yesterday it was still so clear, so fresh. She could still recall the scent of shampoo that clung to her mother's hair. She'd shaken her mother, frantic, only to be met with absolute stillness and quiet that it could have been one of her lifeless dolls beneath her fingertips. And in that single second of comprehension the bottom had dropped out of her world.

"Oh, baby." Jess's voice dragged her back to the here and now. "What'd you do?"

"I ran back to my room, pulled the covers up over my head and prayed I was still having a bad dream. I prayed I'd wake up in the morning and tell Mama about my bad dreams and we'd laugh it away in the light of day. But, of course, it wasn't a dream."

"Why didn't you tell your daddy the next morning?"

"I was scared. Scared because I hadn't done anything to save her."

"Honey, she was past saving."

"I know that now. I probably knew it then, but when you're

a kid…" Maddie drew a deep breath. Now that she'd opened the door, she couldn't seem to stop it from pouring out. "And I was scared because obviously I'd done something wrong if Mama wanted to leave us. What if I did the wrong thing and drove Daddy away, too?"

"Oh, sugar." Jess gathered her close and gave her a long hug. She smoothed her arthritic hand over Maddie's hair. "Your poor mama was emotionally fragile, but also high strung." How many times had Maddie heard that? It was practically tattooed on her brain. "It wasn't anything any of you did or didn't do. It was something inside of Ms. Mary Beth. That poor girl had a sadness inside her that went so deep it didn't seem to have any end. Y'all loved her and she loved y'all, but it wasn't enough to stop her sadness."

Maddie tucked her hair behind her ear and uttered the words she'd never shared with anyone. "She'd told me to clean up my room that day and I'd cheated and just shoved it all underneath my bed." She looked past the broad plantation shutters at the kitchen window to a blue jay fussing outside. "She found my mess and told me 'I'd be the death of her yet.'"

Jess looked at her and Maddie looked back, dry-eyed. She'd probably feel better if she could cry, but she'd cried into her pillow so much at night over the years, her well had run dry. Now there was nothing left but a lingering sadness, guilt and an underlying anger, so fierce she wouldn't allow herself to think about it, that her mother would take her own life and abandon Maddie.

Jess shook her head and rounded the counter. "That's just a saying, honey. She didn't mean it. I've said that lots of times to my kids and my grandkids." She opened the refrigerator and poured milk into a saucepan. "You didn't have anything to do with…what Ms. Mary Beth did." She put the carton back in the fridge, added a smidge of sugar and a splash of vanilla to the milk in the pan and set it to simmering. Warm milk had always been Jess's panacea for all troubles ranging from a skinned knee to a bad date to…this. There was a measure of comfort in the ritual of Jess preparing warm milk.

"Why did Daddy say she'd had a heart attack? How did he get away with that?" The question had plagued her for years, once she was old enough to know that lying about a cause of death was essentially illegal.

"He called his friend and golf buddy, Dr. Henry. Dr. Henry knew of your mother's…problems. He agreed pronouncing her a suicide just meant more heartache for you kids."

"Daddy told the boys, though, didn't he?" She never realized before now, until she uttered the words how much she'd resented that. Because she'd known her brothers knew while she'd been kept in the dark, or so they thought.

"He's a man, and in his book it's a man's job to protect the women in the family. He always thought he failed to protect your mother and he took a vow to protect you. The boys were…well, boys, and he thought if he enlisted their help in protecting you… He'd failed your mother, but surely the three of them together wouldn't fail you." The past's sorrows darkened her blue eyes. "I know he planned to tell you when he thought you were old enough to understand." She shrugged. "And then I guess it just got easier to leave things the way they were."

"I didn't understand it, but I did understand that's what Daddy needed and that was my role." Maddie pushed her hands through her hair. "God, we've all made such a mess of everything. I've been one big enabler." She laughed softly in self-derision. "All my life I've been told how much I looked like *her*. And all my life I've been scared to death I was like her. I let Daddy coddle me and smother me because there was a part of me that was so afraid that I'd shatter and fall apart like Mama and everyone would be left picking up the pieces. It's taken me a long time to figure out that I look like Mama but inside I'm like Daddy—stubborn, obstinate and tough."

Jess poured each of them a mug of milk, sadness still tingeing her smile. "This job with NASCAR is a big step in the right direction. I'm proud of you for doing that."

Nodding, Maddie took the warm mug Jess offered. "It does feel like a step to having a normal life. Daddy and I have to talk. It's time we stopped perpetuating a lie between us. We're going to have to talk about that night and Mama so he can move on and look at having a normal life and a healthy relationship with another woman."

She blew on the milk to cool it down a bit. She didn't want to get burned. And there was absolutely no reason Tucker Macray should pop into her head when she was thinking of developing healthy relationships and falling in love.

THE TUESDAY AFTER A LOUSY race in Texas where Lambert had spun him out in retaliation for Tucker snatching first place at Bristol, Tucker sat behind the yellow-and-blue-draped table set up in the lobby of Sleep EZ's newly renovated location northeast of Atlanta and signed a soft plastic key chain for a brown-haired boy who stood in line with an older woman at the autographing.

"You're my hero, Mr. Macray. I've been watching you race for a long time. I used to go to the dirt track with my Paw-Paw to see you race there. I always knew you'd be famous," the boy said.

Tucker figured the boy to be about twelve. A shabbiness clung to him that spoke of secondhand clothes. That coupled with a look in the kid's eyes reminded Tucker of himself at that age. "Well, thank you. That's always nice to hear. What's your name?"

"Greg Sheffield. And I think that what Lambert did on Sunday was bad sportsmanship."

"It just comes with racing, Greg." He asked a question that he already knew the answer to. "Have you been to a NASCAR race?"

"No, sir."

The gray-haired woman standing slightly behind Greg spoke up. "I'm his grandma. His mama and daddy...they're not around and he lives with me and his paw-paw and we don't have that kind of money." There was a decent forthright honesty and pride behind her declaration.

"I know what you mean," Tucker said, and he did. He felt the kinship of an unhappy childhood with the kid. He'd guaran-damn-tee the parents had skipped or were in prison. He looked at the boy. "Greg, would you like to go to a NASCAR race?"

"Yeah." The kid looked as if he didn't dare anticipate it because it was unlikely to ever happen. Tucker knew that feeling, too.

"How about you come to the Atlanta race as my guests?" he said. Jack and Andy often came, but more often than not, Tucker's allotment of family and friends tickets went unused. Or he handed them out to kids like this. They wouldn't race in Atlanta again until October, but he was pretty sure Greg would enjoy the anticipation nearly as much as the race itself.

"Really?" Cautious excitement warred with wariness in the boy's eyes.

"Really. If y'all want to step over to the side and give your names, I'll get four tickets and a garage pass to you. Bring a friend!" The kid still looked as if he was unsure whether his turn of good fortune was about to be snatched from him. "Really?"

Maddie Felton was standing slightly behind him to the right. He knew exactly where she was without even looking because he could swear his body damn near hummed every time she was around. He looked over his shoulder. "Ms. Felton, would you mind getting Greg's address and phone number?"

"Sure," she said, offering Greg a warm smile.

"Thank you, Mr. Macray. I'll be the one cheering loudest for you that day," the boy said, a smile splitting his face.

"I'll listen for you," Tucker said, and laughed.

Greg couldn't stop grinning and moved over to the side with Maddie.

The grandmother paused in front of Tucker, tears shimmering in her eyes. "Thank you. You don't know what that means to him...he hasn't had it easy."

Her tears and gratitude embarrassed Tucker. Plus he had a long line of fans still waiting on an autograph. "I'm glad I could do it. I hope you enjoy the race. Ms. Felton will take your information."

An hour and a half later they wrapped up the autograph session. Maddie ushered the last fan out as Tucker stood and stretched. It felt good to stretch his legs, but even better to flex his right hand. Tucker genuinely enjoyed meeting his fans, but his hand had begun to cramp the last ten minutes.

Maddie spoke with the manager and then crossed the room again to where Tucker stood.

"Okay. Raoul will take care of the table and the signage. We're done here." She gathered a stylish satchel with a shoulder strap and offered him a smile. "Ready?"

He followed her to the corridor that led to the employee parking lot where she'd met him earlier. They walked down the hall, and Tucker was altogether too aware of how good Maddie smelled and the swing of her hair against her neck.

"Oh, here's the information for Greg and Kate Sheffield you wanted." She pulled a sheet of paper out of the satchel's front pocket and passed him the paper. Her fingers brushed his in the exchange and a surge of attraction flowed through him.

"Thanks."

"That was a really nice thing you did."

Well, damn, she didn't have to sound so surprised. He wasn't a saint, but he was a decent-enough guy. He shrugged. "No big deal. He seemed like a nice kid and I usually have a couple of extra tickets lying around."

"I was thinking…"

They came to the end of the hall and he opened the door and held it for her. They exited to the rear of the building into the employee parking lot and the late-afternoon April sun.

"You were thinking?" he prompted her.

She crossed the parking lot and he fell into step with her. "Sleep EZ could comp them a room the night before the race. We have a location near the Atlanta track and that might be a sort of minivacation for them."

"Sounds good to me." He almost pointed out that Sleep EZ wouldn't get any PR mileage out of it because he'd bet his next race that the Sheffield family barely scraped by and they sure weren't spending any money on travel or motels. Tucker was sure Maddie Felton knew all about the "haves" and equally sure she wouldn't quite get the "have nots." But a compassion and understanding shone in her amber eyes that said otherwise. Just when he thought he had her figured out… "I think they'd be thrilled to stay the night before but—"

A light breeze blew her hair into her eyes. She pushed it away impatiently. "But what?" She stopped next to a silver BMW. What people drove said a lot about who they were, or maybe just who they wanted to be. And the Beemer had Maddie written all over it—expensive and sexy. She hit the button on the key, unlocked the door and tossed her satchel into the backseat.

"I think Mrs. Sheffield was surprised and glad to get the tickets, but her pride may draw the line at a free room. Let's offer the room and the tickets as if they came in a package."

Maddie pursed her lips to one side, considering his logic. "I think you're on to something. And if we did that, we could throw in some gift cards to eat out also."

"Great idea." As if cued by her indirect mention of food, his stomach growled.

"You sound hungry. I'd better let you go."

He was hungry and the prospect of eating alone didn't appeal to him. "Want to grab something to eat and we can iron out the Sheffield details?" he said on impulse.

Today had been a nice travel break. His appearance had been in suburban Atlanta, so it didn't mean a flight out and back. And here it was, the opportunity to demystify Maddie Felton, to solve her puzzle and put her out of his mind.

"I guess that would work."

No one could accuse her of being overenthusiastic.

"If you've got other plans—"

"No, I'm available. I don't mean *available* available...not that way." Okay. He got that message loud and clear. "Sure. I can go to dinner. Where'd you have in mind?"

"I hadn't exactly gotten that far. I just know I'm hungry."

Maddie looked at him and then at herself. "We look like walking advertisements in our team colors, which is, of course, the whole point behind wearing team colors, but we'll stand out like a sore thumb wherever we go."

Tucker nodded. "You're right. Lots of times I can go out in jeans, a T-shirt and a ball cap and nobody notices, but dressed like this...not a chance."

She tilted her head to one side. "Does that bother you?"

"Not really. It's part of what I do, and when I'm getting ready to race and I hear my fans yelling and screaming, it pumps me up. But it's nice to just go out sometimes without being recognized, like a normal guy—" he laughed and shrugged "—because I am a normal guy who just happens to be lucky enough to do what I do."

"Some people might get the wrong idea at seeing us out together…you know," she said, looking thoroughly dismayed at the idea that her name might be linked romantically with him.

"It's a possibility." Not that he wanted that kind of rumor started, either, but Maddie could be pretty tough on the ego.

"I don't live that far from here. If you wanted to we could pick up some take-out and eat there." She looked as if she'd just offered herself up for execution.

Obviously she felt as if she couldn't just opt out. The gallant thing to do would be to tell her to just skip it.

He saw her at least twice a week, always in a crowd or group. Other than the occasional moment, like now, he'd never spent any time alone with her. But she was a sassy, sexy puzzle that he found increasingly distracting. And like it or not, there was an attraction that heated him throughout every time he was around her. This was his opportunity to debunk the mystery of Maddie Felton.

When it came right down to it, curiosity won over gallantry.

"Sure. I'd love to have dinner at your house."

CHAPTER NINE

MADDIE GLANCED IN HER rearview mirror. Yep, Macray had turned into the drive behind her. She drove past the stately white-columned house. Jess was already gone for the day and Daddy, workaholic that he was, would still be at the office.

What was she thinking when she'd invited Macray here for dinner? That was easy enough, she chided herself, she'd thought he wouldn't accept her invitation. Wrong, wrong and wrong. Because here he was driving past the swimming pool, the expanse of manicured lawn, around the side of the stone carriage house to park behind her beneath the sprawling oak that stood at the building's edge.

He climbed out of the truck, bringing two bags of Thai food with him. He'd insisted on footing the bill for the take-out.

"Nice place to grow up," he said, nodding toward the white mansion.

Maddie shrugged. "I guess. It's just sort of…big. Come on this way." She motioned for him to follow her into the garage.

"Is this an ancestral home?" he asked. "It looks like the kind of place that would be passed down from generation to generation."

Maddie shook her head as she unlocked the door. "Someone else's family, maybe. We moved here when I was ten." She kept her tone light, even bland, in an attempt to keep memories at bay.

"After you lost your mother?" Macray asked. His voice reflected a sympathy she'd grown accustomed to when people referenced her mother. How did he know her mother had died? Well, duh. Her death, albeit not the true circumstances, was common knowledge, and it would've been easy enough for him to hear that Louis Felton was a widower. A smart man would make it his business to find out that kind of information about his business associates, and Macray definitely struck her as a smart man.

"Yep. New house, new furniture, new start." Delivered in just the right banal tone with a smile usually satisfied the subject.

"It must've been awfully lonely," he said, and for one stunned second it was as if he'd stripped away all the bandages she'd swathed herself in and found the raw spot blighting her soul.

"Excruciatingly so," she said, responding instinctively to his insight. She recovered her equanimity equally fast. "Jess, you met her a couple of races ago, helped all of us adjust to the new house."

Maddie felt a connection with Macray she'd never experienced before. It was as if he shared not just the knowledge but the ache of a lonely home and memories attached to a place too painful to revisit either emotionally or physically.

Flipping on a light, she led him into the kitchen and quickly steered the conversation out of those emotionally treacherous waters. "And then I moved to the carriage house after I finished college. Well, that was after it was renovated." The carriage-house renovation was a nice, safe topic that didn't contain any emotional nuances. "It was a mess. It had been used as a storage and gardening shed for years. Here, I'll take those," she said, relieving him of the food bags and placing them on the counter. "We'll have to eat at the kitchen table. There's no formal dining room here."

Tucker laughed and it did funny things to her insides. "That's fine. I'm not a formal kind of guy."

No, he wasn't. He was the kind of guy who seemed disconcertingly at home in her house, as if he could easily belong there. He wasn't a big guy but he had such a presence about him, a quiet strength and energy.

Sylvester strolled in and wove in and out of her legs, rubbing himself against her ankles and announcing in a loud feline cry that it was his dinnertime.

"This is Sylvester, and I need to feed him or he'll complain about his lack of dinner until I do." She leaned down to scratch behind his ears…well, make that ear, because the other one was pretty much missing.

"That is one fat cat."

"Shh. You'll hurt his feelings. And he's just pleasantly plump." She pulled a small dish from the fridge and put it on a place mat on the floor. "I actually think he has an eating disorder. He was half starved and beaten up when I got him from the pound. The staff had all voted him the least likely to be adopted." Which was precisely why she'd wanted him.

"Then I'd say he's a pretty lucky cat." Tucker didn't say anything else, but she sensed his surprise that she'd picked her cat up at the pound as opposed to buying from a breeder.

"I'd say we're pretty lucky to have each other." She transferred the food to serving dishes and Macray carried them to the table. "What would you like to drink? There are a couple of beers from the last time my brother Stevie stopped over or there's a nice bottle of Shiraz open."

"You wouldn't happen to have a ginger ale, would you? If not, water's fine."

"I think I do." She personally wanted a glass of wine,

but he was a guest in her house and she felt beholden to ask if it would offend him. "Do you mind if I have a glass of wine?"

"Not at all." He hesitated for a second and ran his hand through his hair. "My parents are alcoholics. I don't touch the stuff. I'm afraid I'd like it too much. But I don't object to other people drinking."

Maddie loved her family, but they were all masters at talking around issues or avoiding them altogether. She found Tucker's direct honesty refreshing and it struck an answering chord in her. "No one talks about it in my family, but my mother had…an issue with pills. I can barely stand to take an aspirin." Tucker nodded as if he knew exactly where she was coming from. "I'd rather be in pain, so I understand why you don't drink."

Maddie dug the ginger ale out of the back of the fridge—a holdover from a stomach virus a couple of months ago—and poured it into a glass. Her fingers brushed Tucker's as she passed him the glass and a tingle ran through her, the same as it had earlier today when she'd passed him the Sheffields' contact information. She poured her glass of wine and joined him at the kitchen table, steering the conversation to the Sheffields.

They ironed out the details quickly enough and Macray told her he was planning to renovate a farmhouse and began asking her about the carriage-house renovation.

Maybe it was the relaxing glass of wine, maybe it was Macray's obvious enthusiasm and interest in her house, maybe it was even that she was actually enjoying his company and wasn't quite ready for it to be just her and Sylvester once again, but Maddie found herself issuing her second invitation of the evening.

"Would you like a quick tour?"

"THIS IS A GREAT PLACE," Tucker said. He meant it. Everything he'd seen so far appealed to him. And if he was honest he'd admit to himself that included Maddie. He forced himself to concentrate on her house.

The kitchen could've been lifted from a magazine, except it had a warmth and comfortableness about it. The outer walls appeared to be original stone while the interior walls, sectioning off the room, were a deep yellow-gold. The ceilings were high, maybe ten to twelve feet, with thick beams running the length of the room. An archway opened to a small foyer and a twin archway opposite led into what appeared to be a den.

"I'm glad you like it."

Ah, there was that smile again that knocked him slightly off kilter. She had the most tempting, what-would-it-be-like-to-kiss mouth.

"It was fun and even when I move out, it's increased Daddy's property value."

"You're moving?" There was no reason that should feel a bit like a kick in the gut.

"I think I have to, one day. I can hardly live in my father's backyard forever."

Did that mean she had a serious man in her life? It was totally plausible that her boyfriend never showed up at the track simply because he wasn't a race fan. It wasn't as if Tucker was personally interested, it was just part of the Maddie Felton puzzle.

He pointed to the exposed beams running along the ceiling. "Are those the original post and beam?"

"Some of it had to be replaced but they did a good job weathering the new stuff to match."

Tucker followed her on the impromptu tour. The house was kick-butt cool and Maddie was captivating in her enthusiasm for the space that was her home. Downstairs housed the kitchen, den and a half bath.

"And there's a small patio out back," she said as she led him to the back door. "I love this door." It was split into a top and bottom half that could be opened together or separately. She opened the top half and the cool air flowed in.

"Awesome," he said, and he meant it. "I'd love to have something like this when I redo my house."

"I kept all the paperwork and the material sources so I can tell you where to find it. Or rather where your contractor can find it."

"That'd be great."

Her shoulder brushed against his and her scent teased around him as they shifted spots so he could look out the open half of the back door.

A fieldstone patio tied the outdoors to the inside. A pergola covered the small area. He heard water. He leaned out and looked to his right. A wall-mounted fountain burbled off the back of the house, a traditional lion's head spouting water from its mouth. Twig furniture, lined with plump pillows, a copper fire bowl and a couple of potted plants kept it simple but cozy and inviting. A riot of flowers and plants sprawled on the other side of the patio. A couple of birds flitted between two pole-mounted feeders in the small garden.

"Mr. Twilley keeps the grounds around the house and between me and the house, but this garden area is mine," she said from behind his left shoulder.

He stepped back away from the door and turned to her. "I like it better. There's a wild and untamed element to it," he said. Yet another surprise from her, another piece of the Maddie Felton puzzle.

"It's therapeutic—gardening, that is." Her smile was a wry

quirk of her mouth. She closed and locked the back door then turned to face him. "Actually, just sitting on the patio can be therapeutic—fresh air, running water, birds singing."

He could tell she loved it and he could see why. It seemed like a quiet retreat. "I bet you spend a lot of time there."

"I do."

An archway opened in the wall to the left of the back door to the hallway. She gestured toward a wrought iron circular staircase at the back of the small foyer, just past the bathroom. "Upstairs are two bedrooms, a bath and a small gym."

He wandered to the staircase and ran his hand along the railing, peering up at the circular twist to the second floor. "I've always thought these were cool, but I've never actually seen one."

Maddie laughed and the sound wrapped around him. "Want to go up? The staircase is fun and it's sort of like a loft upstairs, because the ceilings are so much lower and slope with the eaves." She grinned. "Maybe because it was originally a loft, huh? My bedroom is off-limits because I wasn't expecting anyone and Jess wouldn't be pleased with me—I don't always make my bed."

He followed her up the stairs, her heels making a funny pinging noise on the metal treads. The circular staircase experience was all but lost on him with Maddie's distracting, alluring curves leading the way. He'd have to be unconscious not to notice and appreciate the curve of her hips and the shapely length of her legs. In fact, he was so busy admiring the loving cling of her skirt that he missed the top step, stumbled and damn near fell on his face. He barely righted himself by grabbing the edge of the iron railing.

"Steady there," Maddie said at the top of the small landing, putting her hand on his forearm.

Great! Did she know he'd been busy admiring her...assets?

Nothing for it but to bluster his way through. "I'm okay. Just missed the top step."

"Be careful." She released his arm. "I'll never hear the end of it if you wind up injured. And all those women that fawn all over you would certainly never forgive me."

He wasn't sure how to respond to her teasing him about some of his more enthusiastic female fans. So he made a joke instead. "My ex-wife would probably pay you."

"Nasty divorce?"

He shook his head. "Not really. It was as amicable as a divorce can be. We didn't have any kids so that made it easier."

"What about a girlfriend who'd be upset that her man had fallen at my feet?"

He wasn't always the sharpest tool in the shed when it came to reading between the lines, but he was almost certain Maddie was fishing for information. "Nope. For the same reason I've got an ex-wife. Racing isn't the easiest schedule on a relationship and I've never met a woman I cared about more than racing."

"Well, that's laying it on the line. Is that what's called waving a yellow caution flag?"

"It's called shooting straight. What about you? If I'd fallen at your feet is there some boyfriend who'd be irate? Maybe Marcus Chalkey?" He'd wondered more than once. Now seemed the perfect opportunity to ask.

"No and double no. My father and Mr. Chalkey are business acquaintances. That's all."

"I think Marcus would be open to something more."

"*That's* not even a remote possibility."

He couldn't seem to leave it alone. "Why not? Your fathers are friends, similar backgrounds. I bet you'd have a lot in common. Marcus drives a Beemer, too."

"I don't care what Marcus drives. I'm not attracted to him. I don't need any matchmaking help, thank you."

"I was just saying—"

"Don't. Don't say it again. Topic off-limits." Maddie made a slicing motion with both hands.

He threw up his hand with a laugh. "Okay. But if you-know-who isn't your kind of guy, what is your type?"

"What? Are you looking to hook me up?"

"Just asking."

"It'll be easier for me to tell you what's not my type and that'll pretty much knock anyone out of the running that you might know. It's definitely not a race-car driver or anyone racing related. You're right about the schedule and the level of commitment. Any woman who thought she was interested in a relationship with one of you guys, if she had a lick of sense, would run screaming in the other direction."

"Black-flagged."

"Just putting it on the line."

"Pimo, my tire changer, will be devastated, along with a couple of the other guys. Pimo thinks you have nice legs." For some reason it had irritated the hell out of him when Pimo sat around waxing eloquent about her figure.

She looked appalled and flattered at the same time. "He mentioned my legs—in front of everyone?"

It was sort of cute that she was blushing. He shrugged. "We're guys, Maddie." He couldn't resist teasing her. "And when a decent-looking woman shows up, guys talk."

"Decent?" The laughter sparkling in her eyes belied her outraged tone. "Did you just call me decent-looking?"

"Sure, I'd give you decent." He paused for full effect. "There's nothing *bad* wrong with you."

"Nothing…nothing *bad* wrong with me? I've got an inside

scoop for you, Macray. Your schedule isn't the only reason you don't have a girlfriend."

He laughed in genuine amusement. Maddie was something else. And she had the most exquisitely tempting mouth. "Are you implying my communication skills with the fairer sex are lacking?"

"No, I'm laying it on the line." She tossed his words back at him with a laugh. "So, this is the upstairs. Don't judge. There's my messy bedroom," she said, jerking a thumb over her shoulder. Obviously he needed to carve time in his schedule to get out more, because the rumpled bedcovers and the carelessly thrown gold silk—he'd bet a paycheck that slinky material was silk—nightie with the skinny little straps and the brief amount of material sent his temperature soaring. He didn't have any trouble picturing her in that scrap of a nightgown…or out of it. "And this is the guest room, which is kind of small."

"It's bigger than the bedroom I had growing up."

She looked awkward, almost embarrassed, and that hadn't been his intent at all.

"What's this next room?" he asked, to shift from what had become an uncomfortable moment.

"It's a minigym. I have to work darn hard to warrant a 'nothing bad wrong' rating."

"I told you Pimo said you had nice legs."

She shot him what he guessed was supposed to be a quelling look that left him grinning. "And this is the bathroom."

The ceilings upstairs followed the line of the eaves and were much lower, lending the rooms a cozy, intimate feel. "Very nice."

They headed back down the stairs. "Be careful on the way down."

Since her cute little derriere wasn't at eye level going down, he should manage not to trip himself up. "I'll try not to fall."

They reached the first floor without mishap and he followed her into the kitchen.

"The fieldstone in the entryway is original," Maddie said. "The installer did a good job of matching the rest of the fieldstone, don't you think?"

"Great job. I couldn't tell the difference. It's a good look, but aren't the floors cold?"

She shook her head. "Radiant heat. In the winter, it's like walking around on sun-warmed rocks. And, of course, it's nice and cool in the summer. Kick off your shoes and give it a try. I'll keep it on for another month or so."

She slipped off her high heels, and there shouldn't have been anything sexy about her bare feet. Who knew that slender feet and toenails painted a light bronze would send warmth spiraling through him that had nothing to do with radiant heat.

"Try it," she said.

It was a little strange, but why not? Tucker slipped off his shoes and socks. It verged on a sybaritic pleasure—there was something about warm rocks. In an instant it transported him back to standing barefoot on a sun-warmed rock at the Etowah River. He'd been thirteen and his feet hadn't been the only thing bare. "This reminds me of when my friend Andy and I went skinny-dipping one summer at the Etowah River."

She held up a staying hand. "Don't get any ideas. I only invited you to take your shoes off."

"Well, it's a good thing because I'm not that kind of boy."

The light flirting and playfulness between them shifted, deepened to something potent and slightly dangerous—who was he kidding, she'd been dangerous from minute one on day one.

"I'm not so sure I believe you."

The slight huskiness in her voice drew him to her. Did he lean in or did she or did they both? He just knew her scent became a part of the very breath he drew. The last vestiges of the evening sun slanted through the window, picking out coppery glints in her hair.

Against every instinct of self-preservation, he reached for her. Dammit, if she'd only taken one step back, one step away from him…but instead, it was as if she was as helpless to resist the attraction between them as he was, and she stepped into his arms. He tangled his hands in her hair. It slid against his fingers like fine silk.

"Exquisite," he said.

He felt her tremble. Or was it him? She could've been custom-made for him.

Her whiskey-gold eyes offered a glimpse of want and wariness. She slid her arms around his neck and at that moment he would've traded his win at Bristol for her kiss. He lowered his mouth until her warm breath mingled with his.

"Maddie…" He didn't want to move too fast. He didn't want to take what she wasn't willing to give.

"Macray—" her lips parted in a moist invitation "—for goodness' sake, kiss me."

CHAPTER TEN

TUCKER MACRAY WAS GOING to kiss her. She'd all but ordered him to and every nerve ending in her body quivered in anticipation. He buried his hands in her hair, cupping her scalp, and pulled her closer.

He brushed his lips over hers, and a response fired through her and she brushed back. And then it turned into a full-fledged, lips-clinging-to-lips kiss that melted her bones and fluttered her eyes closed.

Slowly she came back to earth when the kiss ended. One little kiss and her toes were curling against the warm tile and she felt dazed and confused. Tucker dropped his hands to his sides and for a second they simply stared at each other. Maddie said the first thing that came to mind. "And I thought you were only good at driving a car."

Tucker appeared a little dazed himself, but there was no mistaking the glint in his green-flecked brown eyes. "That was only the warm-up lap. I've still got the qualifying run for pole position."

She sent him a flirty, challenging look—at least she hoped it was. "You know, it's not just a matter of how fast you go."

"It never is," he said, his voice low and husky. He reached up and trailed one finger along the curve of her neck. Her heart hammered a response. "It's all about finesse and handling. Every track is different and it's a matter of learning the curves and turns." He smoothed his hands over her shoulders and a shiver shimmered through her. "Some are short and tight." Her entire body tightened in response. "Some run long but fast." He lowered his head and heated anticipation flooded her. His breath feathered warm against her jaw and her own breath hitched in her throat. His mouth hovered just over hers. "But it is never—" she felt his heat "—ever—" the faint brush of whiskers against her chin "—just a matter of how fast you can go."

Then his mouth melded to hers and she lost herself in the touch, the taste, the scent of Tucker Macray. She wrapped her hands around his neck, delighting in the feel of his skin beneath her fingertips, the hard press of his body against her softer curves, the exquisite pleasure of his lips against hers, the sensual exploration of his tongue. She offered a sigh of satisfaction and swallowed his answering groan.

Tucker broke the kiss and took a step back.

Maddie drew a shaky breath. "I'd give you the outside pole position."

"That's nice…except the inside pole position goes to the top qualifier." His breath was as unsteady as hers.

"Well, there is that. Do you put this much energy into *everything* you do?" Just the thought left her weak-kneed.

"Always. Everything." His eyes offered a heated promise. "Otherwise it's a waste of time and energy. I suppose that's why I have limited interest."

Maddie was fairly certain she'd be content standing in her kitchen kissing Tucker indefinitely, which meant it wasn't a particularly good idea. She needed to heed her own advice about moving too fast.

She cleared her throat and deliberately stepped out of reach, because she wasn't altogether sure if he touched her again, she'd have the wherewithal to think of anything other than kissing him. And continuing to kiss him would be a big problem for any number of reasons.

First and foremost, making out with the driver didn't exactly qualify as professional when she was trying to do an outstanding job and prove herself.

"Okay, so I'll get the room info for the Atlanta race to Kelsi and she'll take care of the Sheffields?" It wasn't subtle but sometimes subtle didn't cut it.

"Sure." He ran a hand through his hair. "Listen, I'm sorry—"

"Please don't apologize. I'm not sorry. But I think we both know it can't happen again."

He opened his mouth as if to argue and then nodded instead. "You're right. And it won't happen again."

TUCKER TURNED OFF OF the highway onto the dirt road leading to his house. Lights shone at Jack and Edna's and spilled out of the open garage behind the house. It wasn't late. Nine o'clock. Forty-five minutes from Maddie's house without traffic. He'd only been there a couple of hours but they'd flown by. Good food, good conversation, a helluva kiss, which he'd had no business indulging in, but truly couldn't seem to resist the attraction that flowed between them, and a couple of more pieces as to what made Maddie Felton tick.

He turned into Jack and Edna's, driving past the house to park out by the shop. Might as well see what Jack was tinkering with now and he'd pick Napoleon up, save him the run across the field linking their properties. And after the warmth and coziness of Maddie's place, he wasn't particularly looking forward to going home.

Jack looked up from beneath the hood of a '73 Nova hatchback he'd lovingly repaired, a wrench in one hand, a smile on his face.

"Problem?" Tucker said.

"Nah. Just the alternator bracket. It's just a pain in the butt to get to."

"Need a hand?" Tucker missed being under the hood of a car, and for the most part, his team didn't want him under the 76.

"Sure. Hold pressure on the alternator while I tighten the bolt."

Tucker pushed and Jack worked the wrench in between to the bolt.

"You headed out for Phoenix tomorrow morning?" Jack asked.

"Yeah. Well, tomorrow afternoon."

"The boys got you set up right?" Jack gave the wrench a final quarter turn.

Tucker grinned. Jack never quite trusted anyone to get Tucker's car set up just right—a holdover from the dirt track days when Jack and Andy had been crew chiefs and crew all rolled into one, with Tucker doubling as crew and driver. "Let's hope right enough."

"Grab those spark plugs on the cart behind you," Jack said. "You've got to watch the wall coming out of Turn Two," he cautioned, switching the conversation back to the Phoenix track.

They discussed the tight turns on One and Two and the dogleg in the backstretch, the car's handling and Tucker's odds of finishing in the top five, which was what he and his crew chief wanted.

They installed the spark plugs and a companionable silence

stretched between them as Jack fooled around with the distributor cap.

"I might start renovations on the house sooner than I thought," Tucker said, giving voice to an idea that'd been niggling at the back of his head since seeing Maddie's home. "I stopped by Maddie Felton's place this evening. She lives in a converted carriage house. It'd been used as a storage and gardening shed but you'd never know it. It's nice, without being fussy. It lit a fire under me."

"Isn't that the gal Edna made you send flowers to?"

"Same one."

"Not as ditzy as you thought, huh?"

"No. From what I've seen at the track, she does a good job. The meet 'n' greets run smoothly and there've been no problems with any of the appearances she puts together."

"So, how'd you wind up at her house?"

He recounted the story of Greg Sheffield and the rest of the evening, particularly the details of the house and the renovation.

He did, however, keep his mouth shut about that kiss and the conversation where she'd pretty much laid it on the line that she wasn't looking for a race-car driver—translate: him—as a romantic interest, and he'd told her in no uncertain terms there wasn't room in his life for a serious relationship.

Jack straightened up and wiped his hands on a clean rag. "So now you're inspired? You reckon you can handle it in the middle of the season?" He quirked an eyebrow at Tucker.

Tucker leaned one shoulder against the door frame. "I'm thinking I could get started at least working with a contractor. Ya know, start putting some ideas on paper."

"You liked what she did with her place, why don't you ask the Felton woman to give you some ideas…before someone else gets involved."

Tucker and Jack exchanged glances. Tucker knew exactly what Jack meant but was too loyal to say. Andy's wife, Charlene, was a great woman but Charlene was into froufrou in a major kind of way.

She'd been on a major redecorating bend—lots of lace curtains, flowered wallpaper and borders, busy prints, lots of "stuff" in her and Andy's house. Tucker supposed it was nice enough but it sure wasn't Tucker's taste. He wasn't quite sure how Andy lived there. The simple hominess yet elegance of Maddie's place appealed much more. Charlene had offered more than once to help Tucker with his house when she finished with hers and Andy's. Tucker'd sort of danced around the issue because he didn't know how to get out of it without hurting her feelings, and he'd live with froufrou out the wazoo before he hurt Charlene's feelings. But this could work. He'd explain to Charlene that he was impatient to start but knew she was too busy. And Maddie's animation when she'd talked about the renovation and given him a home tour spoke to how much she'd enjoyed the project. This could kill two birds with one stone—he'd get the ball rolling on his renovation and save Charlene's feelings.

"I think you could definitely be on to something. I'll think about it. Maybe I'll ask Maddie when I get a chance." The worse that could happen was she'd say no.

Damn, why did that thought tie him up in knots? It wasn't as if he was asking her out on a date or anything. This wasn't strictly business, but it definitely wasn't a date.

CHAPTER ELEVEN

SUNDAY MORNING AND THE usual sounds of a track in the grip of race fever filled the air. Maddie scanned the hospitality tent with a critical eye. Everything looked in place and ready.

"It's fine. I'll be fine," said Tamara to her left. "If a problem comes up that I can't handle, I promise I'll call you right away."

Maddie reminded herself part of being a good manager was the ability to delegate.

Tamara had been thrilled when Maddie had asked if she could handle the hostessing at the hospitality tent so that Maddie could check out the garage and pit area. It was harder to turn it over to someone else, albeit temporarily, than she'd thought it would be. And Tamara was right, she was only a phone call away.

"Okay. I'm sure you'll do fine," Maddie said, doing yet one more visual check. "Macray is scheduled to be here in thirty minutes to meet everyone. He's easy to work with."

"I'm looking forward to it," Tamara said. "I've heard he's a really nice guy." Tamara walked toward the front of the tent in a none-too-subtle attempt to herd Maddie out.

"He is a nice guy," Maddie said, getting into the blue-and-yellow golf cart with the Sleep EZ logo on the front and both sides. "Call me if you need me."

Maddie drove the golf cart away from the zigzagged

row of white tents that made up the hospitality "village" toward the tunnel leading to the infield, skipping the credentials office. Since she was a regular each week as a sponsor, she wore a coveted "hard card" on a lanyard around her neck that granted her access to a number of places at the track.

As she stopped at a crosswalk she assured herself she wasn't avoiding Macray because of a couple of kisses. She'd already asked Tamara to fill in for her before that. She just hoped Macray didn't think otherwise. It was only a kiss and it didn't really change anything. Neither of them was looking for a relationship. Granted there was some potent chemistry between them, but chemistry didn't make a relationship, and she'd make sure he knew it when she saw him again.

Maddie passed the tailgaters, the barbecue grills going, the music blaring and all manner of fans, young and old, having a good time, prerace. There was a little bit of everything to be found from the sleek, ultra-expensive new motor homes to the old school buses that had been repainted and decorated as moving icons to stock-car racing and favorite drivers. One of the refurbished school buses boasted a home-welded viewing deck on top and a built-in barbecue grill on the back. A middle-aged couple, cooking at the grill, offered a friendly wave. Maddie waved back.

She checked the facility map and turned into the infield tunnel. Once she was through she made a right-hand turn. She passed three haulers filled with nothing but tires.

A man stood talking to a group and she pulled over to eavesdrop shamelessly.

"These are the tire trucks, on standby. None of the guys are busy now, but they'll be hopping once the race starts. That board lists the recommended tire pressures," he said, pointing to a placard with the information posted. "Of course, the guys don't always run that."

Cool. She drove on and parked outside the gate of the **NASCAR NEXTEL** Cup Series garage. Inside was a hive of activity. Maddie found the excitement catching. This was awesome.

Security checked her credentials and she walked through the gate to the garage area. The garage was one long building with bays lined up on both sides. The team haulers were parked opposite each bay assigned to the teams. Maddie dodged a group of guys moving a stainless-steel cart. Inside each bay the teams were going over the cars, fine-tuning, adjusting, ignoring the people with the passes who wandered in and out. In the middle of the strip, on the right side of the garage, she found the Number 76 team hard at work.

No way she was saying anything to any of them and breaking their concentration. She headed down to the pit road where pit boxes that served as command central for each car sat behind a low wall separating the crew from where the cars pulled in.

It was early yet and the different teams were busy getting the pit areas ready. Maddie immediately spotted Sleep EZ's blue-and-yellow colors and made her way down the pit road to Number 76's box. A guy named Chico, at least that was the name on his racing shirt, squatted on top of the box, putting up the chairs. Two guys were working on tires. Maddie introduced herself.

"Will I distract you if I ask a few questions?"

"Not at all. What do you want to know?" Will said. Those names on the shirts came in handy.

"What are you doing to the tires?"

"I'm getting any dirt off the rims."

"And I'm gluing the lug nuts in place." This from the taller of the two, named Shorty. "It's just enough so they'll stay in place, then the air gun has enough force to unseat the glue when the team puts them on during the race."

"Next we'll put covers over them until they're needed for the race," Will offered.

"Is that to keep out dirt?"

"That and the collectors," he said with a grin and a shake of his head. "Some people don't hesitate to take them as souvenirs, even after they're glued down."

"What?" Maddie said. "But they're used in the race."

Shorty shook his head and laughed. "Trust me. That doesn't matter. Once, this lady stopped and tried to pick one of the lug nuts up. She looks at me and says 'It's stuck' and then she pulls harder. She gets it off, sticks it in her pocket and walks off, stringing glue the whole time." He laughed and shook his head again. "That's when we decided to go with the covers."

Maddie was speechless at the audacity.

Will grinned at her expression. "Hey, it happens. Want to go up top?" He nodded toward the pit box. "Chico's got the chairs up."

"Sure," Maddie said.

"Hey, Chico," Will called from across the walk, "how about taking Ms. Felton up?"

Chico gave the thumbs-up. Maddie thanked Shorty and Will, wished them luck with the day's race and walked over to the pit box.

Maddie climbed the ladder to the chairs mounted up top. Chico followed behind her. They sat and swiveled for a 360 view of the track.

"This is pretty cool," Maddie said.

Chico nodded and explained how Mike Snellings sat up top

wearing a headset and microphone that kept him in constant communication with Tucker, the spotter and incoming stats.

Maddie was impressed. It was an ongoing barrage of input and processing and decisions that made or lost a race. She turned slowly in the chair.

"Quite the view up here, isn't it?" Chico asked with a grin.

"Definitely. And very different from the view in the skybox."

"That's because this is the heart. This is where the action happens," he said, the pride in his job and his team evident.

Maddie nodded, her stomach knotted with a mixture of anxiety and excitement. In less than two hours Macray was going to be out there flying through those turns and hurtling down the straightaways. Not just the Number 76 driver, but the guy she'd shared a meal and a kiss with last week.

TUCKER LEFT THE HOSPITALITY village and headed for the hauler, out of sorts. He'd expected Maddie. He'd looked forward to seeing Maddie—definitely not in a personal capacity, but because he'd wanted to talk to her about helping him out with his renovation. That was absolutely the only reason he'd felt a surge of excitement on his way over. And that was absolutely the only reason he'd been so disappointed to find her assistant, Tamara.

Oh, well, it'd obviously have to wait until some other time.

He walked toward his hauler, signing a couple of hats for fans as he went. That was one of the first things he'd learned— how to walk, talk and sign all at the same time. He had about half an hour before the driver's meeting. He wouldn't mind a quiet spot to run through the track in his head. He'd damn near lost it coming out of Turn Two during Friday's practice run.

"How's it going, Tuck?" Marcus asked, startling Tucker out of his reverie. Guess it said something for his focus that he could block out all the people milling around the outside of the haulers and the garage.

"Fine." He'd practically walked past her before he realized Maddie was standing on the other side of Marcus. "Oh, hello."

A short guy with glasses and dark curly hair sporting a press badge latched on to Marcus, leaving Tucker with Maddie.

"Let's go in." He took Maddie by the elbow and ushered her inside the hauler, her skin soft and warm beneath his fingertips. Once inside he released her, simply because he didn't have a good reason to keep touching her.

"I hope everything went fine with Tamara," she said, pushing her hair behind one ear. Was it just a few days ago that he'd buried his hands in the silky strands of her hair? Just one touch… He shoved his hand in his pocket to keep from reaching for her. *That* would be a really stupid thing to do.

"Like clockwork," he said. He'd bet a dollar to a doughnut that she'd already had a phone conversation with Tamara and knew everything had gone off without a hitch.

One of the guys hurried toward the rear door and Tucker stepped aside to make room, his hip brushing against Maddie's. Like a bolt of lightning in a sudden summer storm, awareness arced between them. He saw it in her eyes. Maddie wet her lips with the tip of her tongue and Tucker felt his body tighten with the memory of her mouth beneath his, the taste of her lips.

Maddie nodded. "Great. I'm really glad to hear it."

"Um, why don't we go to the front? I had something I wanted to ask you."

"Sure."

He followed her down the aisle to the room up front, which was mercifully empty. He had to ask fast because on race day someone would be ducking in sooner than later.

"You know I mentioned renovating my house the other night…"

"Right."

"I had planned to wait on the off-season but your place inspired me. I'm ready to start as soon as possible."

"I'm flattered."

"I was hoping you might come out and look it over. Give me some ideas."

"Seriously?"

"Seriously. Of course, I totally understand if you're too busy or your schedule doesn't allow the time. Not a problem at all if it doesn't work out. I just thought I'd ask."

What the hell was wrong with him? He was practically babbling.

Maddie nodded her head and shrugged. "I'm not sure how much help I'd actually be, but sure, I could take a look at it. When were you thinking?"

"What about next week?" he asked. "Well, actually, tomorrow. Monday is about my only free day. This is really short notice, so if that doesn't work maybe the following week."

"Tomorrow could work. I don't usually stay at the office all day because I've spent the weekends at the track. It'd be after lunch, probably midafternoon."

For as uninformed as she'd been the first time he'd met her, he had to admire what he'd seen of her work ethic since.

"Hey, you're doing me a big favor. I just appreciate you taking the time to do it. Midafternoon would be fine."

"I need directions."

Tucker ripped a piece of paper off of a notepad, wrote out the directions and gave it to her. "It's about an hour from your office out to my place." He knew from meetings he'd attended last year when Sleep EZ had signed on as a major sponsor.

"That's my cell number on the bottom in case something comes up or you get lost."

She tucked it into her pants pocket. "Okay. I'll see you when I get there. Do I need to let you know when I'm on my way?"

"No. I'll be home all day."

"Catching up on laundry?"

It took him a second to realize she was teasing him. Her and her quirky sense of humor. "Yeah. Something like that."

Maddie laughed and Tucker laughed with her. He did not feel an inordinate amount of what bordered on exuberance because Maddie was showing up at his house tomorrow afternoon. Not at all. He was simply excited at the prospect of getting started on the house. Yep, renovation could really wind a guy up.

"Good luck today," Maddie said.

Before he had the chance to respond, Marcus popped in, looking faintly disapproving at the two of them, even though the width of the table separated them. "Ten minutes until the driver's meeting, Tuck. You know missing it means you start in the last position."

What the hell? As if he'd ever missed a driver's meeting. As if he didn't know all of this.

Marcus preened with self-importance. Okay. He got it. Marcus was trying to impress the girl by playing big boss. Whatever.

"I won't miss it. I'm on my way now."

Marcus hovered over Maddie. "Let me show you the cab."

Tucker really wouldn't mind coldcocking Marcus occasionally. This qualified as one of those occasions.

On the way out the door, he remembered Maddie's adamant and sincere declaration that Marcus Chalkey didn't interest her at all. Marcus didn't stand a chance with her.

The idea kept him smiling all the way to the driver's meeting.

MADDIE BIT BACK A SIGH of frustration up in the skybox.

"I'm sorry, Ms. Felton, but that's all we brought," the catering supervisor said.

"You're telling me you only have half of what I ordered for today?" Maddie asked.

"No. I'm telling you we brought what you ordered," the supervisor snapped.

Obviously this person didn't adhere to the philosophy that the customer was always right or that courtesy went a long way in dealing with a mistake. Maddie would pull the contract and check it when she got into the office tomorrow, but there wasn't a thing she could do about it now other than make a mental note to never use this caterer again.

She glanced at the scanty layout of food. At this rate they'd run out of food and drinks long before the race ended.

"Thank you. That's all," Maddie said, dismissing the supervisor. She could send Tamara out to get more food but the race was almost over. There was no point.

Maddie hurried to the front of the skybox. The food situation was a done deal and she was missing the race. That was her real source of frustration. As impossible as it had been for her to imagine a month ago, she was as addicted to the power and finesse of 790-horsepower engines racing around the track, each track offering a different challenge, as the next die-hard fan.

Macray had qualified seventh. Not great, but he'd managed to fight his way up three spots and was holding fourth place.

Thirty laps, one rear-field pile-up and one pit stop later, Maddie gripped the edge of her seat. Macray had gained third, then dropped back to fifth and was now back up at third. Macray and the pack of front six had just come through Turn Four when smoke poured from his engine and he decelerated so fast the cars behind him barely managed to not send him flying across the track.

"This doesn't look good, folks. Let's see if we can find out what's going on."

The network tapped into Macray's audio feed. "Yeah. It was a pop. I'm sure we dropped a cylinder."

Mike Snellings came back with "Bring her in."

What exactly did that mean? Maddie'd learned a lot but she didn't know what a dropped cylinder was. Snellings didn't sound good, but she doubted any crew chief would sound excited at the prospect of losing position. Hopefully, the team would fix it and he'd be back on the track within a lap or two.

Macray had dropped to the bottom of the track and luckily was right at pit road. The car stopped just short of being off track. Maybe not that lucky after all. The wrecker headed over.

"That's a tough break for the Number 76 team. They're done for the day."

"No!"

Maddie didn't realize she'd shouted her protest until everyone looked at her.

She shrugged and offered an apologetic smile. "Sorry."

"Hey, that's how I feel, too," the guy below her, a friend of a friend of the advertising coordinator, said.

Phoenix had turned out to be a bad experience, first the food, now the race—except for Macray inviting her over to his house tomorrow. And now that she wasn't near him being swept up by the force of his personality and the attraction that simmered between them, she wasn't so sure that was such a wise move on her part.

CHAPTER TWELVE

MONDAY AFTERNOON, TUCKER finished watching the replay tape of the race, then walked out to sit on the front porch steps in the sun. Napoleon followed him and curled up on the lower step, soaking up the late-April rays. It was warm today, one of those days when it felt as if they'd skipped spring and gone straight into early summer.

He stood and walked around the corner of the house, double-checking he'd rewound the garden hose after he'd washed his truck earlier. He had.

He paced back to the front steps, ridiculously nervous, and dropped back down to the top step. Hell, he didn't get this wound up for a race. Racing required focus and determination. Maddie Felton showing up at his place required…he wasn't sure.

He wanted her to like his house. He wanted her to see the same potential in it he saw. He'd bought the property because it was near Edna and Jack, but much like his old truck, he saw potential in it with a little TLC.

And…she was here. He heard the quiet growl of the BMW's motor before he saw the car. She turned into his driveway and he stood. Napoleon jumped to his feet, from asleep to alert in mere seconds. He dashed into the front yard.

"Sit," Tucker ordered the little dog as Maddie parked in the dirt driveway.

Napoleon's entire body quivered with the effort of not jumping up and licking Maddie when she got out. Tucker kind of knew how the little guy felt. If Tucker had a tail, he wasn't sure he could keep it from wagging.

"Hello," she said, looking gorgeous and unsure all at once.

"Hi," he answered. He'd never seen her in anything other than business attire. A pair of jeans hugged her curves and a deep gold shirt with a scooped neck brought out the gold flecks in her eyes. She wore a chunky gold-and-bronze necklace and matching earrings. Her painted toenails peeked out of the open toes of a pair of sandals.

"I…uh, changed at the office before I drove out."

"It's a good look." Now that she was here he wasn't quite sure what to say.

"Thanks."

Napoleon, the canine icebreaker, would put her at ease. Either that or send her running, but he'd bet on the first. "By the way, the mass of quivering dog at your feet is Napoleon. His only goal is for you to adore him."

"Done. He's adorable." She leaned down and Napoleon sprang up into her arms. Startled, she laughed and managed to catch him. Good thing she possessed good reflexes.

"Nice catch."

"He's so cute!"

"*Rotten* is more like it. Dump him if he bugs you." Okay, it was a test of sorts.

She shot him a chastising look. "He's fine."

Tucker figured Napoleon was better than fine, considering he was snugged up against her, licking her neck. Whoever said being a dog sucked?

They stood next to her car and Maddie shot him a sympathetic glance. "Sorry about yesterday. You'd done such a great job of moving up. I think you would've won it if that hadn't happened."

Lots of people passed commentary on his driving and his racing from spectators to announcers to his own team, but Maddie's sincere compliment and faith in his abilities warmed him. "Thanks. I think I'd have pulled third, maybe second. Who knows, because a lot can happen." He'd learned a long time ago that second-guessing outcomes could drive him crazy. The best he could do was review the race for how to better handle the car on a particular track and then let it go. "The cylinder was a tough break." It wasn't his driving or the crew's preparation, it just happened. "That's racing. Stuff breaks. Stuff happens." He grinned at her. "When it's the last third of the race, there's nowhere to go but home." He was ready to put Phoenix behind him. "And speaking of home…" He swept his hand toward the house. "This is it. Did you have any trouble finding the place?"

"None at all. Good directions."

Tucker offered a bow from his waist. "My castle awaits your appraisal."

Maddie laughed. "Lead on, royal subject."

Napoleon squirmed, wanting down, and Maddie obliged. Okay, so maybe Napoleon wasn't the smartest dog on the planet after all if he was willing to give up that spot.

She walked up the front steps beside him. "Before we go through the house, why don't you tell me what you see, what you want the house to be."

"What do you mean?"

"Do you want it to be a place for a bunch of guys to hang out? Pool table, card table, games room? Do you want it more orientated to having a family one day?"

He didn't see a family. His own childhood had been a disaster and his marriage had been a wash, as well—he wasn't cut out for the family thing. However, he didn't want a men's club for a house, either. "Okay, I know where you're coming from now. Definitely more like a real house. I'm not into pool or cards. Well, occasionally, but I don't want it at my house. I want comfortable but not stuffy and I sure don't want fussy. I liked your place a lot."

"Thanks. And now I have an idea of where *you're* coming from." She leaned against the post and studied the porch. The floor buckled to the left of the front door, which was off center to the right of the house. "The first thing I'd do is hang a swing." She pointed to the two eyebolts in the ceiling on the right-hand side of the porch. "Looks as if there was one, once upon a time."

Cool. Maybe she was more of a front-porch-swing kind of woman than he'd thought at first. And he was pleased that she hadn't pointed out the buckling floor or off center door. She was looking past the obvious problems to the potential. "That's what I was thinking, too. How about one made out of that twig stuff on your patio?"

A spontaneous smile lit her eyes. "Awesome. And you could maybe do a cushion covered in vintage car material and maybe a nice quilt thrown over the back for cool nights." She pointed to the left portion of the porch, her wrist slender, graceful. "A couple of big rocking chairs over there with matching cushions or a companion print?"

He wasn't exactly sure if he'd know a companion print if it bit him in the butt, but it sounded good to him. "That sounds like just what I'd want." He could sort of see it in his head. "What do you think about a table for playing checkers between the rocking chairs?" he suggested tentatively.

"I think it'd be great. Very inviting."

It felt good to have her approve his ideas. He wanted a home he could be proud of, unlike what he'd grown up in. He carried a seed of insecurity left from his upbringing. He honestly couldn't recall a memory of home that didn't involve dirt and squalor...and violence. He'd always been too ashamed to invite anyone from school to his house.

So, pathetic as it was, when Maddie, the epitome of good taste and class, whose house had felt elegant but comfortable, gave him the thumbs-up, he felt validated and more confident in the plans he'd been sketching out in his head.

They moved through the house, bouncing ideas off of each other, room by room, feeding off each other's enthusiasm. They discussed cabinet finishes and countertops in the kitchen.

"You could do a Dutch door like I have going onto the patio if you wanted to. I think it'd look great," she suggested.

"I'd like that a lot." They actually had very similar taste.

They moved into the den. A crumbling fireplace was in obvious need of repair and Maddie agreed with his idea of replacing the surrounding brick with Tennessee river stone. She suggested built-ins to house the TV, video games, stereo equipment and his books. "You know, one-stop entertainment shopping?"

The place was sort of a mess now, although a damn sight nicer than where he grew up and where his parents still lived, but he was really starting to see the house he could have.

Maddie went crazy when they hit his bedroom and she spotted the fireplace on the wall opposite his bed.

"Oh, this is great! Does it work?"

Tucker was embarrassed to admit he hadn't really checked out whether or not the fireplace was functional. "I'm not sure." The one in the den had obviously needed repair, but this part of the house had been an add-on at a later date and the fireplace was newer.

"Do you have a flashlight?" she asked.

"In the kitchen. Hold on, I'll be right back."

He returned pronto with a flashlight. Maddie lay down on the floor and slid up until her head was in the fireplace. She shone the light up the flue. "It looks pretty good." She glanced at Tucker. "This is exciting."

"What are you looking at? What are you looking for?"

"I'm looking at whether the bricks are crumbling up the flue. I think you can actually burn wood in this. You'll want to check with someone who knows for sure, but I think you can. Here, I'll show you."

She scooted over and he squeezed in beside her. It was fairly tight quarters to fit both their heads. Their shoulders bumped against each other and the scent of her shampoo and perfume teased him. Fireplace. Concentrate on the fireplace. "Now, what am I looking at?"

"See. Look up the chimney. You're looking for crumbling bricks."

"Oh, okay. Nope, don't see any crumbling bricks."

"Isn't that exciting? Is there anything more romantic than a real fire in the bedroom?"

"A fire in the bedroom is always a good thing." Her mouth was so close. "You have a smudge of soot on your cheek." He brushed his thumb over the spot, against her satin skin. Of their own accord, his fingers slid into her hair, cupped her scalp and pulled her closer.

"We're not supposed to do this again," she murmured, but made no move to pull away.

"I know," he said, just as his mouth found hers.

Her warm lips welcomed him. It was like a homecoming and a revelation at the same time. Nothing had ever been more perfect than the melding of her mouth with his. Sweet and hot, offering and demanding, all at the same time.

Somewhere in the back of his mind, Tucker registered a familiar sound. *Click. Click. Click. Whoosh.* Twenty-seven pounds of dog landed on them.

Maddie screamed and Tucker exclaimed, "Napoleon. Stop. Sit."

Napoleon sat. Square in the middle of Maddie. She started laughing and then couldn't seem to stop. It was pretty damn funny. Tucker grinned at what they must look like lying on the floor, practically inside the chimney with one inquisitive dog. Maddie recovered from her bout of mirth and scratched Napoleon behind his ears. "Oh, you bad boy."

She sobered, set Napoleon aside and stood. Tucker stood, as well, his heart still thudding heavily in his chest. She brushed her clothes off with an unsteady hand. "We agreed we weren't going to do that anymore, Macray."

"I know. We did, didn't we?"

"Yeah. We did." Her gaze snared his and he saw something in her eyes, a passion, a wanton disregard that took his breath.

If he had any sense, any measure of self-preservation, he'd send her on her merry way with a promise to never kiss her again and then make damn sure he was never in a position where he could kiss her again. They could work together. He could see her at the hospitality tent, see her at promotional appearances, even sit down for the occasional working lunch—all safely chaperoned by a few hundred folks. But he, who had always been sensible, suddenly failed to see the appeal of sensible. Well, that wasn't true, the appeal of sensible paled in sad comparison to the appeal of Maddie Felton. And the way she'd kissed him, the way she looked at him…he was sure she felt the same attraction, the connection that seemed to flow between them.

"I don't want to lie to you. I can try but I'm not making any promises."

She sighed in self-defeat. "I'm not so sure that I can promise not to kiss you again, either, Tucker Macray. But there is one promise I need from you."

"Okay?"

"My job is important to me…" She hesitated as if she didn't know quite how to say what she needed to say.

He didn't need for her to finish it, he knew where she was going. "Maddie, I don't kiss and tell. Especially not at the track. What happens between us stays between us. No one will ever hear about those two kisses from me. You have my word on that."

"Thank you," she said, and then deliberately changed the subject. "I think it's grand you have a fireplace in your bedroom. If I were you, I'd replace those two windows with French doors and build a private screened patio off this room. And if it were me, I'd put a hot tub out there."

"A hot tub?"

"Sure. Winter's your off-season. Your downtime. That's when you'll spend most of your time here. Just think, a crisp winter night, maybe even a sprinkling of snow on the ground. If you have skylights installed, you can sit in your hot tub with snow around and then come inside to a nice warm fire. And it'll satisfy any latent skinny-dipping urges."

He could handle a car at 180 miles an hour, but listening to Maddie's sensual description was wrecking him. Especially because she painted a very vivid picture and he couldn't seem not to plug her into that scenario right along with him. Her skin…glistening and warm from the hot tub. The snap and crackle of wood in the fireplace. The heat.

He took a deep breath. "Great idea." He had to get her out of his bedroom—and get rid of all the thoughts conjured by a hot tub and fireplace—in record time or he was going to hit the wall. "Let's go look at the laundry room."

Surely, that was safe. Not even Maddie could make a laundry room sexy. She walked ahead of him and he followed the sway of her hips in the snug jeans. Then again, maybe she could.

MADDIE STOOD ON THE TOP step of Tucker's back stoop and listened. Nothing, save the call of a bird and the faint noise of a tractor in a distant field. "It's so quiet here. Very peaceful."

Tucker laughed. "Very unlike the track."

She could see why this place would appeal to him. "No kidding. The track is like one very loud circus."

"Which is why it's so nice to come home to this." He sent her a teasing look. "Hey, if the track's a circus, does that mean I'm a sideshow?"

She laughed. "Now you're putting words into my mouth."

A large bird flew by and landed at the edge of the pond that sat between a small thicket of pines and an open field to the left rear of the house. The bird waded along the pond's edge on long, spindly legs and boasted an equally long beak.

"Blue heron," Tucker said, following her gaze. "He's been showing up for the past couple of months."

"He's huge. I'm used to the much smaller nuthatches and cardinals that visit my feeders."

"Yeah, he's just a little bit bigger than them. He goes down to the pond to fish." Tucker glanced at her. "Have you ever been fishing?"

"Only for the occasional compliment," Maddie shot back, feeling clever and carefree.

Tucker's low chuckle slid over her like a warming blanket, sending heat spiraling through her. "It's the regular guy's version of Zen. Want to give it a try? My next day off is the Monday after Talladega."

Maddie hesitated. She'd sworn to herself after that kiss in his bedroom, when he promised he'd never mention those kisses, that she'd stay the afternoon and then quit while she was ahead. They'd exchanged a few kisses and some light flirting. Game over. No more impromptu dinners. No more visits to brainstorm his renovation. No more private opportunities to steal kisses. They'd keep it friendly but strictly business. She'd sworn that would be her game plan. That was the sane, safe route. She'd say no, he'd respect her decision and that would be that.

"Would I have to touch worms?"

Tucker grinned, sexy and altogether too appealing—cowlicks and all. The man had charisma in spades. "I'll handle the worms."

She could still bail out. "Would I have to touch the fish?"

The look in his eyes sent a shiver coursing through her. "If you manage to catch one, I'll take it off the hook."

She'd spent her whole life—well, since she'd been nine years old—being safe and making darn sure she was sane. Just once, just once she wanted to err on the side of insanity…and this attraction, the heat of his kisses, the sizzle of his touch against her skin…Tucker Macray definitely felt like a fling with insanity.

Maddie felt a sudden burst of pure, unadulterated, unrestrained, in-the-moment happiness. "How can I turn that offer down?"

CHAPTER THIRTEEN

THE NEXT DAY, MADDIE SAT at her desk on the second floor of Sleep EZ's corporate office and double-checked the expense figures for the upcoming race in Talladega against her budget. A little high but she'd come in way under budget in Phoenix, thanks to the catering mistake, which *had* been their fault and had resulted in a complete refund to make amends—and to ensure future business—so the one pretty much offset the other.

She forced herself to focus on the numbers instead of thinking about Macray...the slide of his fingers against her scalp, the sweet heat of his kisses. She and Macray shared some powerful chemistry, and if she was honest, she'd admit neither of them seemed capable of ignoring it. Still, it wasn't a big deal. Keep it light and fun and no harm done.

And she had too much planned for the day to sit around thinking about one very sexy race-car driver.

She ran through her day's "to do" list. One more thing and then she was done. She sent a quick e-mail to Doug requesting additional budget to cover garage tours at upcoming races and copied her father, Stevie and Tamara.

She put a final check in her day planner and took a minute or two to tidy her desk. Five minutes to twelve. She had to hurry.

She stopped by Tamara's cubical on her way out. "I'm taking the afternoon off. And if anyone asks, I came in early this morning to make up the time." Obscenely early, as in she'd been sitting at her desk by 5:00 a.m., but she'd known her father and Doug were traveling out of town this week and it seemed like the perfect opportunity to put her Sharon Makeover plan in action. Makeover today and that left the rest of the week for Sharon to get comfortable in her new look and grow some self-confidence before Daddy was back next Tuesday. "I'll have my cell on if you need to get in touch. Enjoy tomorrow off." Tamara was taking a comp day since she'd worked on Sunday.

Maddie took the stairs to the third floor where Daddy's executive suite dominated one corner. She opened the right side of the matched pair of massive, dark-paneled doors that sectioned his office from the rest of the floor.

Sharon, her brown hair threaded with gray and pulled back into an efficient but severe bun, was on the phone, a pair of wire-rimmed glasses perched on her nose. "Mr. Felton found that clause in the contract unacceptable," Sharon said, and held a staying finger up to Maddie. "Absolutely."

Maddie clicked her tongue against the roof of her mouth. The worst of it was, the gray suit Sharon wore was a dreadful cut and color for her, but obviously expensive. She'd paid a lot of money to look bad. The salesperson who'd allowed her to walk out of the store with that suit hadn't deserved an ounce of commission. Unfortunately, they'd probably earned a huge chunk of change.

Sharon was the model of professional efficiency and looked every day of her fifty-four years. Maybe a couple more. But she had incredible potential—lovely green eyes, nice cheekbones and good skin tone if her hair color and a gray suit didn't wash it out. Ambush makeover Maddie Felton-style was about to hit. "Certainly. E-mail them to me and I'll see that he gets them, Thank you." Sharon ended the call and welcomed Maddie with a smile.

"Hi, Maddie. I'm sorry you had to wait through that call, but your dad's out of the office today."

"I know. That's why I'm here." She was about to dance with excitement, which probably wasn't the best idea, so she elected to perch on the edge of the wing chair to the right of Sharon's dark cherry desk—when guests or employees waited to see Louis Felton, they waited in style.

Sharon paused in closing a document. "Okay. Then what can I do for you?"

While the cat was away, the mice were going to play, and Maddie didn't feel a bit guilty. She'd come in early and she didn't even want to think how many extra hours Sharon had logged in over the years.

"I'd like to take you shopping. You know, update your corporate look on behalf of Sleep EZ."

Sharon was already shaking her head before Maddie finished. "That's nice of you. I know you like to shop, but I've got a ton of work to do. And I just updated my suits last year."

Maddie had formulated a plan, and then a backup plan, because she'd had an idea getting Sharon out of the office wouldn't be particularly easy. Seems it was time to move on to her backup, which substituted honesty for subtlety. Subtlety never seemed to work for her.

Before she could launch her next round, the phone rang. Maddie sat through the phone call and tried to relax, but she was too keyed up. Finally Sharon was off the phone.

"Sharon, I want to talk to you, woman to woman. You've worked for my father for a long time, haven't you?"

Sharon nodded, her green eyes perplexed. "Fourteen years last month."

Maddie nodded. "You know he works way too much. All he does is work and play the occasional game of golf, and that's usually work-related, as well."

"Mr. Felton's very dedicated to his company." There was a note of pride in Sharon's voice.

"Too dedicated. I think he needs to learn how to relax, to develop more of a personal life." Maddie paused for effect. "I think he needs to start dating."

Sharon suddenly busied herself with a document on her desk, but all she was really doing was shuffling papers with a slightly unsteady hand. "Oh. I didn't realize Mr. Felton was interested in someone."

"He's not."

Relief flashed in Sharon's eyes and Maddie knew she was on the right track. "We just need to steer him in the right direction."

"We?"

Maddie drew a deep breath. "Sharon, are you in love with my father?" she asked quietly.

Honestly, she didn't know any better way to approach it than straight on.

All the color drained from Sharon's face and she sat frozen as if turned to stone by Maddie's question.

The phone rang and Sharon reached over, but instead of answering it, she pushed a button sending it to voice mail. Maddie'd never seen Sharon not take a call.

Maybe Maddie'd shot a tad too straight. She backpedaled, trying to reassure Sharon. "Daddy has no idea, by the way." Sharon went from deathly white to bright red and her mouth opened but no sound came out. Maddie continued, "He's a man. He's clueless. I just figured it out a couple of weeks ago."

"How?" The single word came out scratchy. More of a croak than an actual word.

Maddie was just relieved to hear her actually speak. "It's okay. I'm the only one who knows." No need to mention her conversation with Jess and really send poor Sharon into a tailspin. "It was just a crazy thing. For a split second I saw your reflection in the window one day when you brought in lunch and I knew. No one else saw. I promise you."

Sharon drew a shuddering breath and buried her face in her hands. "Why are you bringing this up?"

"Because I think you're a nice person and my dad could use a nice person in his life. But at the rate you're going, it's never going to happen."

Sharon dropped her hands into her lap and looked at Maddie. "It's never going to happen, anyway." The resignation and sadness in her eyes strengthened Maddie's resolve. "I'm like a piece of furniture to Mr. Felton."

Maddie nodded. "You nailed it."

Sharon looked ready to burst into tears.

"That's why we're going to reupholster the sofa," Maddie said.

"Huh?"

"It'll be the same efficient piece of furniture, but from now on it's going to be eye-catching." Maddie smiled encouragement at the other woman. "We've got to get him to notice you. We do a serious makeover in the name of updating your professional look and he'll notice. Trust me, I know my dad." She stood and held out her hand. "C'mon. Grab your purse. We're going for an extended lunch."

"I couldn't." Sharon's eyes reflected the same look she'd seen in Greg Sheffield's. She didn't dare hope in case it was snatched away from her. "I have work to do."

"Then work late this evening. Vivian can cover for you. We'll tell her I need your help with a project. Even though she handles both Doug and Stevie, I don't think she stays as busy as you do," Maddie said. Indecision warred in Sharon's eyes, but the flicker of hope grew brighter and Maddie pressed harder. "I know all about getting in a rut and not wanting to rock the boat, but sometimes you just have to, no matter how hard it is to make a change. You either wither and die or change and grow. This is your chance. It's a win-win situation. You're not going to throw yourself at him—" a blush washed over the other woman's face "—you're just going to update your look, a new outfit or two, maybe a new haircut." Definitely a new haircut, but she didn't want to totally freak Sharon out. "You know, reupholster the sofa."

Sharon stood, indecision fighting a losing battle with hope. Maddie took a step toward the door. "C'mon, we're burning daylight." She'd set a tentative hair appointment with Chantal for this afternoon. They were going to be cutting it close.

Sharon took a deep breath and grabbed her purse. Maddie wanted to hug her because she knew just how much courage it had taken for Sharon to make that decision. Instead, she linked her arm through the older woman's and tugged her toward the door before Sharon lost her nerve and changed her mind. "This is going to be fun."

"IT'S STILL NOT RIGHT," Tucker said, rubbing a hand wearily over the back of his neck. Considering it had gotten off to a great start on Monday with Maddie, this had turned into the week from hell.

"We'll figure it out," Mike said, checking over the spec sheet. They'd busted butt all week and the setup on the car still wasn't right. He had faith they'd get it where it needed to be, but sooner would be much better than later.

They were all tense. Tucker figured the best thing he could

do right now was give the crew some space to do their thing. They didn't need him hovering over them.

"I'm gonna head over to the hauler for a while."

"Good idea. Go read a book."

Tucker laughed. Mike was a good guy. They were all just stressed. There was a lot riding on their performance here. After the spinout, compliments of Lowell in Texas, and dropping a cylinder last week in Phoenix, they needed a good run here in Talladega, and a good run at 'Dega was only going to happen if the car was jam on.

He crossed from the garage area, pausing to talk to a couple of the guys, and then headed to the front of the hauler. Empty. Well, except for Marcus, who surprise, surprise, was on his computer with his headphones on. Marcus always holed up in the corner with the screen angled away and acted as if he was conducting serious business. Tucker suspected Marcus's "serious business" was a serious solitaire addiction.

They exchanged greetings and mercifully that was it. He wasn't particularly in the mood to humor Marcus today.

Tucker dropped to the upholstered bench seat on the side end opposite from Marcus. Truth of the matter was he was nervous as hell. 'Dega had eaten him alive last year when he raced the NASCAR Busch Series here. It had chewed him up and spit him out. Tenth-place qualifier and he still wasn't sure the car was ready. He wasn't sure he was ready. And Mr. Chalkey, the big guy, not Marcus, had made it abundantly clear that after the past two races, he expected a good showing from Team Three at the superspeedway. Tucker reminded himself he just needed to focus and play Talladega as a drafting game.

Three hours later he was back in the transporter, lightning popping all around, thunder booming overhead and rain pouring down in sheets of gray. He wouldn't face down 'Dega today. Nope. Rain delay and tornado warnings had taken care of that. As soon as he wasn't in imminent danger of being electrocuted by lightning, he'd go to the motorhome and hope that the weather and track cleared enough to run the race tomorrow. And, of course, that shot his plans to take Maddie fishing.

His mood grew as dark as the sky outside.

TUESDAY MORNING MADDIE SAT at her desk feeling frazzled. Two days at Talladega had taken a toll. She sincerely hoped for no more rain delays the rest of the season. Not only had it cancelled out her fishing plans with Tucker, it'd been a major pain and had meant scrambling to cover the catering on Monday, as well. The upside had been CRE's second- and third-place finishes. Tucker had drafted into third place behind Team Two's Number 86 car.

She reached for her coffee cup and her office door flew open. Her father stood glowering in the doorway. "Hold her calls," he said to Tamara, and came in, closing her door firmly behind him.

Oh, boy. Daddy never came downstairs. As a matter of course, the lesser beings in the company, herself included, were summoned upstairs.

"Hi, I see you got back okay from your trip," she said as if him dropping into her office like a thunderstorm was an everyday occurrence.

"Yes, I'm back." His expression hadn't lightened. Maybe she could buy herself some time.

"I'm sort of busy, Daddy. Can this wait?"

"If I thought it could wait, would I have walked down here?" he demanded.

True enough.

"Want a cup of coffee?"

"No. I don't want any coffee." He dropped into a chair on the other side of the desk.

Maddie cradled her coffee mug, inhaling aromatic Hawaiian-grown Blue Mountain, and gathered her courage. Might as well get it over with. "So, is everything okay, Daddy?"

"Don't give me that wide-eyed look." His scowl deepened. "You know good and well everything's not okay. What did you do to my secretary?" His eyebrows nearly formed a uni-brow, his frown was so intense. Mission accomplished! He'd finally *noticed* Sharon.

She waved a dismissive hand. "Oh, that. We just went shopping one day. And then I needed a trim, so while we were there, Chantal cut and colored Sharon's hair. Doesn't she look great?"

Sharon had looked even better than Maddie expected. She was truly a beautiful woman. Chantal had given her a shoulder-length cut with some slight feathering around the face to accentuate her cheekbones. She'd taken Sharon's hair a deeper shade of brown with rich auburn highlights that had instantly warmed her skin tone. Next, they'd gone for some new makeup choices with warm colors that complemented her hair and skin and really brought out her green eyes. She'd ditched the gray suit for a tobacco-brown suit with a nipped-waist jacket that showed off her trim figure and accessorized with a silk scarf in mottled shades of browns, greens and golds. She still looked professional and efficient. She just looked gorgeous to boot.

He shook his head. "I don't like it."

"What's not to like? She looks great. At least ten years younger."

His scowl deepened. "She didn't need to look younger."

"Every woman wants to feel like she looks younger than she is. Trust me, it's a woman thing." Maddie sipped from her cup to hide a smile. "And I still don't understand the problem."

"It's like having some stranger around. If I'd wanted a new secretary, I'd have hired a new secretary," he groused.

Maddie was hard-pressed not to laugh. "You mean, it's affected her performance? She's not doing her job?"

"Of course not!"

Her implying Sharon wasn't doing her job certainly bunched his boxers. "Well, I just don't get it. What's the problem?"

He ran a hand across his gray crew cut. "It's damn distracting, that's the problem."

Maddie had to grin. "She's hot, isn't she?"

"She's my secretary. I don't need her to be hot."

Hmm. Interesting that he didn't deny it. "Of course not. You just need her to be efficient and she still is. But she's a woman and *she* needs to be hot."

He crossed his arms over his chest. "I'm not so sure I want to hear my daughter talking about hot."

"Daddy, I'm not a little girl anymore."

"You'll always be my little girl." His tone shifted from gruff indulgence back to annoyed. "But don't go mucking around with my secretary."

"I think you need to stop and think about why this has you so upset."

Good grief. Her father, who looked like a tired prizefighter who'd taken one too many hits, turned a dull red. Her father was blushing.

"Because I may lose a perfectly good secretary." He pushed to his feet and paced across the room, not that he had far to go, her office was tiny. "Sharon understands me. Sometimes she knows what I need even before I do. I'm used to her

Now she's going to start getting invitations to dinner—" he stopped pacing and braced his hands on the back of the chair "—the theater, wrestling—" *wrestling? okay* "—and then she's gonna want to get off early and how am I going to count on her to work late if she's haring off on some date or another? Then the next thing you know she'll be getting married and quitting on me and I'll have to start all over again." He stabbed an accusatory finger at Maddie. "That's the problem."

Whoa. The problem, as far as she could discern, was that her father had a bad case for Sharon. Maddie had wanted to make over Sharon to get his attention. Who knew she'd had his attention all along?

"Well, then maybe you should beat them to the punch and ask her out yourself."

"Don't be foolish." He sat back down in the chair. "I'm her boss. Asking her out would be sexual harassment."

Maddie shrugged. "Then fire her."

"You've lost your mind. I couldn't fire Sharon. It wouldn't be right. She's a great secretary."

"Why not? According to you, you're going to lose her, anyway. So, tell her you're making personnel changes, help her find another job, then ask her out."

"That's the craziest thing I've ever heard. Why should I give up a perfectly good secretary just so I can ask her out?"

"Because she's hot."

"She didn't used to be." Ha. She had him. "This is all your fault."

Maddie shrugged. "I can't undo it. The past is done. And I still think you should ask her out."

"I'm too old for her." He looked uncharacteristically unsure of himself. "Plus, I don't know how to date. I only know how to make money."

"You're just a little rusty. At the dating, not the money-making."

Her father beetled his eyebrows at her. Okay, so the last woman he'd dated had been her mother before they got married, which meant he hadn't had a date in roughly thirty-four years. Maybe he was a lot rusty. "Don't sweat it. Dating's like riding a bike."

"I was never any good at riding a bike. Dating, neither. I'm not a people person. I told you, I'm good at making money."

"I don't know why you'd say you're not a people person. You've always been a good dad."

All his ire and bluster vanished and he simply looked weary. He rubbed his hand over his face. "I wasn't a very good husband."

"You always seemed like a good husband and father to me."

"Your mother wasn't very happy, Maddie, and I never knew what to do to make her happy."

"Have you ever thought that it wasn't you? That maybe Mama just…wasn't happy?"

Had they all sat locked in their own private hells all these years, each feeling responsible for Mary Beth Felton's suicide? Had her father spent the past fifteen years alone because he was afraid he wasn't relationship material? Had he, the man who could outnegotiate, outwit and outlast any competitor, quietly fallen in love with his secretary but never done anything about it because he didn't consider himself husband material? No more. They weren't going to limp along, emotionally crippled by her mother's suicide anymore. Enough.

Should she just say it? Tell him she knew about her mother? Drag it out in the open once and for all? No. Not now. One day. This conversation needed to be about Sharon and new possibilities. Suddenly Maddie understood how days could segue into months and months into years without her father ever finding the "right time" to tell her the truth about her mother.

"Lucky for you, I've got a great idea. It wouldn't really be a date, but it's not quite all business, either."

"Might as well hear it. It can't be any crazier than firing her." He glared at her.

"Invite her to a race."

"A race? Like a NASCAR NEXTEL Cup race?"

"Yeah. You know, that little car we sponsor that goes around the track really fast." Maddie grinned at him. "We were talking when we went shopping and Sharon's a huge fan."

"Sharon?" He looked about as surprised as if she'd announced Sharon was a part-time hooker.

Once upon a time, as in not too long ago, Maddie might've been surprised, too, but not now. Apparently everyone and their grandmother was a NASCAR fan. She'd certainly turned into one.

"Uh-huh. Sharon. I bet she'd love to go to Darlington."

"But that's the weekend after next."

Maddie smiled and nodded. "Yep. You'd better ask fast."

NEARLY A WEEK LATER, the Monday after Richmond, Maddie sat on the bank, at the edge of Tucker's pond, and watched the little red-and-white bobber floating on top of the water off the end of her cane pole. Between her and Tucker, Napoleon lay on his belly in the fragrant grass, front paws stretched forward, rear paws stretched behind him, tongue lolling out, basking in the warm sun.

A soft breeze sent ripples skittering across the murky surface of the pond and blew a few strands of hair across her eyes. In the distance, the steady hum of a tractor sounded from several fields over. Cotton-candy clouds decorated the expanse of robin's-egg-blue sky.

On the other side of Napoleon, Tucker also sat on the bank's edge, the sun glinting in his dark brown hair. She closed her eyes, trying to commit every nuance of the moment to memory. The aroma of clean air, sweet grass, the faint odor of dog, the masculine smell of deodorant and man, the earthiness of the bank beneath her.

She'd made up her mind to throw caution to the wind and live, if not recklessly, at least with a measure of abandon. To seize the day. She and Tucker were operating on borrowed time. She'd replayed their conversation at her house in her head at least a dozen times, maybe more. If and when she decided she was ready for a serious relationship, she'd meant what she'd said, it wouldn't be with anyone involved in racing. She'd led a fairly sheltered, abnormal life up until now. She wanted a normal future. A husband who came home every night. Little League games on the weekends. But for now, for now she'd grab and enjoy every moment. One day she'd tell her children about fishing with the famous Tucker Macray because she was dead certain Tucker was well on his way to carving a name for himself in racing.

"Sleepy?" Amusement tinged Tucker's low, husky question. Added to the moment, the rich sound of his voice.

Slowly, she opened her eyes. "No. I'm not sleepy. I just want to remember every detail of this moment. It's perfect."

He looked at her. His eyes seemed to see straight to her soul. How was it that he was so easy to be with, yet set her heart to pounding at the same time? How had she ever considered him average? She suddenly, desperately, wanted to know everything there was to know about this man before their time was up. And the first place to start was with the most significant thing in his life. "Can I ask you something?"

"You can ask. I can't guarantee an answer, but you can ask."

"You said that you'd never met a woman as important as racing. Why is racing so important? I can't imagine feeling that way about a thing." A frown of concern wrinkled her brow. "That's not a criticism. I'm just trying to understand."

"Racing saved my life."

The quiet intensity, the absolute sincerity of that simple sentence prickled her with gooseflesh. "How?"

"Do you want the PR version or do you want the truth?"

"My whole life has been a PR clip. Let's go with the truth even if it's not pretty." She hesitated. "Except…unless…not if it's painful for you."

"Not anymore. It's the past and it is what it is. Both my parents are alcoholics." His smile qualified more as a grimace. "Mama cries when she's drunk and Daddy hits. She's only sad and he's only mean when they're drunk. Unfortunately, they're seldom sober and the old man thought I made a particularly good punching bag."

His statement sickened her. She hadn't expected…that. She looked at the bump along his nose and knew…knew with a certainty that made her want to weep. "He broke your nose, didn't he?"

The buzz of a bee behind her, the flawless cloud-scattered sky, seemed almost obscene.

Tucker reached up and rubbed the bump at the top of his nose, and Maddie gripped her cane pole tighter to keep from reaching over and taking his hand in hers. "A couple of times."

"What kind of monster breaks his child's nose *a couple of times*?"

Tucker shrugged. "That pretty much sums the old man up.

By the time I was thirteen, I was mad as hell all the time and about one step from running away or turning to drugs and alcohol or both." He relayed how Andy and Jack had introduced him to racing and how he'd wound up behind the wheel of a midget racer one night instead of Andy. "When I'm behind the wheel of that car, it takes me away from everything else. It taps into the best part of me."

The look on his face…the light in his eyes that dispelled the bleakness… Well, she'd wanted to know and now she had her answer. Maddie knew several of the drivers were married and had families, so she knew it wasn't an impossible relationship if a woman was interested—not that she was, well, except as a teammate…friend…whatever. "I can see where that's hard for a woman to compete."

"Yeah. It just didn't work for me. Been there, done that, got the T-shirt. Darlene and I got married pretty soon out of high school. I can't blame her at all for getting tired of it and walking away. All my time, money and attention went to my car."

What had she been like? What had she looked like, this woman that had shared Tucker Macray's life as his partner? It was public knowledge he'd been married before, but to hear about her firsthand left Maddie's stomach knotted. "Do you miss her?"

Tucker's smile seemed ineffably sad to her. "I suppose I should, but, no, not really." He shot Maddie an unsure look. "Does that make me a jerk?"

Relief surged through her that he wasn't pining after an ex-wife. "I hope not, because I've never been married, but I don't particularly miss any of my ex-boyfriends."

"Well, good. I suppose I'm not a total jerk, then, just damaged goods."

Damaged goods. How could she deny it? How could she

even begin to understand the emotional scars he must carry?
"Do you ever see her?"

"Occasionally. Out and about. She remarried. Craig's a nice guy and they have a couple of cute kids. I'm glad she found someone. She's a nice-enough woman and she wound up with the short end of the stick married to me."

"That's lame!"

"What's lame about it?"

"Exactly how were you the short end of the stick? Were you seeing someone else? Did you cheat on her?"

"No. It was never anything like that. I didn't have enough time for her. I sure didn't have time for anyone else. Plus, I'm not like that." He shrugged. "She and Craig got married pretty soon after our divorce. I've wondered...but it really didn't matter. I take full responsibility."

"Wait a minute. Were you or were you not racing when you met her?"

"Well, yeah."

"Were you or were you not racing when you got married?"

"I was. But—"

Maddie cut him off. "There's no *but* about it. She knew what she was getting into. It's not as if you sprang racing on her after you tied the knot. It's not as if you cultivated a new love after the fact." Maddie snorted. "I wouldn't be offering her up for canonization anytime soon."

Tucker's mouth gaped open in surprise.

"Sorry. I just don't think you should be so eager to take all the blame." Well, since she'd just stuck her running shoe firmly in her mouth, she might as well go for broke. "What about your parents? Do you ever see them?"

"I moved in with Jack and Edna when I was fourteen and haven't been back. It was shortly after Jack found out what was going on at home that they took me in. I've never asked and he's never offered, but I suspect Jack had a talk with dear old dad about pressing child-abuse charges. I didn't know and I didn't care. I was just glad to get the hell out of there."

"Have you seen them since?"

"Nope. They live about five miles that way," he said, pointing toward the highway, "as the crow flies. Haven't seen them, haven't talked to them. We don't do Christmas cards." His smile held an edge. "I send them a check every month and it clears my bank every month, so I know they're still alive."

What? They didn't deserve anything from him. "Why do you send them money every month?"

"I figure I owe them. If I hadn't been so damn miserable, I might've never wound up behind the wheel of a race car, or under different circumstances it might not have affected me the same. So I figure if it hadn't been for them, I probably wouldn't be where I am today. And I'm very happy to be where I am today."

She wasn't sure that it made up for a horrible childhood. "I guess so. Adored by thousands…possibly millions…doing what you love…nice place…nice dog. What more could a guy ask for?"

"That's all good, but the best part about being where I am today is that I can make a difference. I sponsor kids in racing that wouldn't be there otherwise. I've always spent part of my racing money on that, even when I wasn't making big bucks. It was budgeted in, but now, now that I'm on the NASCAR NEXTEL Cup circuit, I can really make a difference. And if racing brings to just one of them what it brought to me, then it's worth more than I can tell you."

"You're a good man, Tucker Macray."

"C'mon, Maddie. I was just getting used to being a jerk."

He nodded toward the neighboring property. "Edna and Jack live over there, that white house you can barely see through that stand of trees. You passed it on your way in."

She could take the hint that he'd said enough about himself and was ready for a subject change.

"Do you see them—"

All of a sudden her line dipped and her pole gave a mighty yank in her hands. She screamed and grabbed the pole tighter to keep from losing it and stood up. Her scream and sudden movement startled Napoleon, who leaped up, and it all happened so fast Maddie wasn't sure exactly what happened. One second she was on the edge of the bank with Napoleon racing around her, barking like mad, and the next second her feet were in slippery mud. They flew out from under her and down she went. Pond water went in her mouth and eyes before she could scramble upright. Then she was sitting in a muddy pond, spitting out green water and still holding on to her pole.

Tucker yelled "Maddie, are you okay?" and jumped in after her.

She blinked water out of her eyes and squinted past her dripping hair plastered to her face. "I'm fine." She hauled back on the pole. "Help me get this fish. It's still on the line and even if I'm butt-deep in slimy mud, this sucker's coming in."

CHAPTER FOURTEEN

THE CLOSED BATHROOM DOOR muffled Maddie's voice. "I'm warning you right now, if you laugh, you're a dead man." He heard her unlock the door.

"What if I snicker?"

She cracked the door and gave him the evil eye through the tiny opening. "Any hint of mirth or amusement will not be tolerated."

She opened the door and stepped out. She'd been covered in mud from head to toe when they'd both stumbled back to the house from the pond, dripping wet and laughing. He'd seriously had to hose her clothes down outside the back door, after discreetly turning his back while she stripped down and wrapped herself in a towel before she shagged off to the shower. He'd only had to change his pants and shoes while she showered. The best Tucker could come up with for Maddie while her clothes washed and dried had been a pair of his old sweatpants—drawstring waist—and a T-shirt. The clothes hung on her and she'd wrapped the towel around her head, turban-style.

Her eyes dancing with humor, she drawled, "It's a new fashion statement."

"It's definitely different. And it definitely suits you." He grinned. "Those clothes never looked that good on me."

"Thanks for the loaner."

"Well, you could hardly stand around naked while you waited on your clothes to wash and dry. I mean, it would've been fine with me, you being a decent-looking woman and nothing bad wrong with you…."

A blush washed over her face. "Macray, just shut up and give me the blow-dryer."

"Sorry. No blow-dryer here."

"How can you not have a blow-dryer?"

"In case you hadn't noticed…I'm a guy."

"What? Does it emasculate a man to own a blow-dryer? My brothers use blow-dryers. I bet Tim Lambert uses a blow-dryer."

"Now, that's a low blow." Lambert had spun him out at Texas and Tucker still owed him a payback. "And I'm sure he does…which is all the more reason for me not to."

"Do you have any idea what my hair's going to look like without a blow-dryer?" She pulled the towel off and her hair dropped to her shoulders in wet hanks. She was still a pretty woman, but her hair wasn't looking too hot.

He knew it was the wrong thing to do, but he couldn't seem to squelch his grin. "Not yet. But I think I'm about to."

"It's not funny. It'll dry all freaky and wavy."

"You're talking to me—the king of cowlicks? I wouldn't know anything about hair drying freaky?"

"That's true." She huffed back to the bathroom and pulled a brush out of her purse. He followed at what he hoped was a safe distance. "Don't say you weren't warned," she muttered.

Steam and the fragrance of soap and shampoo lingered in the air. Tucker leaned against the doorjamb.

"Maybe I need to rush out and buy one to save us both the trauma. Or at least the drama." That earned him a haughty glance. "Then I'd have a blow-dryer on hand for the next person that decides to swim after their fish."

"Ya know, I wouldn't consider giving up the NASCAR NEXTEL circuit for the comedy circuit." She dragged the brush through her hair.

"So much for my backup career plan," he said. He thought about pointing out that she shouldn't worry about her hair when she didn't have any on any makeup anymore, but salvaged a brain cell or two and kept his mouth shut. Even if he thought she looked just as pretty, if not prettier, without the war paint, it wasn't likely to earn him bonus points right now. The best thing to do was just apologize for her winding up in the pond in the first place. "Sorry your first fishing experience didn't go better."

He enjoyed the simple sight of her brushing out her hair. He pushed aside the thought that he was growing dangerously addicted to her presence.

She shot him a smile. "Are you kidding? It was great. Didn't you say that's the biggest fish that's ever been caught in that pond?"

Maddie Felton was one of a kind. And by dammit, they'd fished that pond for years, and for years they'd heard or suspected and occasionally sighted the big-mouth bass that had been stocked in there, but no one had ever landed one. Until Maddie. On her first fishing outing. And then she'd insisted on releasing it back into the pond.

He chuckled and stood aside so she could get out of the small bathroom. "Yeah. I meant the falling-in part."

"Oh, that. Don't worry." She waved a hand in dismissal. "I'm sort of klutzy. When I was a kid I was so hopeless in ballet that Daddy pulled me out of the class. And when I was presented at my coming-out at the debutante ball I had to walk down this grand staircase that seemed to go on forever. My brothers had bets on what step I'd make it to before I fell."

He'd worked with Steve before Maddie took over and had met her other brother once. Dave? Derek? Something with a *D.* They both seemed like nice-enough guys. He could definitely see them betting on whether she walked or tumbled down the steps. "Did you fall?"

They walked side by side down the short hall to the kitchen.

"Almost." She grinned. "I made it to the last step and sort of stumbled, but my date caught my arm and saved me, probably both of us, from sprawling on the floor. Ripped the hem right out of my dress, but we were both still upright."

He had to laugh at the picture she painted, which was so far removed from the sophisticated young woman she presented herself as…well, except when she was slip-sliding into a pond.

Tucker pulled a chair out for her at the butcher-block table, a hand-me-down from Edna and Jack. "Well, how the heck do you navigate around so easily in those three-inch heels you wear?"

Her sassy smile tied him in a knot. "Lots and lots of practice."

He laughed again. Funny how if he wasn't busy spilling his guts to her like he had at the pond, he was usually laughing with her over something. "That paints a mental image. I can just see you walking around your house and falling down but getting back up."

"You're not too far off."

Napoleon trotted in and curled up beneath the table, next to Maddie's feet. He'd certainly taken a liking to her. Tucker thought he and the little dog could easily get used to having her around the place.

"How about something to drink?" he offered. "Coffee? Tea? Ginger ale?"

"I'd love a cup of tea."

He opened the cabinet and pulled out a box of assorted teas.
Maddie quirked a questioning eyebrow. "You're a tea
drinker?"

"Not really." He shrugged, somewhat sheepishly. "But I
figured you were so I picked some up this morning."

She selected the Lady Grey and he put on the water to boil.

"I'd thought we might grab some dinner somewhere but it's
going to be a while on your clothes. I make a mean grilled
cheese and ham, but I'm warning you, it's seriously good. It'll
wreck you for any other grilled cheese."

"Hmm. You're telling me it'll be the best I've ever had, but
then you'll have ruined me for any other. I think I have to try it."

"I've done my duty by warning you."

They kept up a light conversation while he made the sandwiches and she prepared her cup of tea. Maddie was good
company, asking questions about Jack and Edna and Andy
and his family. He flipped the sandwiches on the griddle and
killed the heat. The pan sizzled as cheese oozed over the side
of the bread.

"Holy smoke, that smells good," Maddie said. "You know,
you always work up an appetite swimming."

He smiled over at her and for a second lost himself in her
golden eyes. "Almost ready." He slid the sandwiches onto
plates and then neatly cut them in half. "There's a nice sunset
from the back stoop, if you don't mind sitting on a concrete-
block stair."

"Mind? You know I love my patio. What could be better
than a back stoop, a grilled ham and cheese and a sunset?"

He brushed off a few pine needles and Maddie settled on
the second step. He sat on the step above her. It was pretty
tight quarters to sit side by side. His knee brushed against her

shoulder as he settled into a comfortable position and his body hummed from the brief contact. The sun, a blend of pinks, oranges and yellows, dipped toward the pines silhouetted on the horizon.

Maddie bit into the sandwich and sighed with pleasure, which melted him inside as surely as the cheese on the sandwich. "This is sinfully good. I should've paid more attention to how you made it. You'll have to tell me how."

It was about the only thing he was good at making in the kitchen, although he barbecued a mean steak. "Sorry, no can do."

"Why not?"

"Then how would I bribe you back out here again?"

"There are ways."

They ate, sharing a companionable silence, yet he was aware of every nuance of her as the sun set and the light began to fade, the precursor to night. Maddie finished her last bite and then licked her fingers clean. "Delicious. What a perfect day." She shot him a glance. "Perfect except for the lack of a blow-dryer."

Her hair had dried in soft waves. All of the other times her hair was sleek and sophisticated and definitely looked good on her, but this…

"I like your hair like this. It's soft and sexy." She looked as if she'd just climbed out of his bed and thrown on his clothes. This he liked a lot. Too much. They both needed a not-so-subtle reminder of just how different from each other they were. Or at least he did. "Except it's deceptive. A man can forget that you're a princess who grew up in a mansion, a debutante, nonetheless, while he grew up as close to a foster kid as you could get without papers being signed."

"Are you saying that I grew up in a picture-perfect home, adored by all, insulated from the real world and couldn't possibly have anything in common with a boy whose father abused him and tried to make him feel worthless."

"That's the way I see it."

"Maybe you don't see things as clearly as you think you do."

"Maddie, I've seen where you grew up. I've seen the pool and manicured lawns and flower beds all tended by a gardener." He shook his head. "I remember playing out in our yard where the weeds were higher than I was when I was a little kid. Our place looked abandoned. We had a little bit of grass and a whole lot more weeds, but we didn't even own a lawn mower that ran. When I was older, one day in desperation, I used a butcher knife from the kitchen as a swing blade."

"You should know better than anyone that things aren't always the way they seem. The manicured lawn, the gardener… that's the PR version." She had a way of tossing his words back at him. "Do you want the truth? It's not pretty." There was no mistaking the note of steel in her voice.

His gut constricted and his entire body tensed. If someone had laid a hand on Maddie, ever struck her, left a bruise on her soft cheek, blackened her eye…or worse… He felt a sudden urge to find him, whoever it was, wherever he was and tear him limb from limb. His stomach roiled at the thought of anyone hurting this woman.

"The truth." An earlier phrase came back to haunt him. They'd been at the pond and she'd said her entire life had been a PR clip.

She stared out across the backyard, as if she were studying the stand of pines, now shadows against the sky. An owl hooted. "The official sanitized version is that when I was nine my mother had a heart attack and died in her sleep at age thirty-two. The truth is she swallowed a handful of pills." She turned and looked at him in the waning light. "My mother committed suicide."

"Damn."

"Yeah. Damn." He didn't realize he'd spoken until she repeated the phrase. "I spent years thinking it had to be my fault. Thinking if I'd been a better daughter, smarter, prettier, neater, more well behaved, she would've loved me more." Her voice was little more than a whisper. "She would've loved me enough not to leave me."

He couldn't help it. The urge to touch her, to make contact was overwhelming. He gentled her hair back from her face.

"Didn't your father set you straight on that?"

"We've never discussed it. My father told me my mother died of a heart attack and left it at that." She told him about finding her and going back to her room. She told him how she'd been terrified for years she'd self-destruct like her mother or at the least drive her family away.

Maddie's even, matter-of-fact tone tore at him, through him. He recognized the pain it masked. He knew exactly what it was like to anesthetize yourself with detachment to keep from self-destructing with anguish.

"That's messed up," he said.

"It is, but I know Daddy was just trying to protect me. I'm sure he felt like he'd failed Mama. Suicide is a miserable legacy."

Tucker could only imagine the anger, the guilt, the desolation. He'd at least had the ability to walk away. He'd also had Edna and Jack and their family. What had Maddie had except a nice house and one misguided old man? Tears stung his eyes for the girl who'd carried the weight of a mother's suicide all alone. A girl who'd grown into a woman imprisoned by guilt and love and fear.

"You've been like a bird in a gilded cage."

"That sounds so pathetic." She didn't have to attest to its accuracy. "I don't want to sound pathetic—" she lifted her chin and it nearly broke his heart, the courage in that one gesture "—because I'm not."

"C'mere." He pulled her into his arms, onto his lap, offering comfort but not pity. Her hair brushed against his neck as he settled her head beneath his chin and held her against the beating of his heart. "You're way too strong to be pathetic."

He smoothed his hand over her hair and she settled her head back against his shoulder and looked up into his face. "When you told me that at the pond…about your dad and mom. I knew. I knew then you'd understand."

He felt her hurt, her ache, as if it was his own. A kinship of wounded spirits. But instead of feeling like a victim, he found that the more he opened himself to her, the more he offered her solace, the more he felt himself grow stronger, the more his own wound healed.

He cupped her jaw in his hand. "I do understand. And you need to understand this, Maddie Felton. You're one of the strongest, fieriest, sexiest, nonpathetic women I've ever known."

"Honest? You wouldn't lie to make me feel better?"

"Honest. You know I shoot straight. Do you think I'm pathetic because of what I told you earlier? Do you think I'm pathetic because I grew up with an alcoholic, abusive father?"

"Never pathetic. My heart aches because it's just not right that any child should grow up that way, but there's nothing remotely pathetic about you. Well, except your hair." He felt her relax, sensed the release of tension and recognized what was almost embarrassment at having revealed such raw emotion. The same need he'd had at the pond to bring the emotional charge down a notch. It was there in the teasing note she'd adopted. "And I'm not even sure that I still think it's totally pathetic. It's sort of sexy pathetic."

He skimmed the line of her jaw with his lips. "I'll show you sexy pathetic."

She turned her head, her cheek brushing against his, bringing her mouth to his. "Well, a girl can always hope."

SHE'D NEVER FELT SO gloriously alive. Tucker's kiss had started out tender but together they'd taken it to hot. Long, deep kisses that gave as much as they took.

He tore his mouth from hers and murmured against her cheek, "Oh, Maddie."

Her breath came in short, hard gasps. She could only gasp his name in return, "Tucker."

She felt the runaway pounding of his heart against her shoulder, the sensual heat of his skin against hers. He tangled his hand in her hair. "Say it again," he whispered against her mouth. "Say my name again. Please. You've only ever called me by my last name."

"Tucker."

With a soft groan, he pulled her closer and nibbled tiny kisses along her jaw. A delicious heat and lethargy stole through her. She melted against him, into him, as he rained kisses along her neck.

Exquisite sensations chased through her body as his marauding mouth pleasured every inch of her neck and shoulder. "Tucker, please…"

He groaned and rested his forehead against hers. "I think you'd better go, or…" His voice trailed off, but his meaning was clear.

Maddie drew a deep breath and stepped out on a limb. "Or, I could stay." She pressed a kiss against the warm column of his neck. He tasted slightly salty and masculine and she pressed herself against the solid wall of his chest. "I could stay the night…" His jaw rasped deliciously against her cheek. "Or at least a little longer."

"No." It was unequivocal and he pushed her away from him. Maddie felt as if he'd slapped her. Her face burned with a heat that was altogether different from the warmth she'd felt a second before his harsh rebuff.

Humiliation scorched her. Women threw themselves at him constantly, some obviously like the check-out-my-chassis chick and some not quite so obviously like Kelsi, but he had his choice of women. And now a couple of kisses and she was throwing herself at him, too.

She scrambled off his lap. Hot tears of mortification filled her eyes. "Sorry. I…uh…forget I said that. The last thing you need is me throwing myself at you, too."

Instead of letting her go, he stayed her with a hand to her arm. "Wait. I didn't mean it that way. And you didn't throw yourself at me."

"It doesn't matter. It won't happen again and I'm sure my clothes are dry by now."

"Wait—"

"I don't need an explanation."

"Too bad. You're going to get one."

She crossed her arms over her chest, armoring herself with her tattered pride. "Okay."

Tucker scrubbed his hand through his hair. "Today has been one of the best days of my life. I think you've had a good time, too." He suddenly seemed unsure of himself, but Maddie wasn't up for climbing out on another limb right now. She was still winded from her first fall.

"Yes. I had a nice time. Thank you for having me out."

"Dammit, Maddie. I know you're angry, but it came out wrong when I said no and you won't let me explain. It's been a really emotional day. I never talk about my parents or my childhood. I hate thinking about it. Hate talking about them." Who was he kidding? He thought about it, them, almost every day. Damaged goods. "I don't think you like talking about your past, either. You're not pathetic, not by a long shot, but I think you're emotionally vulnerable right now. And as much as I'd like for you to stay—and, yeah, I would—I'd feel as if I was taking advantage of you. And what kind of guy takes advantage of someone when they're vulnerable? A jerk. I don't want to wake up tomorrow morning and have you hate me." And he had to admit the idea of letting her any closer to him scared the hell out of him.

"I wouldn't hate you."

"It's not worth taking that chance. And I don't want to loathe myself in the morning. You're one of a kind, Maddie Felton. You deserve only the best." And God knows, that wasn't him.

She winnowed her fingers through his hair. "And you, Tucker Macray, are one helluva race-car driver, but you are a lousy fishing instructor."

He laughed. "I'm not sure how strong my sense of nobility and self-preservation is when you look at me that way. I think you better leave now. While you still can. Before I forget my noble intentions."

She stood and walked back into the kitchen. "I need to change clothes."

"Just take them with you. You can get mine back to me some other time." He grabbed her clothes out of the dryer.

"But—"

He shoved them in her arms and practically herded her out the front door. "Go while the going's good."

CHAPTER FIFTEEN

TUCKER PULLED THE CAR into the garage at Darlington and left the guys to make their adjustments before the qualifying run. They were in pretty good shape. He crossed to the hauler, autographing a cap and a shirt for a couple of fans who'd come out on a Friday afternoon to watch practice and qualifying runs.

Okay, he gave up. He was calling Maddie. He'd been more than a little surprised when he showed up for a Sleep EZ appearance on Thursday and found Steve Felton there instead of Maddie. Steve had said she was sick and left it at that and Tucker could hardly quiz him.

But not knowing if she was okay was driving him crazy. He couldn't stop thinking about her when he'd been out there on the practice run. He'd damn near scraped the wall and earned himself the Darlington Stripe because of the distraction.

He went to the front of the hauler and speed-dialed the Sleep EZ corporate offices.

"Thank you for calling Sleep EZ, how may I help you to-day?" the receptionist said in a smooth, professional tone.

"Maddie Felton, please." Tucker dropped onto the seat. Marcus sat on the other side wearing his headset.

"I'm sorry, sir, she's not in this afternoon. Could I take a message or put you through to her voice mail?"

"This is Tucker Macray. I really need to get in touch with her. Could you give me her home number or cell?"

"I'm sorry, Mr. Macray, but I'm not at liberty to give those numbers out." Her tone brooked no argument.

"Is Tamara in?"

"I believe she's on another call. Would you like to hold or leave a message?"

"I'll try later," he said, then thanked her and hung up. Tamara probably wouldn't give out Maddie's number, either. At least she shouldn't. He could be any weirdo off the street calling in.

How the hell had he let her leave on Monday night without getting her phone number? Crazy as it sounded, he just needed to hear her voice, know she was okay.

Kelsi strolled in. "Hi." She glanced at Marcus, but he obviously didn't hear her past his headset. One day he was going to ask Marcus what he listened to all the time.

Tucker'd forgotten Kelsi was along for this ride. She was normally one of the "carpet people"—a front-office person who didn't travel, but she had family in South Carolina so she'd flown in with the team. Perfect. Why hadn't he thought of Kelsi before? His day was looking up.

"Hey, Kels, just the person I needed to see," he said.

Her face lit up and she settled on the seat opposite him. "I live to serve. What can I do for you?" she asked, with her ready smile, flipping her blond hair over one shoulder. She did that a lot. He was pretty sure she thought it was sexy. He, however, found it incredibly annoying.

"I need Maddie Felton's number," he said. All his bookings went through Kelsi. Of course she'd have Maddie's number.

She shifted on her seat, crossing her legs. "I can handle anything that needs to be set up with Maddie." Was her smile just a little brittle?

"No need to waste your time. She was supposed to give me some information yesterday, and as you know, Steve did a stand-in for her. I just thought I'd give her a call and get the info. You know, in case she doesn't make it to the race this weekend."

Kelsi laughed. "Inquiring minds are dying to know what kind of info Maddie's giving you. She's not exactly the racing go-to girl."

The hair stood up on the back of his neck and he bit back his temper because, much like the key-ring incident, he had the distinct impression Kelsi was laughing *at* Maddie, rather than *with* her.

He was pretty damn sure his smile held an edge, but he worked to maintain an affable tone. "She has a heck of an eye for renovation. She came out and gave me some pointers on the house I bought last year. She was going to give me some sources she had at home."

"Oh." Kelsi smiled and tossed her hair again. She reminded him of a horse switching its tail to get rid of flies. "You know, *I'd* be *more* than happy to help you with something like that."

Not in this lifetime. "I really appreciate it, Kels, but Maddie's got it covered. I just need her number."

No doubt about it. Her smile got *tight*. "Sure. It's right here." She scribbled a number on a piece of paper and handed it to him.

He glanced at it. It was the 1-800 number for Sleep EZ. He pushed the piece of paper back across the table. "I meant her personal number. Why don't you give me her cell phone?" It wasn't exactly a request.

"Oh, of course. I don't know what I was thinking," she said.

Right.

She slid the paper back to him. "Here you are. Maddie's cell phone."

He tucked it into his book. "Thanks."

"Certainly." She stood and walked to the door, turning to look over her shoulder at him, tossing her hair. Again. "I'm always happy to help with *whatever* you need." She walked out, her heels tapping on the chrome-floored corridor.

"I'd say she has a thing for you."

Tucker damn near jumped out of his skin. He hadn't exactly forgotten Marcus was there, but with his head phones on…apparently he could hear just fine, headphones or not. This was embarrassing.

"Listen, I haven't encouraged her at all. Just the opposite."

Marcus shrugged and grinned. "Hey, she's a beautiful woman. I say go for it." Marcus winked. "Whatever happens in Darlington, stays in Darlington."

FINALLY. TUCKER CLOSED THE bathroom door of the motor coach behind him—and locked it. Dang. Sometimes the things a guy had to do to get a moment of privacy.

He leaned against the sink and dialed Maddie's number. He could've text-messaged her, but he really just wanted to talk to her. It was crazy the way his heart was pounding.

She answered on the third ring. "Maddie Felton." He'd sort of forgotten, or maybe he'd never quite realized until now, how much he liked her voice.

"Hey. It's Tucker. Tucker Macray."

"Hey, you." Her rich laughter floated through the phone. And he loved her laugh. "For the record, I only know one Tucker."

"Okay." Yeah, he guessed he'd sounded pretty stupid. "I… uh…just wanted to check and see if you were okay. Your brother said you were sick earlier this week."

"That's sweet." He'd never considered himself sweet. He could feel his face turn red, even locked in the bathroom

He tucked it into his book. "Thanks."

"Certainly." She stood and walked to the door, turning to look over her shoulder at him, tossing her hair. Again. "I'm always happy to help with *whatever* you need." She walked out, her heels tapping on the chrome-floored corridor.

"I'd say she has a thing for you."

Tucker damn near jumped out of his skin. He hadn't exactly forgotten Marcus was there, but with his head phones on…apparently he could hear just fine, headphones or not. This was embarrassing.

"Listen, I haven't encouraged her at all. Just the opposite."

Marcus shrugged and grinned. "Hey, she's a beautiful woman. I say go for it." Marcus winked. "Whatever happens in Darlington, stays in Darlington."

FINALLY. TUCKER CLOSED THE bathroom door of the motor coach behind him—and locked it. Dang. Sometimes the things a guy had to do to get a moment of privacy.

He leaned against the sink and dialed Maddie's number. He could've text-messaged her, but he really just wanted to talk to her. It was crazy the way his heart was pounding.

She answered on the third ring. "Maddie Felton." He'd sort of forgotten, or maybe he'd never quite realized until now, how much he liked her voice.

"Hey. It's Tucker. Tucker Macray."

"Hey, you." Her rich laughter floated through the phone. And he loved her laugh. "For the record, I only know one Tucker."

"Okay." Yeah, he guessed he'd sounded pretty stupid. "I… I…just wanted to check and see if you were okay. Your mother said you were sick earlier this week."

"That's sweet." He'd never considered himself sweet. He could feel his face turn red, even locked in the bathroom

CHAPTER FIFTEEN

TUCKER PULLED THE CAR into the garage at Darlington and left the guys to make their adjustments before the qualifying run. They were in pretty good shape. He crossed to the hauler, autographing a cap and a shirt for a couple of fans who'd come out on a Friday afternoon to watch practice and qualifying runs.

Okay, he gave up. He was calling Maddie. He'd been more than a little surprised when he showed up for a Sleep EZ appearance on Thursday and found Steve Felton there instead of Maddie. Steve had said she was sick and left it at that and Tucker could hardly quiz him.

But not knowing if she was okay was driving him crazy. He couldn't stop thinking about her when he'd been out there on the practice run. He'd damn near scraped the wall and earned himself the Darlington Stripe because of the distraction.

He went to the front of the hauler and speed-dialed the Sleep EZ corporate offices.

"Thank you for calling Sleep EZ, how may I help you today?" the receptionist said in a smooth, professional tone.

"Maddie Felton, please." Tucker dropped onto the seat. Marcus sat on the other side wearing his headset.

"I'm sorry, sir, she's not in this afternoon. Could I take a message or put you through to her voice mail?"

"This is Tucker Macray. I really need to get in touch with her. Could you give me her home number or cell?"

"I'm sorry, Mr. Macray, but I'm not at liberty to give those numbers out." Her tone brooked no argument.

"Is Tamara in?"

"I believe she's on another call. Would you like to hold or leave a message?"

"I'll try later," he said, then thanked her and hung up. Tamara probably wouldn't give out Maddie's number, either. At least she shouldn't. He could be any weirdo off the street calling in.

How the hell had he let her leave on Monday night without getting her phone number? Crazy as it sounded, he just needed to hear her voice, know she was okay.

Kelsi strolled in. "Hi." She glanced at Marcus, but he obviously didn't hear her past his headset. One day he was going to ask Marcus what he listened to all the time.

Tucker'd forgotten Kelsi was along for this ride. She was normally one of the "carpet people"—a front-office person who didn't travel, but she had family in South Carolina so she'd flown in with the team. Perfect. Why hadn't he thought of Kelsi before? His day was looking up.

"Hey, Kels, just the person I needed to see," he said.

Her face lit up and she settled on the seat opposite him. "I live to serve. What can I do for you?" she asked, with her ready smile, flipping her blond hair over one shoulder. She did that a lot. He was pretty sure she thought it was sexy. He, however, found it incredibly annoying.

"I need Maddie Felton's number," he said. All his bookings went through Kelsi. Of course she'd have Maddie's number.

She shifted on her seat, crossing her legs. "I can handle anything that needs to be set up with Maddie." Was her smile just a little brittle?

"No need to waste your time. She was supposed to giv some information yesterday, and as you know, Steve stand-in for her. I just thought I'd give her a call and get the You know, in case she doesn't make it to the race this week

Kelsi laughed. "Inquiring minds are dying to know kind of info Maddie's giving you. She's not exactly the r go-to girl."

The hair stood up on the back of his neck and he bit his temper because, much like the key-ring incident, h the distinct impression Kelsi was laughing at Maddie, than with her.

He was pretty damn sure his smile held an edge, b worked to maintain an affable tone. "She has a heck of a for renovation. She came out and gave me some pointe the house I bought last year. She was going to give me sources she had at home."

"Oh." Kelsi smiled and tossed her hair again. Sl minded him of a horse switching its tail to get rid of "You know, I'd be more than happy to help you with thing like that."

Not in this lifetime. "I really appreciate it, Kel Maddie's got it covered. I just need her number."

No doubt about it. Her smile got tight. "Sure. It's right She scribbled a number on a piece of paper and handed it t

He glanced at it. It was the 1-800 number for Sleep E pushed the piece of paper back across the table. "I mea personal number. Why don't you give me her cell phor wasn't exactly a request.

"Oh, of course. I don't know what I was thinking," sh Right.

She slid the paper back to him. "Here you are. Ma cell phone."

alone. "I'm fine. Just a touch of food poisoning that lasted a couple of days, but I'm fine now."

"That's good that you're feeling better." Crap. She'd ate his food and then got sick. That wasn't good. "I hope it wasn't my cooking."

"No. I picked up some takeout Tuesday for lunch. I think I had some bad shrimp."

Whew! At least he hadn't made her sick…well, not him, but his cooking. "But you're okay, now?"

"I'm fine. I missed—" she hesitated, as if catching herself "—being at the signing yesterday." Had she almost said she'd missed him yesterday?

"Steve's nice, but it wasn't the same without you there." It was nothing more or less than he'd say to any friend. He'd say the same to Andy or Charlene.

"It's nice to know I was missed. How about you? Are you okay? How're things at the track?"

"Qualifying's this afternoon. We're still working on the setup." He shifted against the counter. "Do you think you'll make it to the race on Sunday?" Yeah, that sounded casual enough.

"I wouldn't miss it for anything. I'll be there. Look for me. I'll be the one in the blue and yellow." He could hear her smile, picture in his mind the way it lit up her face.

He laughed. "Hey, I'll be wearing the blue and yellow, too. So, you got home okay the other night?"

"No problems." Her tone shifted, softened, took on a more intimate note and made him think of kissing her on the back stoop and sharing parts of himself with her that he didn't share with many others. "It was a really great day. And a great sandwich, too."

"Maybe we could do it again." He thought hearing her

voice would be enough, but he knew a sudden, desperate need to see her, touch her. Maybe because she'd seen the real Tucker Macray—the reality of the man outside of the car— and she hadn't run screaming in the other direction. Maybe because when they were together he felt with a certainty that she was kissing him, not Tucker Macray the NASCAR NEXTEL Cup rookie. Maddie grounded him in what could be a very crazy world of fast cars and constant travel. When he was with her he almost believed he could be the man she seemed to think he was. He cleared his throat. "You know, de- pending on your schedule and my schedule."

"I'd like that…a lot."

"Yeah. Me, too." And because he felt the equal urge to shift away from feeling so intense, he lightened things up. "I'm not sure if you noticed when you got home, but you left your panties."

"Great. That's just peachy. How embarrassing. No, I hadn't noticed. How stupid was that?"

"Not stupid at all. They were stuck in my blue jeans. Guess they got in there with the dryer tumbling or something. I pulled my jeans out and…well, your panties were in the leg."

"I hope you threw them away."

"Of course not." Maddie was fun to tease. She always rose to the bait and was a good sport about it. "No sense in wasting perfectly good panties. Actually with all that lace, they were better than just good. I brought them with me on Thursday to give them to you. I wasn't sure about giving them to your brother, but I've got them with me now. I'll return them on Sunday. If I forget, just remind me."

"Tucker!" He chuckled at the predictable way she gasped his name. "Please tell me you're kidding. You don't really have my underwear at the track, do you?"

He had her going. "Right here in my back pocket."

"You're teasing."

Ha. She wasn't quite sure. "Wait a minute. They were just here." He pretended to feel in his pocket, just to get the timing down right. "Maybe I dropped 'em in the hauler or the garage."

"Now I know you're lying."

Suddenly someone banged on the bathroom door. "Hey, man! Did you die in there?" yelled Tiny, who cooked for all three teams. On any given weekend, Tiny cooked about twenty pounds of bacon and at least thirteen dozen eggs.

"Hold on a second," he said to Maddie. "Give me just a minute," he yelled back through the closed door.

"All right, man, but I've got to go." Tiny sounded sort of urgent. The motor coaches of the guys with families were mostly off-limits, but since Tucker was single, wasn't dating anyone and pretty much didn't care, Tiny and a couple of the other guys made themselves at home in his motor coach. It'd be nice, however, if Tiny had made himself a little less at home about now.

Maddie burst into laughter on the other end of the phone line. "Are you calling me from the bathroom? You are, aren't you?"

Okay. He'd teased her about having her underwear at the track, he supposed she deserved a turn over him hunkering down in the bathroom to make a phone call. "Do you have any idea what it's like to try to find a little privacy around here?"

"Oh, my God. That's hysterical."

He grinned into the phone. "As long as you're amused."

More banging on the bathroom door. "Hey! Sometime today."

"I'll be right out," he called to Tiny, and then got back to Maddie. "Obviously I've got to go. See you on Sunday."

"See you then. Tucker…"

"Yeah?"

"Good luck on the qualifying. Drive safe."

"I will." He paused. "I've got my good-luck key ring… and panties." He laughed, clicked off the call and opened the door.

Tiny stood squirming in the hall. "You were in there forever. You okay?"

"I'm fine."

Oddly enough, talking to Maddie had improved his bad mood immeasurably.

CHAPTER SIXTEEN

SUNDAY, MADDIE SAT IN THE golf cart and waited on her father and Sharon to arrive. Her father had followed her advice and invited Sharon "as a valued Felton Enterprises employee," Maddie had rolled her eyes at that, but, hey, at least he'd asked Sharon to the race.

Sharon had promptly accepted and she and Maddie had promptly rushed out on another shopping spree. Sharon was classy through and through. Maddie was keeping various and sundry body parts crossed that things worked out the way she thought they would between her father and Sharon. She had a sneaking suspicion Daddy better start looking for a new secretary now.

It was a glorious spring day and Tucker's meet 'n' greet earlier in the morning in the hospitality tent had gone well. Better than well. She'd been ridiculously happy to see his bed-head hair and smiling eyes when he'd shown up. The sun slanted in the side of the golf cart as people streamed by. If she was brutally honest with herself—and what was the point in being anything less—she hadn't been ridiculously happy to see Tucker, she'd been frighteningly happy.

She'd had boyfriends off and on. None of them serious because she'd never allowed it to get serious. She'd never allowed herself to get too involved or care too deeply. Now she could look back and see that she'd just been too unsure of herself and too frightened to allow someone to mean too much to her. And she'd never meant to feel this way about Tucker Macray. She hadn't even wanted to like him, much less…feel giddy when he showed up.

Was she caught up in some weird celebrity fixation? No. It'd almost be a relief if she was, then this, too, would pass. But she wasn't impressed by his celebrity, which she thought was fast-tracking to expand exponentially because he was a talented driver and he did have a great team on the car. Nope, his celebrity didn't impress her. Somehow, somewhere, the man beneath the hype had slipped beneath her radar, had slid beneath her skin, had become increasingly important to her.

The truth hit her like a semi rear-ending her on I-75. Somewhere along the route, she'd been dumb enough to fall in love with annoying, slightly arrogant, endearingly funny Tucker Macray.

Tucker, who'd shot straight and made it clear he didn't have a relationship and didn't want a relationship. Tucker, who considered himself damaged. Sure, he'd called her and sure he wanted to see her again, but that was all after he'd made it abundantly clear that racing was the only love he had room for in his life.

And what had happened to her assertion that any woman with a brain would run screaming in the other direction if they thought they were remotely interested in a guy who was on the road and at a track thirty-eight out of fifty-two weeks in a year? What had happened to her need for a "normal" life? Obviously her heart had bypassed her brain.

She'd pushed Sharon to make a change, to seize an opportunity before life rendered the opportunity gone or too late. Maddie had pushed her father and brothers to see her in a different light. To see her as strong and capable. But did she have the courage to see herself as truly happy? As the successful half of a relationship? As a partner who gave and took rather than someone who only complied and played the role they thought required to engender loyalty and love?

Did she have the courage to reach for what she now realized she'd always thought could never be hers? Maddie stiffened her spine. Damn straight she did. She was her father's daughter. No. She was her father's daughter, but she was more than that.

She was Madeleine Suzette Felton, strong and brave, and by God, she loved Tucker Macray. She might come out of the fray bloody and wounded, but he was worth fighting for. She would not sink her ship and leave those aboard floundering in icy waters as her mother had.

A hired car pulled up outside the credentials trailer. The driver got out and opened the door. Sharon, followed by her father, climbed out. Sharon definitely looked shell-shocked. She might book travel on the private corporate jet all the time, but it was something of an eye-opener to actually travel that way. She also looked great in the dark blue slacks, yellow silk blouse and lightweight yellow-and-blue cardigan, accessorized with great chunky jewelry they'd found on their shopping trip. Sharon radiated elegant sexiness, which Maddie suspected was as much a combination of her own newfound self-confidence and her father's attentions. And Sharon definitely had his attention, judging by the slightly panicked look in her father's eyes.

She walked them through the credentials trailer to pick up garage and pit passes, compliments of Kelsi, and then they were on their way. Her father took the backseat, giving Sharon the front. Daddy was such a good guy! And he and Sharon made such a cute couple.

Maddie pointed out Hospitality Village along the way to the west tunnel to the infield. "Here it is. The infield. Sort of crazy, isn't it?"

Sharon glanced around as if to absorb it all. Maddie glanced back at her father. He was busy watching Sharon. Maddie pointed to one of the refurbished school buses that boasted a homemade viewing deck on top and a built-in barbecue grill on the back. This bus was at every race. She waved at the family she'd begun to recognize since she saw them every weekend. "That's my favorite. I love the reworked school buses. To me, they represent how passionate some of the fans are about the sport."

Sharon nodded and finally seemed to find her voice. "Wow. It's so big. And I can't believe I'm actually in the infield."

Maddie grinned at Sharon, being sure to include her father. "Just wait until we get to the garage and the pits. That's incredible." Actually, Darlington's infield was much smaller than Talladega's. Too bad Sharon had missed that.

Sharon pushed her sunglasses to the top of her head and swiveled her head from left to right, as if unsure where to look first to take it all in. "It's so…overwhelming."

Maddie smiled, charmed by Sharon's enthusiasm and also loving the feeling that she herself wasn't such a novice anymore. She parked outside the gate of the NASCAR NEXTEL Cup Series garage.

Maddie led her father and Sharon to the Number 76 car bay.

"I'm not sure how the guys concentrate with so many people around when they're trying to get things ready, but they do. And it makes it sort of crazy for them, but I think it's remarkable how accessible this is to the fans. Think about it. In less than two hours this car's going to be racing around that track and the folks who have garage passes get to come in here and see these teams getting ready to make it happen. I think that's a really cool aspect of the sport."

Her father shot her a funny look. "What?" she asked, feeling suddenly self-conscious. "Did I just say something stupid?" It had been known to happen. She was still learning, and there was still a whole lot more about this sport that she didn't know than what she did know.

"Not at all. I'm just listening to what you think is cool." Her father winked at Sharon.

Sure. Her father could tease her all day if it gave him a way to flirt with his secretary. She wrinkled her nose at him.

"Where's the crew chief?" Sharon asked.

"He and Tucker are at the driver's meeting right now. After that there's a rookie meeting for all the rookie drivers. It shouldn't last long and then Tucker'll be heading back to the hauler to suit up for the driver introductions. Want to check out pit road?"

"Absolutely."

In the next bay the Number 82 team had the tires off and had cranked the car. With all the people around and a car cranked right next to them, hearing was only possible by talking very close to the other person.

Sharon spoke next to Maddie's ear. "What are they doing there?"

Maddie recognized opportunity when it knocked at her door. She shrugged and leaned in to speak in Sharon's ear. "I'm not sure. Ask Daddy." She pointed toward her father just to alleviate any doubt.

Maddie watched the Sleep EZ crew busy at work instead of staring while Sharon leaned in to ask her father and he in turn had to get close to answer. And it was a pretty long-winded answer considering the amount of time her father spent with his head close to Sharon's. This plan was working out just fine.

Another team came by pushing their car, and Maddie pointed out the end bay where the car would be checked over by the NASCAR officials. The scent of grilled peppers and sausages and chicken wafted past. Maddie pointed to a tent tucked into a back corner between the last hauler in the row and the fence. "That's lunch for the teams."

She heard the rumble and started moving, pulling Sharon and her father along with her, even before she heard the "Heads-up" call. A two-tiered cart filled with tires passed them, one crew member pulling, two other guys pushing from behind. "They're taking it to the pit road. Why don't we stop by the hauler first."

They found Marcus and Kelsi in the lounge. They both stood to be introduced to Sharon.

"You just missed Dad," Marcus said. "He'll be back in about a quarter of an hour."

Maddie suggested they go to the pit road and then head back to the hauler to try to catch Dan Chalkey. It was already hot outside. She dropped her backpack purse next to the stereo system. She'd learned her lesson at Phoenix with the discrepancy with the caterer. Now she brought along information pertinent to each particular race she was attending. She'd picked up a stylish backpack purse to keep the paperwork and her day planner in. Might as well leave it there and she could pick it up when she came back. It was going to be plenty warm out on the pit road.

"Let me show your father and Sharon the rest of the hauler first," Marcus suggested. "I think they'll be impressed with our state-of-the-art equipment."

Marcus was doing his self-important routine so Maddie

simply stepped aside and let him have at it. She'd discovered that was the best way to handle Marcus.

Maddie stayed behind. The hauler was tight quarters.

"So, I guess Tucker got in touch with you on Friday?" Kelsi asked with a friendly smile Maddie didn't trust at all.

"He did." The less said, the better. And how did Kelsi know he'd called her?

"He mentioned the renovations you're helping him with. You can just send that information through me from now on. His plate's full and I've offered to handle it." Kelsi stood and tossed her hair over one shoulder, "If you'll excuse me, I've got a phone call to make."

"Sure."

Maddie was glad Kelsi left. Ugh. The woman was so obvious. Honestly, she'd rather deal with Marcus and his self-importance than Kelsi and her cattiness. And that was a sad day when Marcus came out the better proposition.

Marcus's computer sat at the other end of the table. The laptop was on but the cover was closed. Okay, so she admitted it. She was nosy. But every time she visited the hauler, Marcus was in the corner on his computer.

Maddie lifted the laptop lid and peeked at the screen. Solitaire. And he was losing to boot. She shook her head and lowered the screen.

Within a few minutes Marcus returned with her father and Sharon. Marcus resumed his seat in front of his computer. "If you'll excuse me, I have a few things that need to be taken care of before things get too hectic around here."

Maddie bit back a smile as they left. Solitaire was pretty pressing business.

Once they reached the pit road, Maddie introduced her father and Sharon to the guys at the pit box. Sharon looked exactly the way Maddie had felt the first time she'd come down here. Heck, it was still exciting.

She hadn't noticed that her father had stepped aside until he returned. "Come on, ladies. This gentleman is going to take you up on the top deck of the pit box."

"Why, thank you, Mr. Felton," Sharon said.

"Sounds ridiculous for you to call me Mr. Felton when we're here. Why don't you just call me Lou?"

Lou? No one had ever called her father Lou, it'd always been Louis. Hmm.

Sharon smiled shyly. "Okay, Lou."

Her father smiled back at Sharon and Maddie knew without a doubt that for at least a few seconds the rest of them ceased to exist for Sharon Connelly and Louis Felton. Her father took Sharon's elbow and escorted her to the ladder steps that led to the top deck. Rick, one of the over-the-wall guys, scaled the ladder first. Louis held Sharon's arm until Rick helped her the rest of the way. Maddie ascended next, followed by her father. They sat, Maddie leaving the seat next to Sharon open for her dad, on the chairs mounted up top.

They only stayed up top for a minute or so before "Lou" helped Sharon down.

"Do you want to head over to the hauler now?" Maddie asked.

"Is that what you want, Sharon?" her father asked.

"That would be lovely, Lou."

Maddie bit back a laugh. She didn't think these two much cared where they were as long as they were together—pretty much the way she felt about Tucker Macray.

TUCKER FINISHED UP WITH the rookie driver meeting and headed back to the garage area. He really needed a few minutes to just think through his strategy.

He made his way through the throng of fans and entered the back of the hauler. He walked into the lounge area, and it was a nice surprise to find Maddie inside, along with her father and a woman she introduced as her father's secretary. He didn't remember this woman, Sharon, at all from the few meetings he'd attended at Felton Enterprises. Kelsi and Marcus, in his usual spot, rounded out the numbers.

"Good luck out there today," Louis Felton said, engulfing Tucker's hand in a bear-sized paw and offering a firm shake.

"Thank you, sir." He'd thought a lot about what Maddie had told him, about her mother's suicide and her father's and brothers' silence on the subject to protect her. Maybe Tucker was cynical given his own childhood, but he'd wondered this past week if her father's silence all these years had been to protect Maddie or to keep from dealing with a situation painful to him. But face-to-face once again with Louis Felton, he dismissed the notion that her father had anything other than Maddie's best interest at heart. Maddie didn't look a thing like her old man, but there was a sense of purpose, a firmness in his handshake and a directness in his gaze that echoed Maddie's.

After a minute of chit-chat, everyone headed for the door so he could get ready for the race. Without thinking it through Tucker spoke up. "Maddie, could I see you for a moment?"

"Sure." She waited behind while everyone else emptied out of the front of the hauler. Tucker closed the door and turned to her. Did he pull her into his arms or did she go there on her own? Tucker was pretty sure she met him halfway. He framed her face in his hands and kissed her. She sighed against his mouth, wrapped her hands around his neck and kissed him back. Hard. Longing. Intense.

Reluctantly, he released her. "I've wanted to do that all day."

She smiled into his eyes. "Me, too."

"I want to kiss you again."

"Me, too, but I'm sure everyone already wonders what you wanted to see me about."

"Just wanted to up my quota of good luck." Kissing her again was a bad idea with everyone waiting outside, but he still couldn't bring himself to release her. He contented himself with brushing his thumb over the fullness of her lips. She caught his wrist in her hand and brought it to her mouth, pressing a kiss to it, setting his heart thudding against his ribs.

"Good luck." Her voice was as quiet and intense as the kiss they'd just shared. "Drive safe today."

"Always."

Maddie left. Tucker opened his locker, pulled out his racing gear and suited up. He took a second to think about kissing Maddie because he was going to be one hundred percent focused on the track and the car, but he wanted that good-luck kiss with him.

The Feltons and Sharon had already left when he came out of the hauler. Marcus and Kelsi stood nearby with a couple of secondary sponsor district managers. It was only mid-May but it was already hot.

He made his way through the crowds holding hot passes toward the track along with the other drivers. They'd just wrapped up the driver introductions when a prickling started at the back of his neck. Damn! Was he letting the track get to him that bad?

As he put on his helmet and the rest of his safety gear and got in the car, his arms began to itch. What the hell was wrong with him? And whatever it was he'd better get over it fast because they were about to start an important race. Okay, they were all important, but Team Three needed a good showing at Darlington.

Two laps into the race and Tucker knew he had a problem. "Something's wrong," he said to Mike via his headset.

"Talk to me," his crew chief came back.

"It's not the car, the car's handling fine. It's me. I'm itching."

"Itching?"

"Yeah. Like I rolled in poison ivy or something."

"Do you need to bring the car in?"

"No. My concentration's a little off but I'm not coming in. The car's handling good. Nice and tight on Turns One and Two."

Hours later he finally headed back to the garage. It was without a doubt the longest race of his life. He wasn't even excited that he'd come in sixth on a track that last year had seen him limping in thirtieth. He didn't give a crap. He just wanted out of this uniform. The car had barely rolled back to the garage when he was out of it and heading to his motor coach to strip down and shower.

CHAPTER SEVENTEEN

"MADDIE, DO YOU KNOW anything about this itching powder in Macray's driving uniform?" her father asked her on Monday. Sharon had called with a midafternoon summons. Doug and Stevie were already in the conference room when Maddie arrived. All three men looked worried.

"I know it happened." Tucker had called her about an hour ago when they'd gotten the test results back on his uniform. It infuriated and worried her that someone had done something like that.

Her father sat forward and planted his arms on the conference table. "This is awkward, princess. Dan Chalkey called me. Apparently an empty can of itching powder was found in your backpack."

"What?"

"He said it was found in the hauler, and when an employee looked inside to see who it belonged to, he found it belonged to you, but he also found an empty can of itching powder."

That explained Kelsi's smug satisfaction when she'd dropped off the backpack Maddie had forgotten and left in the hauler.

Daddy, Doug and Steve all stared at her with a mixture of anticipation and apology. They couldn't…

"Mr. Chalkey thinks I did that?"

Her father looked uncomfortable but stared her straight in

the eyes. She returned his gaze without flinching. "How uncomfortable do you think it was for him to make that call to me? But they found the empty can in your purse."

"I'm assuming you assured him I wouldn't do something like that," she said.

She saw the answer in his eyes before he spoke. "I needed to check with you first."

Her heart sank and her ire rose. "I didn't do it. But I think I know who did." She explained the Kelsi situation, the other woman's cattiness and veiled hostility. Even as she spoke, she could see from their expressions they didn't get it. Another woman would get it straight away, but men didn't get it, and Kelsi was always careful not to show that side of her personality around men—Maddie had noted that. "I think she's setting me up."

Her father and her brothers traded looks. "Honey, why would she set you up? Why would she have something against you?" Her father's tone was that of a parent soothing a distraught child.

This felt as if it were disintegrating from bad to worse. "Because she's got a crush on Tucker. She has had from the beginning and now that he and I are friends, she's jealous."

Stevie looked apologetic. "Maddie, don't take this the wrong way 'cause I think you're really pretty, but you know Kelsi's sort of gorgeous."

Maddie clamped her lips tight. Thanks a whole bunch, Stevie. She was the one coming off poorly here and Kelsi was looking like a saint.

Daddy interrupted. "Most people would look at your job and think it was a piece of cake. They don't realize the travel and coordination and the stress involved."

She wasn't a child. "I love my job." And she did. It wasn't a piece of cake. It was a bit of a logistics and coordination effort, but she loved the challenge and she'd become quite addicted to the racing itself. "And I'm good at it," she tacked on.

"You've done a good job, Mads—" her father used her childhood pet name "—until the powder...and the dead flowers. Dan told me about that, too."

"I didn't do either, but someone's trying to make it look like I'm guilty." She'd be damned if she'd mention Kelsi again.

"We want you to take a break. Get away from the stress for a little bit," Doug finally spoke.

Stevie jumped in, as well. "Do the things you enjoy. You know, go shopping, get your nails done." He actually reached across the table and patted her hand. "Just a little break from your busy schedule."

They wanted to yank her from her job? "You're firing me?"

"No, no, no," Daddy assured her. "It's more of a...hiatus. Dan's agreed to keep this quiet if you take a little break and stay away for a while until this all blows over."

The Maddie she'd been two months ago would've complied. No more. "I don't need a hiatus."

"Just a little break from the stress—" Stevie almost looked ready to cry.

Dear God. It was all of their worst nightmares manifesting right before their eyes. They all thought she was cracking up.

"I wasn't behind those two incidents, I don't need a break and I'm not paranoid delusional."

"Maddie, be reasonable."

Tucker's words echoed in her head, giving her strength, lending her confidence. *You're one of the strongest, fieriest, sexiest nonpathetic women I've ever known.* She stood, planted her hands on the table and stared at each one of them. "I'm not her." She spoke clearly, enunciating every word, imbuing it with quiet conviction. The moment of reckoning was upon them. "I'm not Mary Beth Felton. I'm Maddie Felton. I look like her, but I'm not like her. I'm not manic depressive or bipolar or whatever she was, and I'm sure as hell not suicidal."

Maddie sat in her chair, straight and defiant. She hadn't planned to approach it this way. But there it was, laid out on the table. In the words of Tucker, she was shooting straight. Her father and two brothers, who had been her whole life, looked positively stricken. She anticipated the question that would follow once their shock wore off and answered it before it could be asked.

"I've always known. I found her and the note."

Her father seemed to age ten years on the spot. "You found her and the note?"

Maddie explained the night and the days that followed. Doug stared out the window, past her, as if looking back at a past he'd tried to forget. Stevie kept his eyes trained on the notepad on the table in front of him. Her father, however, watched her intently as she recounted her story. "And it's taken me a long time to figure out that I'm not like her. I've spent my whole life doing what you wanted me to do because I was so scared I'd been part of the reason she…left." She squared her shoulders. "But I'm not giving up this NASCAR job. I love it and I'm good at it. I'm not having some delusional breakdown and I'm not sabotaging the team with pranks."

They all stared at her then, as if she'd grown a third eye. Sure, she was spoiled and she'd always got her way…as long as it was their way, as well. They weren't used to Maddie taking a stand.

"We've needed to clear the air about Mama for a long time. I'm not taking an ad out in the paper, but I'm not perpetuating a lie any longer, either. She wrote a note that pretty much said nothing, swallowed two bottles of pills, and left us all to fend for ourselves and wonder where we went wrong. I won't pretend anymore that she had a heart attack. She made a horrible choice and each of us need to acknowledge it so we can get on with our lives. Daddy, you weren't a bad husband. Stevie and Doug, we weren't bad kids. I'm not asking us to talk it to death, but for goodness' sake, let's just call it what it was. I know the three of you were trying to protect me and I was trying to be what you needed me to be, but I think we've all stunted our emotional growth."

She pushed to her feet and picked up her purse.

"And now I'll leave so you can discuss the best way to handle me. Good day, gentlemen."

She closed the door behind her on the way out. And then she started to shake.

DAMMIT, HE SHOULD HAVE driven into the city instead of waiting on Maddie to come here. Tucker ran his hand through his hair. She'd obviously been upset when she called him on his cell phone. Not crying upset. But he'd heard the tension in her voice. He forced himself to sit on the front steps, waiting, instead of pacing the front yard. This had something to do with that damn itching powder in his uniform. He knew it. Mr. Chalkey had been very closemouthed, but Tucker felt as if there was more than he was willing to say.

He was on his feet the moment he heard the car and saw the telltale dust cloud that came from driving fast on a dirt road. Napoleon abandoned chasing after squirrels and followed Tucker. They were both at her door before the car was in Park. Tucker gave the sit command to Napoleon just in time.

Maddie opened the door and launched herself at him. For a second or two he merely held her close, tight against him, her heart thudding against his. Traces of old tears had left tracks down her face. He smoothed her hair and nuzzled at her temple. "What's happened? Tell me what's wrong."

"Can we sit on the back stoop?" She pulled away from him and pushed her hair behind her ear with a shaky hand.

The stoop was dirty and she had on a nice suit. "How about the kitchen table? You're dressed so nice."

"I don't care. I want to sit on the back stoop." She looked ready to cry. Please not that.

"Then we'll sit on the back stoop."

He was tempted to pick her up and carry her there, but he knew, knew as inherently as he knew his own name, that she needed to walk there on her own. He could support her along the way, but she needed to make the journey under her own steam.

She took a deep breath and picked up the quivering little dog sitting impatiently at her feet. "Hey, Napoleon." Napoleon licked her face eagerly, coaxing a smile from her. Halfway around the house, he'd finished greeting her and she put him down. He was off like a rocket, intent on chasing squirrels he never caught.

They walked to the back in silence. Tucker settled on the top step and pulled Maddie down onto his lap. She wasn't exactly a lightweight, but her curves fit against him as if she belonged there. "Talk to me."

She relayed the conversation and he bit his tongue, difficult as it was, until she was through. "Dan Chalkey called your father, told him you did it, and agreed to keep it quiet if you were pulled off the job?"

She nodded. "That's it in a nutshell." Tension radiated from her with every word. "Do you think I had anything to do with either of those?" The very thought seemed to horrify her.

"No." He felt some of her tension ease when he uttered that

single word. "I accused you of the flower thing, but honestly it never felt right to me. And Mike and I agreed not to tell Chalkey. I don't know how he found out. And this thing with the itching powder—there's no way."

"Thank you."

"For what?"

"For believing in me."

It wrenched at him that she hadn't known a whole lot of that—of people believing in her. For a girl who'd had everything money could buy, she'd done without a lot of other things. "It occurred to me that I could announce that you couldn't possibly kiss me the way you kissed me and do what they accused you of doing. But I thought it probably wasn't a good idea."

"Probably not." A shadow of a smile curved her lips and then faded. "My father…my brothers…they thought it was me. I think they still aren't sure it's not."

"I know that hurt," he said quietly. He could all but feel the hurt rolling off of her. "I'm sorry, Maddie."

"I know it's not me. You know it's not me. But that doesn't do a whole lot of good when the rest of the world thinks I'm some spoiled nutcase running around pulling potentially dangerous pranks. I'm sure it's Kelsi." She nestled in close to him, her head fitting in the crook of his neck and relayed Kelsi's comments regarding the renovation.

"I never told her she'd be involved at all."

"I know that," Maddie said. "Remember the dead flower? Kelsi was part of the garage tour that day, but then when I came back from getting my day planner out of the garage, she wasn't in the hauler with everyone else. In fact, I never saw her again that day until I was leaving the building on my way home."

"I remember. And I tried and tried to solve that mystery. You know, she didn't want to give me your number on Friday."

"You know, she's got a major thing for you. Have you... you know, dated her? Spent time with her?"

This was a mess. He rubbed his hand over his head. "I know she does, but, I swear, I've never encouraged her." Kelsi didn't do a thing for him. "Date? No way. We went to lunch once, but it was strictly business to go over my schedule. And that was at CRE's cafeteria."

"She obviously has a serious thing for you and a serious issue with me. She's the one who arranged the garage and pit passes."

Which would've put Maddie in the hauler at some time during the day. And she'd been pretty unhappy when he insisted she give him Maddie's number. "Damn. Then this all comes back to me. I should go talk to Dan Chalkey."

"And say what? You can't go to him until you've got some kind of proof. I'm the one that had an empty itching powder can show up in my backpack. But thank you for believing in me. You're sweet."

"You said that once before. You've got to quit calling me sweet. Men don't want to be sweet."

"Really? This is interesting. What do men want to be?"

This conversation was much better. She no longer looked as if she was about to burst into tears. He could do this for Maddie, distract her by flirting. "They want to be tough, rugged, sexy."

"I'm sticking with sweet. You've already got a big enough ego. I'm not telling you all that other stuff."

"Ah. But you think it, don't you?"

"Are you fishing for compliments from me, Macray? If I was assessing you on the grounds of tough, rugged and sexy—" she leaned her head to one side and pretended to study him "—I'd have to say there's nothing *bad* wrong with you."

He cupped her chin in his hand and lowered his head until

her warm breath fanned against him. "Then I suppose I'll just have to work on that."

"Hmm." Maddie wound her arm around his neck, her fingers curling into his hair. "Sounds like a good idea to me."

She drew his mouth down to hers and within seconds he was lost in the taste and scent of Maddie. Time lost meaning. All he knew was the beat of her heart in sync with his own, the heat of her skin, their mingled breaths, and the fire that burned between them.

"Nana, they're kissin'. Yuck!" Bobby's shrill disgust washed over them like a tossed bucket of cold well water.

Maddie sprang up, her hair sticking out, her face flaming red. Tucker stood at a little more leisurely pace.

Edna stood at the edge of the house, holding two-year-old Melanie, while Bobby stood making a face.

"Maddie, this is Edna Matthews, my favorite princess, Melanie, and the town crier and champion fisherman on the hill, Bobby. This is Maddie Felton."

"It's nice to meet everyone." Poor Maddie looked as if she'd like for the back stoop to open and swallow her.

Edna smiled. "It's nice to meet you, too. Now, you just quit being embarrassed because we saw y'all kissing. That's a perfectly natural thing to do. And how were you supposed to know a nosy old woman and two rotten kids were gonna show up?"

"Nana says we're rotten all the time, but she don't really mean it. It's a *good* rotten the way she says it."

Maddie laughed, her awkwardness dissipating with Edna and Bobby's chatter. "I'm sure it's a good rotten."

Melanie squirmed, holding out her arms toward Tucker. Edna put her down and she toddled over. Tucker met her before she reached the hard steps and scooped her up. "How's my girl?" Melanie snuggled against his neck and promptly popped a thumb in her mouth.

For one crazy moment, the scenario took on an intimacy more intense than sitting on the back stoop kissing Maddie. He and she standing on the stoop, he holding a cherub-cheeked princess, a rough-'n'-tumble little boy watching them. For an instant he thought this was what they could have. Together. And how crazy was that? It was dangerously crazy because he knew the dark blight on his soul. He knew that when push came to shove, he wasn't meant for this. How much more proof did he need than one failed childhood and one failed marriage?

Edna looked at them, and for an instant he could've sworn the same thoughts were running through her head. "We walked down to invite y'all to eat supper with us. Nothing fancy, but we've got plenty. Andy and Charlene are coming. We saw your car go by and we thought we might be able to waylay you."

Maddie glanced at him and he realized she wasn't sure how he felt about Edna inviting her. A dose of the Matthewses was exactly what she needed after her own family had let her down today. It'd be a damn sight better for her than going home to her empty house. Well, Sylvester was there, but he wouldn't inundate her with enough curiosity and goodwill to take her mind off her problems.

"Edna's a heck of a cook," Tucker said with a smile. "It's worth putting up with all of us, just to get the food."

"Well, in that case, I'd love to join you for dinner."

"But she invited you to supper," Bobby pointed out.

Maddie laughed. "You're right. Supper. I'd love to."

"Good. Why don't y'all walk down in about two hours?" Edna said. She took Melanie from Tucker. "And it's naptime for you, Miss Melanie."

Melanie's head sank onto Edna's shoulder like a tired flower wilting in the sun. "You want me to carry her back for you?" Tucker offered.

"Nah. She's not heavy, and she'll be asleep before we make it back to the road." Edna smiled warmly at Maddie. "I'm glad you can make it tonight."

"Thank you for inviting me. I'm looking forward to meeting everyone."

Edna and the kids rounded the house and Bobby's chatter drifted farther and farther away. Maddie looked at Tucker, then started down the stairs. "I'll be back."

He was confused. "Back? You just said you'd stay for supper."

"No. I'll be back for supper. I'm going shopping. There is no way I'm showing up for supper dressed like this." She indicated her suit and heels with the sweep of her right hand.

"You look nice."

"Tucker! I went into the office dressed for work. I'll be severely overdressed if I show up in this. Let's talk about sticking out like a sore thumb."

"A pretty sore thumb." He laughed at her narrowed eyes. "Okay. You're going shopping. Wait. You have a pair of panties here."

"You're so helpful."

"I try."

"Try harder."

"You're always bossy, aren't you?"

"Pretty much. I'd have thought you'd be used to it by now. I'm almost used to what a pain you are."

"I ought to kiss you for that comment." He pulled her to him.

"You mean, if I stand around and insult you, you'll kiss me?" Her lips parted.

"You might as well save the insults. I'd pretty much decided to just stand around and kiss you regardless." He started to kiss her and she foiled him with her hand to his mouth.

"Hmm. Hold that thought until I get back. I'm not sure if I start kissing you now, I'll stop in time to go shop. I tend to lose track when we're doing that." It was good to know he had the same effect on her that she had on him. She stepped out of his embrace, putting some distance between them. Smart woman. "Now, real quick, tell me what Charlene's like."

"She's nice." When she wanted to be and Tucker wasn't too darned sure Charlene was going to play nice with Maddie tonight. Charlene and his ex-wife had been best friends. Still were. Even though Darlene had remarried posthaste, Charlene would more than likely be prepared to dislike Maddie on Darlene's behalf in the convoluted rationale of the mysterious female mind.

Maddie exhaled an exasperated breath. "What's she going to wear to dinner...I mean, supper...tonight?"

"She'll be dressed."

"I'm about two seconds away from braining you with my stiletto. Is she a blue jeans kind of person, a dress, a long dress, a miniskirt—what kind of clothes is she going to show up in?" She drew a deep, steadying breath. "I want them to like me. I want to fit in."

Her quiet sincerity touched him. His bossy, fiery little Maddie was worried she wouldn't fit in. She wanted his surrogate family to like her. "There's no way they won't like you, but Charlene'll probably have on blue jeans and a frilly shirt. There's lots of lace and ruffles in her house. Is that what you mean?"

"Yeah. Is that why you haven't asked her to help you with your house?"

"Exactly. She's nice, but I'm not into all the froufrou."

"No. I don't think you're a froufrou kind of guy." She dodged past him and waited until she was out of reach. "You're just sweet."

"I'll get you for that when you get back."

"Promise?"

"Count on it."

CHAPTER EIGHTEEN

MADDIE SUCKED IN HER breath and buttoned and zipped the jeans. They fit in the butt, but a fat roll spilled over the top edge of the jeans. That was the problem with the low-cut jeans.

She unbuttoned and unzipped, but before she peeled them off, her cell phone rang. She didn't recognize the number. She answered, "Maddie Felton."

"Hi, Maddie. It's Marcus."

She almost asked Marcus who, but caught herself in time. Oh, yeah. Marcus Chalkey. "Hi, Marcus."

"I hope I didn't catch you at a bad time?"

Only half undressed, wearing her bra and with her pants undone. "No," she lied brightly. The hair stood up on the back of her neck, not just because she was talking to dweeby Marcus when she was half naked—which did totally hit her ick factor, but because she was pretty sure this call was about the track "incidents" and it had been darn nice to put that behind her for a while. She might as well get this over with even if she was standing in the Wal-Mart dressing room—she'd have never made it into the city to Neiman's and back in time for dinner… make that supper. "This isn't a bad time. What can I help you with?"

"I just want you to know I support you one hundred per-cent. I know my father called your father, but I told him you couldn't possibly have anything to do with it. I just wanted you to know that."

She'd take support wherever she could find it. "Well, thank you, Marcus. That's good to know. I was very disappointed to hear your father thought I might be responsible."

"Absolutely preposterous. And I told him so. I'm using all of my influence to stand behind you on this. You can count on me to champion you. I believe in you, Maddie."

The way he said it sent chills down her spine. Or maybe she'd just caught a draft of air-conditioning. "Thank you, Marcus. That means a lot to me."

"I thought maybe we could go to dinner to talk about it."

It didn't mean that much to her. Nope. She wasn't sure whether "it" was the incidents, his backing or her gratitude or a combination thereof. Regardless, she didn't want to do dinner with Marcus and discuss any of it. She was glad she had a legitimate excuse. "I'm sorry, Marcus. I already have a commitment."

"Maybe another night?"

Maybe never. She sort of felt bad about that, but there was something about Marcus outside of his dweebiness. Something she couldn't quite put her finger on, but she had no intention of alone time with Marcus Chalkey. "I'll have to check my calendar." Mercifully, the loudspeaker went off, the announcer requesting all associates perform a zone defense. "Sorry about that. I had to pick a few things up and it's noisy in here. Thank you again for your support, Marcus. I'll talk with you later."

She hung up, fairly certain she'd not shown the appropriate level of appreciation for Marcus's support. She was pretty sure he'd counted on her going to dinner with him. No. She'd muddle through this without resorting to sucking up to Marcus.

She switched her attention back to her impending fashion disaster. She had an hour and so far all the jeans looked hideous on her.

TUCKER LOOKED AROUND the noisy dinner table and felt a moment of sublime happiness and contentment.

It had been touch-and-go at first. Much as he'd suspected, Charlene had walked in ready to dislike Maddie on Darlene's behalf, and because she knew Maddie's family had money out the wazoo. It'd been seven years and he'd gone out occasionally, even had the occasional bed partner since Darlene, but Maddie was the first woman to meet the family.

He could've warned her earlier today, but he'd let her walk in blind because otherwise he was afraid she would've backed out, and Maddie needed the comfort he knew these people would give. The turning point had occurred when Melanie had climbed up in Maddie's lap...and promptly thrown up on her. There were a whole lot of ways that cookie could've crumbled, but after one startled moment, Maddie had handled it just right. When it was apparent that Melanie was okay, Maddie had laughed it off. And it hadn't been a fake oh-gross-some-other-woman's-kid-just-puked-on-me laugh. It had been genuine, just like Maddie was, and Charlene had been sunk by the charm and laughter that defined Maddie's indomitable spirit.

Charlene had dragged Maddie off to her house. "No one should have to eat dinner in puke clothes. Heck, none of us can eat dinner if you don't change." They'd gotten on like a house afire since then.

Bobby squirmed in his chair. "Nana, I'm done. Can I go play?"

Charlene gave an almost imperceptible nod to her mother-in-law's questioning glance. "Okay. Clear your plate on the way."

"Yes, ma'am." Like a car coming up on the straightaway out of a turn, he was up and gone, his plate barely making it to the counter instead of the floor. Once her brother vacated the premises, Melanie was clearly of the same mind. "Out. Please."

Edna laughed and nodded. "You boys take the kids out to the swing set. The girls can help me tidy up."

Tucker saw the flicker of happiness that crossed Maddie's face over being included as one of "the girls." He could've kissed Edna for including Maddie in the cleanup plan.

He pushed back from the table and carried his plate into the kitchen on his way out back to swing-set duty. Napoleon, who'd waited patiently by the back door for him, dashed outside, eager to play. It wasn't that Edna thought cleanup was women's work and below the men. Quite the opposite. Edna maintained she didn't want some inept man bumbling around in her kitchen.

Jack and Andy followed him out to the backyard and the wooden play set they'd all spent a weekend building for the kids last year. Andy carried Melanie to the toddler swing and strapped her in. Bobby climbed the rock wall to the slide.

"Nice gal you got there," Jack said, offering his seal of approval in his quiet way of few words.

Andy shot Tucker a glance as he pushed Melanie. "Charlene likes her."

Andy, much like his father, was a man of few words, which was a good thing because Charlene talked plenty, and then some. They complemented each other, completed each other in a way he and Darlene never had.

"Maddie's good people," he said.

"How's she like racing?" Jack asked.

Tucker shrugged. "It's grown on her."

"Better than pretending," Jack said. They all knew he was

referring to how Darlene had paid lip service to his racing commitment and then done a one-eighty after they'd tied the knot.

"Mama likes her, too," Andy commented. The women were visible through the kitchen window and through the window on the back door. They were laughing and chatting as if they were old friends.

"They was kissing when we walked up to Uncle Tucker's," Bobby offered. Unfortunately, Bobby didn't share the "man of few words" characteristic of his father and grandfather. "Daddy kisses Mama sometimes. Lots of times. She closes her eyes. Aunt Maddie had her eyes closed, too."

"That's Ms. Maddie," Tucker corrected.

"Well, if Daddy kisses Mommy and her eyes close and you're my uncle and you kiss Aunt Maddie and her eyes close, then why isn't she my aunt?"

Andy laughed at Tucker and shrugged. "You're on your own on this one, ace."

Jack shook his head, "Don't look at me."

Damn. They were hanging him out to dry.

Bobby launched off the slide and took off toward the house. "I'll go ask Nana."

"No!" Tucker snagged him and caught him up in the air. Bobby squealed and giggled. "She's not your aunt because I'm not married to her, you little troll."

"Why not?"

"'Cause I haven't known her long enough. You have to know someone a long, long time before you decide you want to marry them."

Jack and Andy laughed. Good to know you could count on them to be helpful.

"So maybe you should kiss her some more," Bobby pointed out with four-year-old rationale.

"That's an idea."

"Can you give me a ride to the monkey bars on your shoulders?"

"Monkey bars for a little monkey? Sounds right to me."

The kids played while the talk turned to the Charlotte race in a couple of weeks.

A few minutes later the women drifted out the back door to join them. Maddie looked happy and relaxed and right at home with Edna and Charlene.

"We've got to go, snooks," Charlene said to Andy. Snooks was short for snookums and if Charlene was *snooks*-ing Andy in front of Maddie, she definitely liked her. "The kids need baths and tomorrow's gonna come early."

Everyone exchanged goodbyes, Maddie promising to return the borrowed clothes via Tucker.

Bobby's voice carried on the night loud and clear as his mother herded him to the car. "Mama, Uncle Tucker's gonna kiss Miz Maddie some more so he can marry her and *then* she'll be my aunt."

Andy laughed while Charlene admonished both of them.

Edna and Maddie looked at Tucker. He chuckled and shook his head. "Don't ask. Trust me, you really don't want to know."

Andy and Charlene's taillights faded in the distance as Tucker and Maddie started down the dirt road, back to Tucker's house.

A sliver of a moon hung above the trees, as if suspended by a thread. Stars washed the night sky in pinpricks of light. Tucker caught Maddie's hand, warm and capable, in his, and they walked down the dirt road holding hands. Napoleon scampered ahead.

"Have you noticed that every time you come over here

you wind up wearing someone else's clothes home?" Tucker said as they strolled along, neither in a hurry. A breeze whispered through the night, carrying a leftover remnant of winter chill. Tucker felt Maddie's involuntary shiver. Letting go of her hand, he put his arm around her, pulling her close, sharing body heat. She slid her arm around his waist. "Why'd you let her drag you to her house for a pair of sweatpants when you had your suit at home...I mean, my house?"

"Because she obviously needed to take care of me after Melanie threw up on me. And here's a better question for you. Why didn't you tell me she was your ex-wife's best friend and was going to come in loaded for bear? Not fair, Macray, not even a little." She pinched him where her hand rested on his waist. Not hard, but a pinch nonetheless.

"Ouch. No, it wasn't, was it? It was unfair and very selfish of me. I didn't tell you because I was afraid you'd change your mind about going and I really wanted you to go."

"Why?"

He was glad it was dark. Some things were easier to say in the dark. "Because I wanted you to meet them. I wanted them to meet you."

They turned into his driveway and walked past her car.

"I'm glad I did. They're wonderful."

"Sometimes..." He stopped, but then he knew Maddie would understand. They seemed to share a connection. "Sometimes I'm sitting there with all of them and I have to pinch myself that I'm a part of that. That people that good really care about me."

They climbed the front steps and she stopped him at the door, her palm flat against his chest over his heart. "That's because you're a pretty wonderful person, too, Tucker Macray. You've lived with the same thing I have all these years. Both of us, thinking if we'd been more of what they needed us to be, they would've loved us more. My mother wouldn't have overdosed and your father wouldn't have beat you while your mother let him."

It was as if she'd crawled inside his head, peered into the dark corners of his soul. "For the longest time I didn't know who I hated more. Him or me."

"I was angry with my mother for years. I'm not sure if I can ever let it go completely." She traced her fingers over the edge of his jaw, as if memorizing the line. "The Matthewses love you because you're you. Neither one of us is our parents. We're not our childhoods. They shaped us, but they don't define us. It's the decisions we make now that make us who and what we are."

She turned her head and pressed a kiss to his chest that seemed to brand straight through to his heart.

He braced his hands on either side of her, trapping her against the wall next to the front door. He ached for her touch, her taste. He kissed her and she kissed him back with an intimate, exploring hunger that left him on fire. She pulled his T-shirt out of his jeans and slid her hands beneath the hem, her fingers scorching the bare skin of his back, kneading his tense muscles.

With a groan he scattered kisses along her jaw, moving down to the tender skin of her neck, nibbling at the sensitive spot beneath her ear. A wanting, a need fiercer than anything he'd ever known before, shook him. A need for her.

He rasped her name against the hollow of her throat, "Maddie…"

"Tucker…" She splayed her fingers against his back, her breath mingling with his, becoming his. "I need you. I want to stay tonight."

He felt her need all the way to his soul. Her family had hurt her today. God knows, the day was coming, and he knew it with a dark inevitability, when she would ask more than he could give, when she'd tap that part of him that was dark and hollow and realize at the core he didn't have more to give, but this, this he could do for her. He could hold her through the dark night, light her way with the passion that burned between them.

"Stay with me," he whispered against her ear, her hair feathering against his face, her scent wrapping around him.

"Yes." She dropped her head back.

"I have to fly to Charlotte early tomorrow morning for a meeting. I'm not sure I'll still be here when you wake up in the morning."

"As long as you're here tonight."

CHAPTER NINETEEN

MADDIE LET HERSELF IN through the kitchen door and greeted Sylvester as the sun began to edge over the horizon. "Morning, sunshine," she said.

Sylvester twined about her legs, paused, and then offered a baleful glare in return.

Maddie had called Jess on her way to pick out clothes yesterday and asked her to stop by and feed Sylvester. Maddie suspected Sylvester was more in a snit over Napoleon's scent on her rather than her actual absence.

She started the coffeemaker and headed upstairs for a shower. She'd been awake when Tucker got up to leave for Charlotte. Actually, she'd never gone to sleep. She'd been so utterly content, so absolutely happy, that she'd wanted to hold on to the feeling for as long as possible. It had been a magical night, and if the magic vanished with the dawn, she wanted to jealously guard every precious moment until then.

She was halfway up the stairs when someone knocked on her door. Maybe Tucker had gotten a phone call en route to the air strip that his Charlotte trip was canceled and had decided to surprise her. She flew back down the stairs, across the stone floor, and threw open the door.

"Oh." Definitely not Tucker. "Daddy."

Her father wore his usual suit and tie, obviously ready for work. "I saw your car go by a few minutes ago."

Maddie nodded and glanced down at the suit skirt she'd worn at yesterday's meeting. She'd put on her own clothes to wear back home. "I was out."

"I know. Jess said you were having dinner with Macray."

"Supper. I was having supper with him." She was still punch drunk from the night before.

"Looks like supper ran on to breakfast," he offered dryly.

If they were going to discuss her spending the night with Tucker, it was probably best if they were both caffeinated. And yesterday's conversation still hung between them— definitely requiring caffeine. "Actually, I just put some coffee on. Want a cup?"

Her father, who usually bulldogged his way through everything, hesitated at the threshold. "Is there enough for me?"

"I can always make more." She linked her arm through his and brought him inside.

Sylvester, his tail in the air, stalked past. Her father sat in one of the heavy wooden chairs at the rough-hewn table. A comfortable quiet settled between them as Maddie poured two coffees in thick mugs and put on a backup pot to brew. She'd never joined the frappe, latte, chocowhatamatte crowd. She liked her coffee straight up, strong and black. She put his cup on the table in front of him and wrapped her hands around the hot mug.

He stared into the cup. "You know what I was thinking about last night?" He looked up and across the table at her. "I was thinking about how you used to climb up in my lap when you were just a little thing." Sadness marked his smile and shadowed his eyes. "You'd say 'Fix it, Daddy' and look at me with those big golden eyes, certain I could make it all right. And I would whether it was a broken toy or a scraped knee. And then when I found your mother that morning, I knew I couldn't fix it." He shook his head, as if his inability all of these years later still baffled him. Maddie reached across and rested her hand on top of his. "I couldn't fix it. I couldn't make Mary Beth happy. I couldn't bring her back for you or your brothers." He rolled his hand and grasped hers. "You had her smile, her laugh. I was so afraid for you." His grip tightened painfully for a heartbeat. "I just wanted to protect you. And all these years I've been so afraid for you that I couldn't see what was so clear, that you've grown into a strong, capable woman despite my misguided intentions."

She squeezed his hand where it still held hers. "Daddy, I love you."

"I love you, too, princess." He relinquished her hand and picked up his cup, as if his emotional display had embarrassed him and he was ready to move on to something else. "Are you okay?"

Maddie nodded. "I'm good, now that we've got it out in the open. It's like a huge weight has been lifted. What about you?" She took a swallow of coffee and felt the burn all the way down. Wonderful.

"I'm a whole lot better than I've been in a long time." Daddy took a coffee break. "Hey, this is good stuff." He shifted and a dull red crept up his face. "I wanted to talk to you about something else."

"Okay…."

He took another fortifying swallow of coffee and looked at her over the top of the mug. "I've asked Sharon to marry me."

She could've fallen out of her chair. "I like Sharon, but don't you think this is kind of fast?"

Her father smiled rather sheepishly. "I suppose it might look that way or it might look as if we've wasted a lot of time. Part of what makes me successful is that once I've figured out what I want, I don't second-guess, and I sure as hell don't wait on someone to beat me to the punch. Sharon and I talked. She's still the same person she's always been underneath that new look, and so am I. She knows me better than I know myself, Maddie, and she still loves me. I'm not willing to waste any more time."

"Then go for it. I'm thrilled for you both."

He put the mug on the table, relief in his eyes and his smile. "We've already wasted so much time." It was as if he simply couldn't stop talking about them, which was kind of cute and endearing, especially since it was so unlike her father. "Can you believe that crazy woman says she's been in love with me since she came to work for me?" The tips of his ears turned red.

"I can believe it. And how about you? How long have you been in love with her?" It felt good, but weird, to be teasing her dad about his love life.

"A long, long time, princess. So you don't mind? Me getting remarried?"

Maddie put aside her teasing for the moment. "I'm so happy for you both."

"Sharon said she thought you would be."

She recalled his initial indignation after Sharon's makeover. "Guess you'll have to break in a new secretary, after all."

"Nope. Sharon said the way she figures it, she's marrying a workaholic, so the only way she's going to see me is if she keeps her job. Plus, she said she'd either work for me or someone else, and she didn't particularly want to break in a new boss, but she wasn't willing to do nothing. She said I fell in love with a career woman, so I could marry a career woman. She's pretty darn amazing."

"I think you both are. And I think you're going to be deliriously happy."

"I hope so. I'm supposed to meet her mother on Wednesday." He drained his coffee.

Maddie grinned all over herself. Her father, who commanded a multimillion-dollar operation looked as nervous as a schoolboy. "She'll love you."

"I hope so."

"Trust me. You love her daughter and your prospects are pretty good. It's not as if you're exactly a bum." She patted his hand. "You'll do fine."

"There's one more thing, Maddie. You're not going to like it." Judging by his expression and faintly apologetic air, she had a feeling she wasn't. "I compromised with Dan Chalkey. I'm not pulling you off the job, because I don't know what the hell is going on, but after I thought about it, I know my daughter wouldn't do either one of those things."

"Thank you. So, if I'm not off the job, what's the compromise?"

"Restricted access. You'll turn in your hard card and be restricted to the hospitality tent and the suite."

"That's fine."

"Fine?"

"It's Kelsi, Daddy. But neither Tucker or I can say anything until we have proof. Restricted access means we narrow the playing field because she'll slip up sooner or later and we'll catch her when she does."

"Is that where you spent the night? With him?"

She nodded.

"I don't want to see you get hurt, honey. He seems like a nice guy but…"

"But?"

"He's in a position, a job, if you will, where there's a hundred more waiting in line behind Kelsi. And that boy's just a rookie this year, but he's taking off. He's going all the way to the top, and that just means there'll be more and more Kelsis."

She knew it came with the territory. "That's a chance I have to take."

"Have you told him how you feel about him?"

"Not yet." She thought about walking the dirt road holding hands beneath the stars. "But I've had a glimpse of what we can have together and it's good. It's better than good."

"You're as much of a fighter as your old man, aren't you, princess?"

She grinned at him. "You haven't seen nothing yet."

TUCKER PUT IN HIS EARBUDS and stared out the window of CRE's corporate jet on the return flight from Charlotte. Last night had been great—and probably one of the biggest mistakes he'd ever made. He didn't want to hurt Maddie, but he couldn't seem to stay away from her, he couldn't seem to resist her. He knew his limitations, he'd tried to make sure Maddie knew them, but dammit, things all got so tangled up when they were together.

He wondered how she was this morning. Did she have a job when she'd shown up at work? He'd had zero opportunity to contact Maddie today, other than the one time he'd escaped to the bathroom and text-messaged her that he'd come by her place on his way home. Even when they weren't in meetings with the secondary sponsor who'd signed on, he'd spent the rest of the day with Dan and Marcus Chalkey.

Marcus was jumping up and down on his last nerve. Unfortunately, Marcus had the perception of a garden slug.

"So, Tuck, what's happening with you and the Kelsinator?"

The Kelsinator? Tucker counted to five and reminded himself he worked for Marcus's family. "Nothing's happening. She does her job. I do mine."

"I'd say she was all for expanding her job description with you." That was the thing that sucked about Marcus. Tucker tended to overlook that Marcus was there...but Marcus was there and taking it all in. Damn, why'd Kelsi have to say that stuff in front of Marcus? Because she thought he'd been wearing that goofy headset and she hadn't thought he was paying attention. "Maybe you could double-date with us sometimes."

Okay. Marcus had totally lost him this time. "Double-date?"

"Yeah. You and Kelsi. Me and Maddie."

"Maddie?" This was getting interesting.

"Tuck, come on, dude. Maddie Felton. We're keeping it sort of quiet until this stuff at the track blows over, but she's had a thing for me for years. Can you believe it, she was just too shy to do anything about it? I'm afraid she's been pretty obvious lately with the way she looks at me. I think she's been a little reluctant to mix our pleasure with our business, if you know what I mean." Marcus winked at him. "But now that she's not working at the track anymore, I think it's going to be a different story. She wants me bad."

Tucker sat speechless. One of them was nuts...and Tucker knew for sure it wasn't him.

CHAPTER TWENTY

"HE SAID *WHAT?*" Maddie swiveled her head so fast she nearly whiplashed herself.

Tucker had shown up with dinner and they were sitting out back on the patio. It was a good thing they'd already eaten or she'd have very likely choked on her chicken.

"Yeah. Are you carrying some secret torch for Marcus?"

She couldn't believe Marcus had had the nerve to say that about her. "That little worm. The first time I met him at the track he came up and asked me if I remembered him. It was kind of embarrassing because I didn't. Then he was irritated by that. He remembered going to dinner with my family once. It must've been five or six years ago. He recited exactly what I'd had for dinner and even what I'd had for dessert. I thought it was sort of creepy."

"Well, his story is you've been jonesing for him but were too shy to pursue him," Tucker said. "According to him, you want him bad, and now you can have him since business doesn't stand in the way of pleasure."

Yuck. "If it wasn't so scary, it'd be funny. But I'm not laughing. Are you serious? I know you like to tease. Is this a joke?"

Tucker shook his head, his hazel eyes somber. "I wouldn't kid around about something like this. I think the guy's seriously unhinged."

"But why frame me?" She pursed her lips, thinking. She sat up straighter and snapped her fingers. "Wait a second. I'd forgotten all about this. Yesterday afternoon when I was out shopping, he called me. He told me that his father was sure I was the culprit. Marcus assured me he knew I'd never do anything like that and he'd 'champion me.'" Maddie rolled her eyes in disgust. "Then he asked me out to dinner to discuss it. I told him I had other plans and he asked me to set another date."

"Did you?"

"What do you think? Of course not. So, he's delusional... very delusional. But it doesn't mean that he's behind any of this." Maddie shifted and her bare foot brushed Tucker's. Heat curled through her. "Although he did take my day planner from me that time in the garage and he never did go in the hauler. But how would he have known about the flowers?"

Tucker looked sheepish. "Because he was there when I ordered them. He's like a permanent fixture in the hauler. He's always sitting in the corner, Internet-surfing with his headphones on. You sort of forget he's there. And you figure with the headphones on he's not paying attention to what's being said. He *could've* heard me order them. It doesn't mean he *did* hear me order them."

"True. And there's still the matter of why? If he's got a thing for me, why frame me? Why try to get me in trouble?"

"What did he tell you last night? He'd champion you?"

"Yeah. That's exactly the word he used—*champion.* I thought it was weird, but then again, Marcus *is* weird. It was like I was supposed to see him as my hero—my knight in shining armor. I think he was disappointed I didn't leap at the opportunity to go to dinner with him to show my gratitude."

"Okay, the guy is a little out there. So we've go to think a little out there to figure him out. Say I'm a strange little guy who alternates between being overlooked and strutting around telling everyone how important I am," Tucker said.

Maddie took up his thread of reasoning. "And my business is a sport where the drivers are macho—"

"Really, you think macho?" he interrupted with a smirk.

"—shut up, and somewhat idealized—"

"Macho and idealized?"

He was incorrigible and she shouldn't encourage him by laughing at him, but she couldn't bite back a snicker. She picked back up where he'd interrupted. "Macho and idealized, despite bad hair. What chance do you have of competing in that environment? How do you set yourself up as a hero?"

Tucker put his feet on the ground and leaned forward in the chair, bracing his forearms on his knees. "By producing a damsel in distress. If he set you up, then he could come in and save you. When everyone else turned on you and was pointing a finger at you, who stood beside you? Who *championed* you? Who assured his father you couldn't have possibly done those things?"

Maddie shivered in the warm evening. "That's freaky."

"Yeah, well, it's Marcus we're talking about here."

Maddie stood and paced over to the edge of the patio. This entire conversation was unnerving. But necessary. Someone had set her up, darn near got her fired, and at the least she was banned from the garage area. And it wasn't likely to end with that. She'd been so sure it was Kelsi, but now she just didn't know. The whole thing with Kelsi was much more straightforward. This was getting a little convoluted with Marcus. "So, he's riding to the rescue on his trusty steed. What's his next move?"

"He gets rid of the competition." Tucker's stark words held a sinister note.

Maddie wrapped her arms around her middle. "How does he do that?"

Tucker stood and wrapped his arms around her from behind, resting his chin against the top of her head, enveloping her in his scent, his warmth, his strength. "I don't know exactly, but I think we'd better figure it out pretty soon."

TWO WEEKS LATER, ON A Saturday night at a Sleep EZ in Charlotte, Tucker stood talking to a group of Sleep EZ district managers in a meeting/ballroom. A dozen round tables draped in white tablecloths were set up about the room. Two bars flanked either side of the doors that led to the hallway. Dinner, the culmination of a four-day sales meeting, would be in about half an hour, and until that time, Tucker's job was to chat with the three dozen or so district and regional managers scattered throughout the room.

Tucker listened with half an ear to a guy from South Carolina who was about one beer away from too many, especially for a business event, offer his assessment of the other NASCAR NEXTEL Cup Series teams. Tucker scanned the room in search of Maddie. Ah, there she was, across the room looking professional, elegant and heart-stoppingly sexy in a curve-hugging black cocktail dress, her hair swept up in a smooth chignon revealing the tempting line of her neck, the smooth round line of her shoulder.

He couldn't see it from across the room, but she had a tiny birthmark right at the base of her neck, and when he kissed that area she turned inside out. Her breath would quicken and she'd utter a satisfied noise, half moan, half purr in the back of her throat. His temperature spiked half a ballroom away as he simply thought about that sweet spot on the back of her neck.

As if she sensed his glance, as if she'd felt the brush of his lips on that nerve-rich expanse of skin, she glanced over her shoulder. For one second her gaze locked with his as if they were the only ones in the room, and then she looked away, turning her attention back to her group's conversation.

They weren't any closer to figuring anything out about the itching powder or the dead flower. Nothing unusual had happened trackside, but he didn't believe for a minute that it was over. He was still sure it had to be either Kelsi or Marcus or the two of them working together, behind the pranks. He and Maddie had talked with her two brothers, who were now convinced it was either Kelsi or Marcus. Both Doug and Steve were showing up at as many races and functions as possible and keeping an eye out for anything suspicious. Amateurish as it was, they'd even developed a signal if one of them thought something suspicious was about to happen.

Mr. South Carolina punched him in the arm. "Isn't that right, Macray?"

He steadied the guy with one hand. "Sorry, what was that?"

"I said the Number 76 car is kicking butt and taking names. It you don't screw up the next couple of races, we're gonna make the Chase, aren't we?"

Tucker laughed. The guy was slightly drunk but really excited at the prospect of them making the Chase. Heck, so was he. "I'm going to try really hard not to screw it up. We've been holding steady and building points. We did well in Charlotte last week and we've got a better qualifying position this weekend. I think you guys are going to see a heck of a race tomorrow."

They talked another minute or so about the particulars of running on the one-and-a-half-mile quad oval in Charlotte versus next weekend's "Monster Mile" in Dover. The guys took off to answer nature's call, offering Tucker a brief break.

He was strung tight, because it all felt as if he was waiting on the next shoe to drop. There was a sense of inevitability. Something else was going to happen.

He sipped his ginger ale and let his gaze sweep over Maddie for just a second. His gut tightened as he thought about the hang-up phone calls that had begun to plague her. Even with phone technology, it simply came up Unknown Name without any identifying number. When she was at Tucker's house, she'd come home to find twenty or more calls, all hang-ups. If he was at her house and she answered, the caller never identified her or himself, but the calls would stop. It was as if the caller wanted to make sure she was home. It was more than a little creepy.

Tucker'd thought about having a little talk with both Kelsi and Marcus. But he lacked proof. And a conversation with Marcus without benefit of proof could be career suicide. Flinging accusations at his team owner's son without proof seemed a pretty sure way to find himself without a job as a driver. It'd be one thing if he had the clout of several good seasons behind him to feel Marcus out, but if he turned out to be wrong, a rookie sure as heck couldn't afford to make that kind of mistake.

Kelsi had continued her pursuit of him and Marcus hadn't given up on Maddie, issuing a weekly invitation, which she always declined due to her busy schedule. Desperation was bound to drive one of them to the next move, to screwing up. If it was Kelsi, she still hadn't totally eliminated Maddie from the scene. And if it was Marcus, he still wasn't Maddie's hero.

Tucker rubbed the back of his neck where tension knotted his muscles. It was like the lull before his father tied on a good drunk and then beat the living daylights out of him. A lull when everything took on a semblance of normal, an illusory time that fooled him into thinking the bad stuff was over and done with. He'd learned not to trust the lull, because as sure as the sun rose and set every day, another beating was going to come his way as long as he lived with his father.

Tucker didn't trust this lull. He couldn't shake the feeling something was about to go down.

As if conjured up by his thoughts, Marcus appeared by his side. "Hey, how about a drink, Tuck? Beer? Wine? Something a little stronger?"

"Nah. I'm good."

"Oh, come on. One drink won't hurt the night before a race. Let me pick something up for you from the bar." Marcus eyed the nearly empty glass. "You know, this won't happen that often, me serving you. What are you drinking?"

Marcus was awfully eager to get him a drink and Tucker could've sworn there'd been a flash of malice in his eyes, but then again Marcus was alternately ingratiating and arrogant. "Sure. I'll have a ginger ale. Thanks, Marcus."

"Got one coming your way in just a sec. We want to take care of you." Marcus's smile oozed self-satisfaction. "We want you in top form tomorrow."

The hair on the back of his neck stood up. Maybe because he'd had thirteen years to fine-tune it, but he had an internal radar for when someone was about to send bad stuff his way. And his radar was going crazy. Marcus was up to something.

Tucker scratched behind his ear, the sign they'd come up with. Maddie was across the room, her back to him, engaged in a lively conversation with a couple of managers. Steve stood in the opposite corner of the room, but Doug was fairly close to the bar. Doug brushed his hand down the front of his jacket, as if smoothing a wrinkle. Signal received. He'd keep an eye on Marcus.

Tucker looked around the room, forcing himself to relax

his stance. His buddies, done with nature's call and a cigarette or two, wandered back in. Within a couple of minutes, Marcus was back. Winking—guys just didn't need to wink at other guys, it was just wrong—he handed Tucker the fresh drink, even going so far as to take his empty glass from him. "There you are, big guy."

In less than two minutes, Steve Felton joined them. "Hey, sorry to interrupt, but can I snag Marcus and Tucker for a minute?" He smiled at the Felton employees. "Business. You know how it is. But you guys relax."

Marcus seemed nervous. "Emergency executive staff meeting. Doug's getting Maddie," Steve told them. Tucker shrugged and followed Marcus and Steve out of the ballroom to a smaller conference room. Louis Felton and Dan Chalkey were waiting in the room. Louis looked grim, Dan perplexed. Maddie and Doug slipped in behind them and Doug closed the door.

Dan Chalkey didn't look particularly pleased to be there. He and Marcus were at the dinner as CRE representatives, but he sure as heck wasn't happy to have been dragged into a conference room. Tucker wasn't exactly sure what had happened, but Steve wouldn't have brought them here without good reason. Tucker suspected Dan Chalkey was about to be a whole lot less pleased.

"This better be good. What's going on?" Dan said.

"We're going to turn the floor over to Marcus," Doug said. He reached into his jacket pocket and pulled out a clear empty glass vial, taking care only to handle it with the cocktail napkin around it. "Go ahead, Marcus, you take it from here."

Marcus turned a very wormy white and his hands began to tremble. He shoved them into his pockets and puffed himself up, a pathetic show of bravado. "I don't know what you're talking about."

Doug shook his head. "This can go down easy or it can go down hard, but it's going down. I saw you drop a napkin, bend down with that drink—" he nodded toward the drink Tucker held in his hand, the one Marcus had just handed him in front of three other guys "—pull that vial out of your pocket, dump it in the drink and pick up the napkin. When you straightened back up, you tossed both the napkin and the tube in the garbage, then you walked over and handed the drink to Tucker. It was pretty smooth. You must've practiced it for a long time."

"You can't say those things about me." Even his voice shook.

Maddie tag-teamed him. "Your fingerprints are on both glasses, Marcus. It'll be a pretty easy thing to have the tube and the drink analyzed. Seems you could save everyone the time and just fess up."

Marcus glanced toward the door. Tucker all but saw Marcus's wheels turning as he assessed his chances of making a dash for it. Doug Felton positioned himself in front of the door and crossed his massive arms over his chest, radiating hostility. Doug smiled at Marcus. It wasn't friendly and it wasn't nice. It taunted and dared, screaming that Doug wanted one good reason to beat Marcus's ass.

Tucker definitely wanted Doug on his side, rather than against him, in a fight.

The whole room saw the moment Marcus made his decision—a wise decision in Tucker's opinion because Doug would've decimated him. Marcus's shoulders sagged and his bravado crumbled beneath him.

"What the hell have you been up to?" Dan Chalkey's question hissed through the quiet like the lash of a cat-o'-nine-tails biting into bare flesh.

Marcus flinched as if it had.

"Tell us, Marcus," Maddie said, her voice soft, soothing. "The worst thing you can do is keep it bottled up inside you."

The expression in Marcus's eyes, adoration and accusation, said it all before he opened his mouth. "It was all for you, Maddie."

She didn't blink and the rest of the room seemed to hold a collective breath. "What was in the vial, Marcus?"

"Sleeping pills and laxatives. Even if he'd managed to stay awake, he wouldn't have been in any shape to drive."

"You slipped him sleeping pills?" Maddie swayed on her feet and Tucker stepped closer, steadying her with a hand to her elbow. He knew how she felt about pills.

"Not enough to hurt him." There was a whining note in Marcus's voice. "But he wouldn't have been behind the wheel of a race car tomorrow." Marcus giggled, an eerie sound from a grown man. "It would've been too messy."

Ugh. Sleeping pills and laxatives. Talk about a combination sure to leave a man with no dignity.

Marcus shot Tucker a triumphant glance. "Then he wouldn't have been the big race-car driver hero."

Maddie nodded and pressed him. "And the itching powder? The dead flower? Did you do those things?"

Another one of those creepy giggles. "Of course it was me. The flower was really easy, but the itching powder—" he made a frustrated face "—I carried that around for weeks waiting until the right opportunity."

Maddie had more questions. "But what if I hadn't left my bag behind? What if Kelsi hadn't looked in it?"

"That worked out well. If it hadn't, I would've stopped by and asked you a scheduling question and then you would've looked in your bag and I would've seen it. Considering Kelsi's so jealous, it worked out really well for her to find it." He actually preened.

Anger flushed Doug Felton's neck and face. "You little creep, you set my sister up. You wanted everyone to think she did it."

Marcus crumpled in the face of Doug's anger. "I told them she wouldn't do something like that." He looked at Maddie. "I stuck up for you."

Marcus took a step behind Maddie, and Tucker shifted to put himself between them. He thought Marcus was only trying to hide behind a woman, but Tucker wasn't taking any chances that the little nut job might grab her as a hostage or something equally twisted.

Marcus shot Maddie an accusatory look. "I just wanted you, but you didn't even remember meeting me."

Maddie had called it right. And Marcus needed some help. Of course, Doug looked just about ready to hammer some help home.

Maddie looked at Marcus, her expression firm, "I'm not your girlfriend. I'm not going to be your girlfriend. Ever. Got it?"

Marcus sighed, defeated. "Got it."

Dan Chalkey ignored everyone else in the room and stepped up to Maddie. "I owe you an apology. I misjudged you and I'm sorry for that." He offered his hand.

Tucker had the distinct impression they were witnessing a historic moment. Chalkey was a nice enough guy, but apologies weren't in his regular bag of tricks.

Maddie took his hand. "Apology accepted."

Dan finally looked at Marcus. "You need help, Marcus. I think the signs have been there for a long time, but I chose to overlook them. We're going to get you some help." Dan took Marcus's arm. "We're going to leave now. Please apologize to your guests for me, I'm not feeling well."

Tucker had always admired Dan Chalkey, but no more than at that moment. And Marcus was no longer a threat to Maddie, but what about him, Tucker? Inside he knew they were running on borrowed time.

CHAPTER TWENTY-ONE

"THIS IS THE LAST ONE," Maddie said. She sent the flying disk across the backyard, Napoleon in hot pursuit. One leap and the little rascal caught it in his mouth.

He promptly ran over and dropped it at Maddie's feet, looking up at her expectantly. She shook her head, laughing. "No way. I'm exhausted and I've only been throwing. I'm done."

Tucker grinned from his seat on the back stoop. "Haven't you figured out by now that Napoleon never wears out before you do?" He loved watching Maddie play fetch with the dog. In the weeks since Marcus had been caught, they'd stolen every moment together possible, and for Tucker the time had an almost frantic quality. Sometimes he knew Maddie felt the tension, too, as if a thunderstorm was brewing on a perfect summer day. He patted the spot beside him on the stoop. "C'mon. I saved a special spot just for you."

She plopped down beside him, Napoleon settling on the step below their feet. He put his arm around her, pulling her close to his side. She settled her head in the crook of his shoulder.

The panting of the dog accompanied the symphony of crickets and the distant hum of an air conditioner. This was one of those perfect moments when he wished he was outside of time—that time wouldn't end. Contentment flowed between them like a lazy, winding river.

She pressed a kiss to his chest. "I love you."

He felt as if he'd just had a blowout at 180—the sensation of spinning out of control, the instinctive, reflexive reaction of not banging into the wall and flipping end over end a couple of times.

She pulled slightly away from him. "I can see that went over big. Let's try this again. I love you, Tucker Macray." She elbowed him in the ribs. "That's your cue to say something like, 'Wow, Maddie. That's some good news. And by the way, I love you, too.'"

He said nothing because he couldn't tell her that. This was it. The moment he'd dreaded. The raging storm. The moment when she wanted from him what he didn't have to give.

She nodded slowly. "Or not."

She pulled away from him and he took his arm from around her shoulders. "Maddie, what do you want from me?" He fought to keep his breathing steady, fought to keep panic at bay.

"I'm pretty sure I just told you what I wanted."

"Why are you doing this?"

"You say that as if me telling you I love you is a bad thing. How can you not know I care about you? Don't you feel it every time I touch you, kiss you, say your name? I thought I felt those same things from you. I guess it was my turn to be wrong." She laughed, a dry, wry sound at odds with her usual mirth. "My wrong just turned out to be a biggie."

"I'm damaged goods, Maddie. I was honest with you. I told you from the beginning."

"You did, didn't you?" She looked away from him and studied her sandaled feet. "I just thought that when two people found something real, something special, they were supposed to go with it."

He reached out to touch her but dropped his hand back to his lap. "But it's not real. It's the lull, Maddie. The lull is the time in between the bad times, when you think the bad times won't come back and bite you in the ass. But they do, every time. So you can't trust the lull."

She shook her head and looked at him, her eyes clear and direct. "No. I don't believe that."

"Why are we even having this discussion? Why can't we just enjoy what we have right now?"

"Because we are, as Edna would put it, 'making do,' getting by. I've gotten by my whole life, Tucker. I took what I was given and didn't ask for anything more because I didn't think I deserved it and because I was scared what I had would be taken away if I asked for more—and I'm not talking about material wealth. You talk about how different we grew up. In some ways, yes. In others, no, because I think you were exactly the same. I think that's why you still pinch yourself at dinner with the Matthewses. I'm not willing to settle for half measures anymore. I want it all. I want to hear 'I love you' when I go to bed at night and when I wake up in the morning. I want commitment and promise. I want a future with you. Children. A family. A baby to put in the high chair when we go to Edna and Jack's for supper."

She made it sound so easy, so real. "Maddie, I can't…"

She jumped to her feet and Napoleon took off for a safer spot. For a moment Tucker thought she was going to plug her ears; instead she snapped at him. "Shut up, Tucker. Yes, you can. You just won't. There are a hundred women out there who'll settle for a whole lot less from you. Of course, if that's what you really wanted, I guess they'd be standing here instead of me."

He stood. "Dammit, Maddie—"

"Oh, no, you didn't! You didn't just *Dammit, Maddie* me. Let me tell you a thing or two, Tucker Macray. You're the one creating illusions. You say racing saved you and it's your true love and there's nothing left over. I say bogus. Racing may have saved you, but it's also been a big door for you to hide behind. That's an absolute load of crap that there's not enough room in your life for a relationship and racing. It's a convenient excuse to avoid a relationship. And every month when you send that check to your parents, at least be honest with yourself why you're sending it. It's not a thank-you. It's a great big slap in the face. And that's fine. They deserve it. But at least own up to it. Call it what it is."

That cut way too close to home and he lashed out. "I think it's time for you to leave."

She stomped down the last two steps. "I'm sure of it. But I've got one last thing to say."

"I think you've said plenty."

"Almost. In spite of all your faults you're the part that completes me. I didn't want to fall in love with you. I didn't want to find the part that made me whole. I wasn't looking for a soul mate. I wasn't looking for someone who knows me as well as I know myself because, quite frankly, I've kept my own counsel for a long time. I didn't want any of that, but somehow it happened." She sucked in a deep breath and so did he. He'd hoped she was done because she was tearing him apart, word by word. "For richer, for poorer, in sickness and in health, for better, for worse, I love you. I'm not offering any less and I'm not settling for any less."

She turned on her heel and marched to her car, her nose in the air. Tucker sank back onto the stoop and remained there long after the sound of her car's engine had faded away.

The lull was over. He'd known it wouldn't last.

IN THE MIDDLE OF AUGUST, Maddie sat back on her heels and surveyed the room full of packed and taped boxes. Just her desk to go and then she'd be ready for the moving van tomorrow. A lifetime of change had been crammed into the past couple of weeks.

A knock at the door startled her out of her reverie. Jess opened the door and stuck her head in. "Want some company?"

"Of course." She moved aside a box that had wound up on the sofa so Jess could have a seat. "One more orange soda in the fridge and it's got to be cleaned out by tomorrow."

She returned with the drink and Jess's hands weren't quite steady when they took it from her. "It'll be nice to have another woman in the house again. But, Lord, child, I'm going to miss you when you move."

Maddie blinked back the tears that threatened and steadied her voice. These were all good, positive changes. "I'll miss you, too, but it's the right thing to do. Daddy and Sharon need their privacy."

They'd been married last week in a simple ceremony in the garden of the assisted-living facility where Sharon's mother, Mrs. Betty, lived. Doug and Stevie had stood up for their father as best men. Mrs. Betty, in a wheelchair, had served as Sharon's matron of honor and Maddie her maid of honor. Jess and her family had attended, as had Sharon's brother, Curtis, who lived in Jacksonville, his wife and their two kids. "Having a grown daughter living in your backyard isn't exactly private. Plus, the carriage house'll be a nice place for Curtis and his family to stay when they come to visit." They were nice people. They'd enjoy the carriage house. The kids would love the wildness of the back garden.

"I know you're right, but it doesn't mean I'll miss you any less. Why'd you have to move so far away?"

Maddie grinned. "I can't afford the rent in this area. But I'm only half an hour away. And I still know when silver-polishing day is."

She'd decided if she was going to talk the talk, she needed to walk the walk. No more allowance from Daddy. She had a real job, where she made real money, and she'd live within the means of a real budget.

Jess smiled through a sheen of tears. "I hope so. Silver-polishing makes for fine conversation. I didn't think I'd ever see Mr. Louis so happy again."

"Sharon's good for him." Maddie was fairly certain her father had never been this happy before—especially with her mother. Happiness with Mary Beth had come in snatches, reprieves from what Maddie now knew had probably been incorrectly diagnosed manic depression or maybe bipolarity.

"Still no change in the other…situation?" Jess asked. Jess had offered a shoulder to cry on and Maddie had done some crying. She'd nearly cried a river when she'd walked away from Tucker. There'd been so many times, especially late at night, when she sat on her patio and let the twilight settle around her into the night. When she missed him with an ache that nearly rendered her in two. When something funny happened that she wanted to share with him. Those were the times she was tempted to settle for less. To call him and offer to take him on whatever terms he was willing to offer. And then she'd pull herself together. She'd love him, she'd support him, but she refused to short-change either one of them.

"No change in that situation." She started to pack the files from her desk. May as well finish up while they talked. "Still overcast and cloudy."

"He'll come around, honey."

She'd thought so at first. She still hoped he would. But that was the hard part about loving someone, offering a partnership. You could make the offer, but you couldn't make their decision for them.

Maddie shook her head. "I see him every week at the track. I'm polite and friendly. He's polite and friendly. The only thing that keeps me going is every once in a while I see a look in his eye, a glimmer, and I know I can't give up on him."

She pulled out the last two files that contained brochures she'd acquired during the renovation. A glossy pamphlet slid to the ground. She picked up the brochure with the attached pricing sheet of the twig furniture. She and Tucker had talked about him ordering the swing. His sad front porch needed this swing. *He* needed this swing. An idea took hold.

She looked up at Jess. "I'm going to send him something. Something he needs. Well, what he needs is me, but this'll be the next best thing."

She looked at the price. It would blow her budget to smithereens. What the heck? She'd eat beans for the rest of the month.

CHAPTER TWENTY-TWO

TUCKER TURNED DOWN THE ROAD that led home, trying to ignore the hollowness inside him. Racing, the one thing guaranteed to bring him joy and satisfaction, had grown stale and flat, like a carbonated drink left open overnight.

The team was doing a great job on sending him out in the right car with the right setup every week, and he was doing a fine job of driving. Every week he went through the motions of high-fives and the celebrations as their standing in the points rose and they moved closer to solidifying his spot in the Chase. But none of it seemed to really touch him.

Maddie was there each week, offering support, cheering him on, one of the Number 76 Sleep EZ team members, but that felt hollow and insubstantial, too. Racing, which had always felt real and grounded, now felt illusory.

The only thing Tucker knew to do was stay the course. This, too, would pass.

He drove by Edna and Jack's place and turned into his drive. What the heck were they doing? He threw the truck into Park and hopped out at the corner of the house. Jack folded up a ladder and Edna finished tying a cushion in place and then stepped back.

A twig swing hung from the eyehooks in the ceiling. A long cushion covered the seat, another was tied along the back. The cushion material was dark blue with vintage muscle cars printed on it and trimmed in blue-and-yellow gingham.

"Where'd this come from?" He knew before he asked, but he asked, anyway.

"Maddie. She asked us if we'd install it for you if she sent it," Edna said, giving the cushion a final tweak. She straightened and faced him. "Jack's told me to keep my nose out of your business and I have. But I love you like a son, Tucker, so I'm going to speak to you that way. You've not done right by that girl." Edna walked down the steps. "Ya'll come on to dinner when you finish up here."

Tucker waited until Edna had crossed the yard before he said to Jack, "She doesn't understand what racing's like. It doesn't leave a lot of room for anything or anyone else."

"Especially not if you don't let it. I'm going to ask you a simple question and all I want is a simple answer. Do you love her?"

"I do love her. But I also love racing, and mixing the two works for some people, but I just don't see that it'll work for me."

"You can love it. You can love it all day long. But you can't *need* it to be the man you are. You've got to find that in yourself because the sad fact is one day you're gonna be too damn old to climb behind the wheel of a race car and when that day comes, if you can't be the man you need to be without it, you're gonna be in a helluva bad spot. If you can't be a man without it, you're no better than a junkie waiting on his next fix."

"The problem is you've never thought you could have it all, son, and you can. Maddie's not a princess, she's a steel magnolia, and that's the kind of woman who'll stand with you."

It was almost more than Jack had said collectively in a lifetime. He carried the ladder down the front steps. "We'll wait supper on you. No hurry."

Tucker sat in the swing. It was just what he'd wanted for the porch, just what he and Maddie had discussed. She had done this for him. He swallowed a hard lump in the back of his throat, but it refused to go away.

This felt as lonely and empty as every lap he'd driven around every track for the past five weeks. He knew as surely as he knew his name that without Maddie it would always be this way, this empty, aching hollowness. But the absolute worst of it was Edna had hit the nail on the head. He hadn't done Maddie right. He'd turned away her love because he was a coward. Because he was too damn scared to admit he loved her. She deserved better than him. What if he let her down? Hell, he'd already let her down.

But he could try. He wouldn't offer her half measures. And maybe, just maybe she was right. He deserved the same for himself.

He had the swing. Now he just needed the girl.

"HE'S DONE IT. HE'S DONE IT. Race fans, the Number 76 car, with driver, Bed Head Macray, has scored its third win at Bristol! And if there was any doubt, the 76 is now in the Chase for the NASCAR NEXTEL Cup Series Championship."

Tucker did a burnout, threw it in reverse until he was heading in the other direction and took his lap around the track, driving in the opposite direction. He pumped his hand in the air as he made the lap and the crowd went wilder than ever.

He hit Victory Lane and climbed out. Mike and the team were there, Dan Chalkey, and the only person he was really interested in, Maddie.

The network announcer was on him when he climbed out of the car. "You've got to be feeling pretty good now."

"I hope I'm about to be feeling a whole lot better." That got the media's attention. "And I want the fans to hear this, too." He found Maddie in the crowd and held out his hand. "Maddie will you come over here?"

She wore a we're-so-proud-you-won smile for the camera but he saw the question in her eyes as she joined him in front of the car, in front of the cameras and the crew and the fans. He looked into her whiskey-gold eyes that he'd known were trouble the first time he'd glanced into them. "I used to think there was nothing I loved more than racing. I used to think nothing could possibly be sweeter than pulling into Victory Lane. I was wrong. I want the whole world to know that I love Maddie Felton." The stands erupted. Maddie's smile bathed him in sunshine. He dug in his pocket and pulled out the Sleep EZ key chain. "A couple of races into the season, Maddie gave me this for good luck. I want to give it back to her now." He dangled the key chain from one finger and the crowd really roared when the camera zoomed in on the diamond ring attached to the key chain.

He dropped to one knee. "Madeleine Suzette Felton, will you have me for better for worse, for wins and losses, for richer or poorer, in sickness and in health? Will you be my partner, my best friend, my wife?"

Laughing, crying, nodding yes, she pulled him to his feet and kissed him in front of God and everybody. Then crazy, incredible woman that she was, she turned and grinned into the camera.

"Take note, girls. Send the man a swing, get a ring."

TUCKER WALKED OUT THE front door carrying two glasses of Edna's homemade lemonade and a sweet joy blossomed inside Maddie. "Nectar on a summer night."

Maddie patted the seat cushion next to her on the swing. "C'mon. Let's take it for a test drive. I guess that would be test swing."

Tucker put the lemonades on the rail and settled in the swing next to her. "I was just thinking that the first time I met you, I thought about sitting on a front porch swing with you."

"You're making that up."

"Honest. I saw you and I thought about sitting on a porch swing with you, just like this. And I thought I needed my head examined because you weren't a front porch swing kind of woman."

He slipped his arm around her and she snuggled up close. "Guess you were wrong."

"Doesn't happen often."

She snorted inelegantly and he set the swing into gentle motion with his foot. Maddie loved the rhythmic creak of a swing. It offered a music all its own.

"So, you didn't mind me proposing in front of the cameras?" Tucker finally asked.

"Are you kidding? It saved me the trouble of telling all the other women to back off because you're taken." She sent him a lazy smile. "That was the most perfect proposal a woman could ever have. Of course, you put me through hell before we got there, but I suppose I forgive you."

He stroked a lazy circle against her shoulder with his finger. "I thought about what you said. I thought about it a lot. And Jack gave me a couple of home truths. I kept thinking I had to be more than I was because who I was couldn't possibly be enough. I am enough. Racing doesn't define me, my parents don't define me, and much as I love you, you don't define me. I decide the man I am and the man I want to be."

She pressed a kiss to his cheek. "You're one of the finest men I've ever known."

"I love you so much, Maddie, it frightens me."

"I know. Me, too. You know, I think we're mostly going to have lulls, but you know there's going to be storms, as well."

"I know. But we'll ride the storms out together." He cleared his throat. "What were you thinking in the way of a wedding?"

She had, in fact, been giving it a little thought. Well, that was a lie. She was a woman, and she had enough self-awareness to admit that she was bossy. She had the wedding planned down to the last detail. But there were some things the man in your life, even if he was your soul mate, simply didn't need to know. "I was thinking something in the fall. Maybe when the leaves are changing, but before it gets too chilly. Something small. Maybe down by the pond."

"That would be nice," he said. *Whew. Saved her having to talk him into it.* He cleared his throat. "I thought I'd invite my folks."

Maddie's heart caught in her throat. "Are you sure?"

"I need to make peace…with myself. I don't think we'll ever all be sitting around a Thanksgiving dinner together, but I realized I can't keep hating them. It wasn't the childhood I wanted. Neither was yours. And our kids' childhood will be different, we'll see to that. But I don't hate them anymore. They're just sad people with terrible problems, but they're my parents."

"Then we'll invite them. I can't invite my mother, but I'm finally not angry with her, either. I carried that anger for years. It was a companion to my guilt. It's hard to love someone completely and allow yourself to be loved when you're harboring hate and anger. I never realized how heavy it was until I let it go."

"So, you think we can go ahead and start the renovations even with our travel schedule?"

"Definitely. My job is challenging, but give me a break. I can handle both. You can move your stuff in with me and then we'll both move back into the renovated house. It should be finished in time for the off-season."

He threaded his fingers through her hair. "Well, what will we do with all that extra time on our hands once the renovation is done and the racing season is through?"

A sweet heat unfurled through her and she nuzzled the faint stubble along his jaw. "The hot tub will be finished. I bet we'll think of something to keep us busy."

EPILOGUE

Twelve weeks later, Miami, Florida

"STEADY, 82, LOW. Watch for a bump-draft out of Turn Two," Bart, his spotter, said through the headset.

Two laps. The Number 82 car was going to make his move for third place. Damn. Tucker was riding the wall.

The 82 car bumped and made his move, but it was too soon. Both the 82 and the 63 spun and Tucker was out of places to go. He gripped the wheel. This was going to hurt.

Afterward, he never could say how he made it through. "That was some driving," Mike Snellings yelled though his headset.

"That was some luck." An adrenaline rush had him shaking.

Green flag. White flag. Checkered flag.

His rookie NASCAR NEXTEL Cup Series season had officially ended. "We did it. We did it, guys!"

"We'll see you down front."

Tucker climbed out of the car and reached for Maddie, who was waiting on him, a smile wreathing her face. "NASCAR race fans, here he is, your NASCAR Raybestos Rookie Champion of the Year, the 76 Sleep EZ driver Tucker 'Bed Head' Macray."

Contentment underscored the adrenaline rushing through him. He kept one arm firmly planted around his wife and hoisted the trophy in the air with the other hand.

"Thank you. This means so much to the team and me. This was a great rookie year in a lot of ways. I learned a lot. And it's just going to keep getting better and better."

He'd been more of a rookie than he realized when he first started. A rookie to NASCAR NEXTEL Cup Series, but even more of a rookie in love. And he'd wound up with a heck of a winning season.

* * * * *

*For more thrill-a-minute romances set against the exciting
backdrop of the NASCAR world, don't miss:*

OLD FLAME, NEW SPARKS *by Day Leclaire*
ALMOST FAMOUS *by Gina Wilkins*
Available in August

THE ROOKIE *by Jennifer LaBrecque*
LEGENDS AND LIES *by Katherine Garbera*
Available in September

A CHANCE WORTH TAKING—*by Carrie Weaver*
TURN TWO—*by Nancy Warren*
Available in November

*And for a sneak preview of TURN TWO, featuring a cameo by
real-life NASCAR driver Carl Edwards, just turn the page…*

SUNDAY WAS A PERFECT DAY for racing. Sunny but not too hot, the sky so clear and blue there was no danger of rain, and the air shifted with only a slight breeze. Taylor hoped that a perfect day was a good omen for Hank's first NASCAR NEXTEL Cup Series race.

She was so nervous she could barely stand still. She felt as proud of Hank as if he was her brother or son, and so nervous she thought she might throw up.

Her driver was fortunately made of sterner stuff. If he was nervous it didn't show. He stood proudly in his brand-new fire suit with the name of the chain of hardware stores sponsoring him prominently identified.

"How are you feeling?" she asked him.

He grinned at her, and she could see the excitement shining in his eyes. "I feel good," he said. "Real good." He glanced around as though he couldn't believe that he was here. "Today is going to be a great day."

They made their way to the staging area where drivers were milling around, each with his PR manager. Fans watched from the perimeter.

Carl Edwards caught sight of Hank and immediately walked over.

"How you doing?" he asked Hank.

"I'm doing fine. Not too nervous." He stood there for a second and asked, "Do you have any advice for the rookie?"

"Yeah. Drive fast. But not faster than me."

They laughed and even that little release helped dim Taylor's stress level. She took a quick glance around and thought that most of the PR managers looked more tense than their drivers.

"Really, what I would say is just, you know, enjoy the moment. I'm guessing you've dreamed of this day since you were a little kid."

Hank nodded. She could picture him hanging around cars as a little guy, watching races, finally getting a chance to try a cart and falling in love with the sport.

"There's a lot more guys who dream of going out there than will ever get the chance. You have to drive like you mean it. Drive with your heart and your guts and all your dreams right out there. Keep your focus and—" he shrugged, looked up at the sky as though for inspiration "—do what has to be done."

"Okay."

"What we do is amazing, right?" He looked like he'd pumped himself up with his pep talk. "This is so cool."

"It sure is. I've been practicing my backflips, in case I win."

Carl treated him to his toothy grin. "Stick to something you can handle. Like a cartwheel."

The picture of Hank in his blue-and-yellow suit, turning cartwheels was so ridiculous she had to laugh.

He appeared to take the suggestion seriously. "Think that's too flashy? Maybe I should stick to one of them…what do you call them? Somersaults."

Carl gave him a mock punch. "You're going to be okay."

Then the drivers were being introduced. She heard Hank's name called and felt another swell of pride. This was it. While he made his introductory lap, she walked back to the garage.

The air was buzzing with excitement. She took a moment to look up at the stands and enjoy the spectacle of one hundred and sixty-eight thousand or so fans all set for one of racing's premier events. The stands were a sea of color. Fans sported racing gear, most of which was in bold, primary colors. It was a rainbow of caps, jackets, T-shirts, coolers.

Hank arrived, looking pretty colorful himself in his brightly hued fire suit. He stood by his car, chatting with his crew chief. Photographers were everywhere, snapping photos from every conceivable angle. Hank, like most of the drivers, did his best to pretend he didn't notice.

As drivers walked by, they'd give him a good-natured shove or mumble something that she assumed meant good luck in some incomprehensible sports-guy speak.

As he continued talking to his crew chief, Taylor was thrilled to see a broadcaster walk by for a quick interview.

"How do you think you're going to do out there today?" Hank was asked. A no-brainer question and one she'd prepared him for.

"I'm going to do my best. I've got a great team behind me, a company I'm proud to race for and sponsors and fans who believe in me." He broke into his infectious grin. "I have to tell you and everybody out there who's rooting for me today that I feel ready for this."

Taylor stood by while he climbed into his car, put in earplugs, pulled on his helmet and plugged it in. She watched him strapping in, putting the steering wheel on—getting ready to go.

When she heard the words *Gentlemen, start your engines,* she though she might hyperventilate. This was it. Not only Hank's rookie race, but hers, too.